AF228095

HEY THERE
slugger

by USA TODAY bestselling author
GINGER SCOTT

HEY THERE SLUGGER

BOOK 2

THE BOYS OF SWEETWATER SPRINGS

GINGER SCOTT

**Text copyright © 2026 Ginger Scott
(Little Miss Write, LLC)**

No part of this book may be reproduced in any form or by any electronic or mechanical means, including information storage and retrieval systems, without permission in writing from the author. The only exception is by a reviewer, who may quote short excerpts in a review.

Without in any way limiting the author's exclusive rights under copyright, any use of this publication to "train" generative artificial intelligence (AI) technologies to generate text is expressly prohibited. The author reserves all rights to license uses of this work for generative AI training and development of machine learning language models.

This book is a work of fiction. Names, characters, places and incidents either are products of the author's imagination or are used fictitiously. Any resemblance to actual persons, living or dead, or events is entirely coincidental.

Ginger Scott

Cover design and formatting by Ginger Scott

E-book cover photo by Sydney French, Broken Compass Photography

For moms and dads in all wonderful forms.

ONE
BROOKS CALLAHAN

I haven't slept in thirty-seven hours. I can feel it, too. I'm on the brink of going a little bit crazy. I've seen videos of those sleep deprivation tests. Lack of z's messes with the head, and I'm right in the middle of being messed with. But I have a three-month-old baby who is on her second-to-last diaper, and if I want any shot at sleeping in the next few hours, I need to have more clean diapers ready. I may be undergoing a self-taught crash course on this whole parenthood trip, but I learned one lesson real quick—there are *never* enough diapers within reach.

"What do you think, Holly? Are you a size one? A five? You're three months old, so does that make you a three?" A tiny spit bubble forms on her lips as her mouth contorts into the sweetest yawn. She's tired, fed, and dry. I need to get us both home, stat.

"You look a little lost." The voice of a woman is accompanied by a soft giggle, and I turn around, expecting to see someone who looks like my mom did when she was alive. Older, worn out, hungover perhaps. Instead, I'm instantly knocked back on my heels by a pair of green eyes, light brown hair, and lips that stretch into this awe-striking smile. Did I die just now? Is this an angel?

"Uh, sorry. I'm . . . exhausted."

I laugh and shake my head, pinching the bridge of my nose as I squeeze my eyes shut tight, working feeling into my face.

It strikes me that I may be hallucinating, so I crack a lid open, half expecting the vision to be gone. Instead, she's still here—very real, very beautiful—and she's smiling down at the now sleeping baby in the carrier hooked over my forearm.

"*Shh*, I think you finally lost her," she says, her pale-blue-polished fingernail touching the curl of her top lip.

I'm briefly mesmerized. It's lips like those that got me into this situation, though, so I shake my head, waking myself up by patting my open hand against my unshaven cheek a few times.

"Would it be weird if I just lay right here, in aisle"—I lean to the right to check the number hanging above the end cap where prune juice is on display—"fourteen. Good ole aisle fourteen. My favorite."

The mystery angel laughs softly again and shakes her head.

"Not to those of us who know what you're dealing with. First babies are the toughest. I went and had twins," she says in a hushed tone. She holds up a finger and lifts on her toes to reach a package of diapers labeled 2-3, then hands them to me.

"You want to go by weight. She's probably about twelve pounds, maybe thirteen. Next week, you'll want the threes." She leans her head to the right toward the red diaper packs with the bright blue number three emblazoned on them.

I exhale, and it spills out of me with enough force to send me back a step and force my hiked shoulders down to a normal position for the first time since Holly showed up on my doorstep less than a week ago.

It was just before midnight, and the knock at my door was loud enough to wake my ass after a full week of conditioning with the team. And there she was, with nothing more than a blanket, a couple of onesies in a plastic bag, and a note from a college one-night stand. My *only* one-night stand. Ever.

"Thanks. I seriously have no idea what I'm doing." I take the package from this kind woman, my hand brushing hers on the exchange, her cheeks flaring to a really sweet pink when we touch.

What is happening? I go years without a girlfriend, for obvious reasons, then let loose a little bit my senior year of college and bam—the universe makes me a single dad. And now this—the perfect woman—is actually upping my flirt game, and I am in no shape to act on any of it. Plus, she has twins. She's probably married.

"You should get her home while you can still take advantage of this time," she whispers, and winks.

I nod and smile with relief.

"Seriously, thank you again . . ." I hold out my free hand, the diapers tucked under my arm and the carrier clutched against my hip.

"Lindsey," she utters finally. Thank God I didn't have to come out and ask. I don't know if I have the nerve in me. Again, not that I'll ever follow up or do anything with this knowledge. But at least I'll know what to call her in my mind later when I replay this and pretend things went a different way.

"Lindsey," I say, my mouth forming an instant smile at the feel of her name on my tongue. "Good to meet you. I'm Brooks."

"Oh, I know who you are. I'm sure I'll see one of your games again soon. You better rest up if you want to keep that hitting streak alive." Her cheeks redden. More flirting. Fuck me, why is this my luck?

"Right. Well. I'll try. Got my hands full." I lift my shoulders and arms, showing off the baby and diapers, as if I need to.

"Right. Well . . ." She waves with a flicker of her fingers, then turns her back to me as she heads down the aisle waving her own grocery list. Meanwhile, I spin on my heels and head to the register, calling myself a dumbass the entire way.

Got my hands full.

I shut my eyes briefly and take in a short breath, too tired to feel the full burn of embarrassment by my behavior. Besides, what could she possibly think about me? I made it pretty clear I wasn't babysitting. And I'm a rookie making league minimum, which is less than a substitute teacher here in Oklahoma. I looked that up last night.

By the time Holly and I get back to my apartment, we're both ready for a nap, though she got a decent head start. I crash hard and fast while I can, and neither of us stirs until midnight. After a fresh diaper and bottle of formula—and a protein bar for me—we're both back in slumberland within an hour.

I can do this.

I cannot do this.

I've felt the unbelievable highs and lows of parenthood a dozen times over the last seventy-two hours, and what I've come to terms with is the cold, hard truth—something is going to have to give. And it might just be baseball.

My last shot is this Hail Mary from Hunter, my former teammate. He got called up to the majors last week and came to Sweetwater to pick up his truck and meet Holly. He also gave me a tip on a great nanny. I thought it was strange that the woman he recommended was named Lindsey. I haven't stopped thinking about the angel from the grocery store since we locked eyes during my diaper meltdown. But what are the odds this Lindsey is *that* Lindsey?

I shot her a text right away, and we agreed to meet for coffee this morning to see if we can work something out. But she's ten minutes late, and with every passing second, my doubts grow that she's going to show at all.

Holly coos in her carrier beside me, so I tuck the thin blue blanket around her body a little tighter, then let her hold on to my finger. She's gotten into gripping things lately—my hair, the collar of my T-shirt, my face. She's fascinated by my fingers, always pulling one into her tiny mouth.

The chimes sound at the coffee shop's door, pulling my attention away from my daughter in time to catch sight of my angel and two very loud, incredibly hyper toddlers rolling their way into the shop. I swallow hard as I scooch out of the booth in time to catch one of the boys as he launches into my side as if I'm a piece of playground equipment.

"I got him! Riggs, get his feet!" The other boy wraps his arms around my legs as he worms around my feet on the floor.

"Deacon, get off of him. Riggs, off the floor. You're filthy now. Oh, my God, boys!" Lindsey blows up at the loose hairs that have fallen over her face, then shrugs, offering me a crooked grin while peeling one of her children from my right oblique.

"What's fill-fee?" The boy around my feet crinkles his nose as he cranes his neck to look up at his mom.

"Dirty, Riggs. The floor is dirty. Get up. Just . . . ugh!" Her smile morphs into a strained jawline as she lifts the boy from the brightly colored linoleum, all while wrangling what seems to be his twin into the booth seat. The two of them settle in finally and pull menus from the wooden holder pushed against the window.

"So, in case you were wondering, yes . . . we did meet already. And I completely understand if you decide all of *this* is too much for you to be in business with." She blows up at her hair again as she motions her hand toward the side of the booth where her boys are kicking their feet with enough gusto to somehow shift the large double-sided booth backward a few inches every time.

I chuckle and hold her gaze for what feels like several seconds but is probably less than a blink. Holly's bubbling cry kicks in a moment later, and reality crashes right back in.

"I'm sorry. I'm sure it was the zoo I brought in that woke her up," Lindsey says as I lunge into the booth to scoop her from her carrier and cradle her against my chest.

"No, I was gambling with time. She slept most of the night for once, so this morning nap was bonus time." I feel her bottom as I bounce on my feet and try to hush her back to sleep, but every time I lift my heels seems to only upset her more.

"Can I . . ." Lindsey reaches toward me, and I transfer my crying daughter into her waiting arms. Within seconds, Holly is staring up at Lindsey with wide eyes, her quivering mouth frozen on the verge of a smile.

"I swear I'm not really magic. Sometimes a change of position, or a different view, is enough to distract them from the fact they're upset. Doesn't it?"

Lindsey drops her face close to Holly's and blows raspberries with her lips as she bends her knees and quickly pops back up into a full stand. I'm not sure if it's the motion, the funny sounds, or the exaggerated expressions that have Holly rapt—maybe it's a combination—but whatever the magic, it seems to work instantaneously.

"When can you start?"

I chuckle when Lindsey looks at me with a smirk, but I'm not kidding. I'll send this superhero a deposit right now if she's willing to take the gig and buy me an ounce of breathing room.

"You got a car seat in that beast out there?" She tilts her

head toward the window. My Suburban is parked outside. It's a nice ride, and I'm sure it looks like I'm swimming in cash, but that SUV was my home for my last year of college. It was the only damn thing my mother had left when she died, and I'm sure it was bought with drug money. Something good should come my way after my shitty childhood, so when the state of California notified me after probate, I picked up the keys, drove my ass back to Iowa, and never looked back.

"I got a car seat, yeah," I say, exhaling with my words. I think that's relief I feel. Or exhaustion. Perhaps both.

"I can start today, then. As long as you don't mind this sweetheart being around a couple of terrors, I mean toddlers." She glances to the booth where her boys are now taking turns smacking each other on the top of the head with the menus.

"I play minor league baseball. Your boys seem more grown up than the guys she's been around in the clubhouse. Believe me."

"*Hmm*, probably true," she says, twisting her lips into a crooked, tight smirk.

She shifts her gaze to me and holds out a hand, and we shake on the deal . . . despite the fact we haven't discussed a lick of detail. Hunter said he filled her in on my story, aka how I ended up here with a baby, but he doesn't know all the particulars. Hell, neither do I, honestly. I'm sure Lindsey and I will have those conversations, and hopefully she won't judge me too hard. Truth be told, I'd pay her the balance of my signing bonus to help me get through this season. But leading with that probably isn't the best negotiating tactic.

"I can pay you for today, of course. Or for the week? I don't really know how this whole thing works." *Yeah, I'm bad at bargaining. They should have agents for this stuff.*

"Weekly would be great. Let's say a thousand every Monday, and extra for overnights. And I'll need a key to your place. And access to the Suburban, of course."

I arch a brow.

"And why the Suburban?" I can see her minivan parked outside. She has plenty of room to haul the three kids wherever she needs to take them.

"No real reason. I just want to drive it. Test out the sound system. See how it thumps. You know . . ." She holds my gaze for a beat, then cracks into heavy laughter.

"You're fucking with me," I say through a massive exhale as I glide my palm from my forehead into my hair.

"I'm fucking with you. About the Suburban, at least. The key and the cash are nonnegotiable."

"Done," I say with a nod.

We swap mobile payment info, phone numbers and addresses, and I load Lindsey up with Holly's go-bag of formula and diapers. I've been a single dad for less than two weeks, but for the first time since she showed up at my door, I can see a path forward. Until now, I've been piecing my life together, staying up all damn night and fitting in a few hours of sleep when I can between practices, then racing from the local church preschool to the stadium and back again to make everything fit into my limited free time. I've gotten lucky so far with the times they're open, but that luck is running out. Church daycare and triple-A ball schedules aren't necessarily in sync.

I carry Holly to Lindsey's car and get her locked into the seat. I tuck the small blanket she arrived with around her body and press a soft kiss to her precious forehead, and as I back out of the gray minivan littered with Cheerios and Hot Wheels cars, I'm suddenly overwhelmed by relief. So much so that I wrap my arms around Lindsey and hug her against my chest, tucking my face into her hair and willing myself not to cry like the exhausted nutcase I've suddenly become.

"Oh . . . okay, then. It's . . . it's okay," she says through a soft giggle, her hands rubbing gentle circles on my back.

Her touch snaps me back to attention, and my eyes fly

open wide. I clear my throat as I back away, wincing through the embarrassed burn on my cheeks.

"Sorry about that. I'm a bit—"

"I get it. Trust me. I've been there . . . a few times." Her gentle smile barely reaches her eyes, and it's in that moment I see how tired she is, too.

"It's nice not to be alone." I shrug, but my words seem to hit us at the same time, our gazes widening. Lindsey's chest fills with a deep breath, and I feel this urge to somehow rearrange my words so they seem less needy.

"It is," she says before I speak. And there's a rawness to her tone that makes me think our stories might not be so different.

Or I'm so fucking tired that I'm delusional and reading into things that don't exist.

Either way, this is the best grand I've ever spent.

[illegible]

TWO
LINDSEY BLACKWOOD

Okay, I can do this.

I forgot how nice it feels to lie down with a sleeping baby against my chest. I'm so used to the trampling of feet over my body and the sharp elbows of my twins as they race to be first to the van when we're going anywhere. This baby, though . . . she is sweet. And so quiet.

For now.

"Mom, Mommy, Mom, Mom, Mom . . ." Deacon is bouncing on his knees on the only open cushion on my parents' sofa. Meanwhile, Riggs is rolling around the floor, claiming he's so hungry he might die. We all literally just ate full-ass meals.

How Holly sleeps through this onslaught of neediness baffles me, and I must admit I'm jealous. I wonder what would happen if I shut my eyes and simply pretended to be sleeping too? I'd try, but I'm afraid the boys would drag Holly and me into the front yard and spray us with the hose to get my attention.

"Boys, hey . . . boys!" I whisper shout, waving them to sit on their knees on the floor beside the couch. They both drop their pointy chins into my gut.

"Remember how we talked on the way home about how Holly would be hanging out with us a lot, and she needs more sleep than you two because she's growing faster, and that we need to try whispering when she's asleep?"

My boys shake their heads. Liars. They remember. Though it's possible they weren't really listening.

I groan softly and work myself back into a sitting position. Two minutes of rest will have to do. I carry Holly to her carrier and tuck her in, then place her next to my father's chair, shielding her from the chaos on the other side of the room as my sons bound into the kitchen and begin jumping in attempts to reach the cabinets. They're not even close to tall enough.

"You've got your hands full." My mom chuckles lightly as she walks in with a few grocery bags slung over her arms.

"I've got my life full," I relent, leaning against the fridge door and handing over two slices of Kraft cheese to amuse the rabid toddlers.

I brought my parents up to speed while the kids and I slammed down breakfast at the diner this morning. They have a strange tale of their own, having lived apart for most of my life, but they recently got back together. My mom slowed her career down to help my dad through the rest of his stroke recovery. She moved back into their home, and they act like newlyweds, together on the sofa each night, taking morning walks, and running every errand together. The only reason they are apart right now is that my dad is at his physical therapy evaluation and has to undergo several tests. Plus, they knew I was coming back here with, well . . . my hands full.

My mom sets the grocery bags on the counter, then crouches so she's on my sons' level. They come in close enough for her to place a hand on their shoulders as they chew their way through the pieces of cheese.

"Boys, do you want to go play with the hose in the yard?"

She glances up at me and winks, as if she's letting them in on a secret.

"Yeah!" Deacon shouts. My mom hushes him quickly.

"Remember, *shh*. It's nap time for Holly," she says, and my boys instantly quiet down.

"Oh, right. I mean, *yeah!*" Deacon's whisper isn't incredibly quiet, but it's cute, and it melts my tired heart.

"Okay, you can unwind the side hose, and as long as you keep it on the grass, you can run around as long as you want." She's barely through her instructions before the boys jet out the door and rush to splash in the grassy mud.

"We need to water the lawn, and it's hot out today. I think they'll tire themselves out in twenty minutes. Maybe thirty." My mom winks at me, this time as if she and *I* are the ones in on the secret. And we very well might be.

"Where's the little one?"

I lead my mom into the living room, and she bends down next to Holly's carrier, balling her hands together and holding them over her grinning lips. It's hard not to melt when looking at this baby.

"Your dad takes plenty of naps over here, too, you know," she whispers.

I smirk and sit on the ottoman.

It's strange having my parents so . . . *together.* But I like it. I had more time with them like this than my sister Renleigh did, and maybe that's why she's been so resistant to their reunion. As much as I like this big-family feeling, however, I would also very much like a place of my own. My parents have been gracious enough to let me crash here for the last few weeks, ever since I caught my cheating-ass husband with another woman. It's going to be a while before the divorce paperwork goes through, and I'm sure Brandon, my ex, will make custody an issue. Not that he actually *wants* to spend time with our kids. He rarely has since they've been born. He's far more interested in spending time with grad students at his college, it seems. Young, pretty ones.

I shake my head and pull myself out of the mental death spiral that's been plaguing me for days. It's time to focus on the good news. Forward movement. *My life.*

"We agreed on a thousand a week," I say, drawing my mom's attention to my face. "It should be enough for me to get a small place and pay the bills, at least to start the boys in pre-school. Then, when they get to kindergarten, I can finally look for something part-time or maybe hybrid."

"Lindsey, relax. You can stay here as long as you need." My mom's eyes drift back to the baby, and her smile inches deeper into her cheeks. She might not think so when Holly is fussy. I've heard the set of pipes on this girl.

"I appreciate that. I'd like to be independent, though. You know . . . show Brandon how unnecessary he is."

My mom glances back at me with a soft, empathetic smile. She knows I'm hurt. We don't need to say that part out loud. I'd rather move right on to hating the asshole. He stole my spirit, and I'm resentful as hell over it. I had my own dreams, and as much as being a mom was one of them, so were a lot of other things. I feel foolish for giving up my schooling so he could finish his doctorate and climb the academic ladder. I have loved every minute with my boys, even the trying ones that probably cost me some of my hair. But maybe we *both* could have found a way to finish our degrees. Instead, Brandon gets to play the part of a cheating, married professor while I'm the advertising school dropout.

"Whatever speed works for you, Linds. Dad and I have your back, is all," my mom reminds me. She's said it a few times since I loaded my belongings into the tiny spare room I was sharing with my sister until she moved to Texas with her boyfriend.

Holly begins to fuss, and before I'm able to scoop her up,

my mom does, instantly patting her back to sleep as she wanders around the house.

"I'm not saying you won't be able to do this job. I know you will. But while I'm here to help, and while the boys are outside, why don't you lie down and shut your eyes for fifteen minutes. You're gonna need to bank every ounce of shut-eye you can."

She's right, because I'm too tired to object. I nod softly and mouth, "Thanks."

I pull the thin throw blanket from the back of the sofa and wrap myself in it from head to toe, and for a blissful seventeen minutes, I don't think of a damn thing. I don't even dream. Life is easy and wonderful, until a bony elbow sinks into my diaphragm, and the urgent voice from one of my sons asks when he'll get to see his dad again.

I crack an eyelid and meet Deacon's frowning face.

"I miss him. I want Daddy. I want to sleep in my old bed," Deacon whines.

He rubs his tired eyes, his tears smearing together with dirt on his cheeks. Riggs is standing just over his brother's shoulder, and he starts to cry, too. They both need a bath, and their muddy romp didn't buy me nearly enough time. But for a few minutes, they did have fun. Even if it's over now. For the time being, that's the best I can do for all of us. A few minutes here. A few there.

And anything that's left . . . that's for me.

Holly is fast asleep, and Deacon and Riggs are finally worn out from climbing everything in sight. It took three trips to the community park down the street, but that last one finally did them in. It did me in, too. I forgot how heavy a three-month-old baby is. They're too fragile to prop on the hip, and so very hot against the shoulder.

But damn, is she sweet. And I see her daddy in her looks. A lot of people think you can't see it when they're this young, but I can. Just like I saw Brandon's high cheekbones in the twins from day one. Holly has her father's sweet lips, and I bet it's a wide smile too. She hasn't done that much, but her yawn spans her face every time. Brooks has the same yawn. His mouth stretches up on the ends, teetering on a grin before deflating with a heavy sigh. It's one of the first quirks I noticed when I ran into him in the diaper aisle at the grocery store. I thought it was cute then. I still do.

"Linds, someone's in . . . the driveway." My dad has a mirror on the wall opposite the front window so he can spot people coming and going when he's sitting in his favorite chair. He's been rehabbing from a stroke and was making great mobility progress, but then a few weeks ago, he fell and broke his leg. He hates being surprised, so my mom yanked the mirror from the downstairs bathroom and put it up on the far wall. It's ugly as sin, but my dad loves splitting his attention between that mirror and whatever sport he's watching on TV.

"It's Brooks. Keep an eye on these two," I say, pointing toward my now-lazy boys as they hang off the edge of the sofa with their heads upside down. My dad points to his eyes, then to them, making a fierce face as if he's the cop and they're the bad guys. They giggle. I giggle, too.

"If he's hungry, invite him in," my mom says from the kitchen. She's making a roast, and the house smells of beef stock and cooked carrots. My mouth is watering. It's nice to have another cook in the house, honestly. Brandon always preferred to order in, and when my sister Renleigh and Dad were living here alone, they counted on me dropping in to cook a few times a week. Turns out, though, I like being fed without slaving over a stove.

"I'm sure he's got things to do," I say, waving her idea off.

I don't need this to turn into anything beyond a business relationship.

I know how my dad is with ballplayers. He was one. If we get Brooks in this house, suddenly he'll be dropping by for drinks and making himself comfortable. And then I'm going to start getting ideas about him. It's better to keep the few fantasies I've had about the man tucked deep in my head.

"Hey, sorry I'm a little late," he says as I sweep the door open wide. And of course he's wearing a tight, sleeveless shirt and shorts that sit on those handlebar muscles that frame his sides. I don't even know what those fuckers are called, but at a quick glance, I can't help but figure they're made for gripping.

I shake my head and right my gaze, hopefully before he catches me gawking.

"You're fine. My mom was just making dinner. You're invited, but that's because she's nosy, so . . ." I wave my hand, urging him to say no while my mom hollers from behind me.

"I made plenty, Brooks. You're welcome to stay." I glance over my shoulder and shoot her a glare.

"I'm pretty zonked, actually. How was Holly today? She's been good for the sisters down at—"

"You've been taking her to the sisters at Countryside, huh?" I sway Holly in my arms as I hand her over to Brooks. He picks up my movement naturally and continues to rock her. She doesn't stir a peep. He's better at this than he thinks.

"Out of desperation, really. They don't get a lot of babies at the preschool, so they were pretty excited to have her. But their hours don't exactly jive with a baseball schedule." His gaze flickers up to me, but only briefly before dropping back to his daughter's angelic face.

"I bet not. If you run into one of them, I maybe wouldn't mention I'm her nanny now. They'll triple bless her and warn you to run," I say through a chuckle.

"Oh, I doubt that," Brooks says, his eyes lifting and his

gaze sticking to mine a little longer this time. His crooked smile strikes a tender nerve in my chest, and my cheeks heat.

"She's not kidding," my dad says, ruining my moment. I was rather enjoying being admired, even if it's meaningless and brief. It's something I shouldn't indulge in. Brooks glances over my shoulder, toward my dad, so I brace myself for the truth.

I am a bad girl. And not in the sexy way I'd prefer all single men to assume moving forward. Bad, as in, name on the chalk board, as well as a police report or two.

"They kicked her out . . . of Sunday school," he whispers loudly. It's not even really a whisper when he does that. His damn speech is getting better, so I can't hope Brooks doesn't hear him clearly. He's clear as a goddamn bell.

"What does a kid have to do to get kicked out of that?" The twitch in Brooks's lip as his gaze flits to me strikes that nerve again, and this time the heat in my cheeks spills down my back.

"I'm not going to stand here for this," I say, walking away from the doorway and heading to the kitchen table where I have Holly's bag of extra diapers and formula packed and ready to go.

"For starters, she blew her nose . . . on Sister Mary's skirt," my dad says.

"That's not so bad," Brooks says, giving me a sideways look.

I may as well be the one to break it to him.

"I was twelve," I clarify.

His mouth hangs open for a beat before he begins to quake with silent laughter.

I shake my head and roll my eyes as I scoop up Holly's carrier and bring it to the door, along with her bag.

"She picked on me. And I don't care what these two tell you, she had it out for me and maybe deserved it a little."

She totally didn't.

Nobody deserves the hell I gave that woman. I was young, and my parents were sort of splitting up, so I started acting out. Plus, adolescence was a bitch. I got curves early, and boys are dicks. I got sent to the timeout corner for putting gum in her hair. I did that because she took my soda away from me, which I snuck into the youth room after lunch, and promptly spilled on the new carpet.

"And then this devil-child cut Sister Mary's shoelaces off with her craft sisters. Then cut a hole in the back of her skirt, right about . . . here," my mom says, rounding the corner as she draws a line along her own buttocks.

I sigh loudly.

"What can I say? I failed at Jesus*ing*."

"Ha! That's an understatement," my dad coughs out.

I roll my eyes until my gaze meets Brooks again, and his amused smirk is both irritating and alluring. I have to get him out of here.

"I'll come to your place tomorrow. Lest these two get me fired by revealing *all* my secrets." His hand wraps around half of mine as he takes the diaper bag from me, and we both utter an awkward, "Sorry."

"I don't know. I kind of like hearing your secrets," he says.

My eyes dart to his just in time to catch them flicker. I don't think he meant to say that out loud. And if he did, he probably shouldn't. I don't even know his story, at least not completely. Neither of us should be flirting.

I clear my throat and take a half step back while he kneels to tuck Holly into the carrier.

"So, seven tomorrow? You report at eight, am I right?" You don't grow up in Sweetwater without having the Mavericks practice schedule memorized.

"Yeah, seven is good," he says as he stands, lifting the carrier to his side.

When our gazes meet again, I struggle to maintain eye contact, and I know my flustered behavior is obvious to everyone in this room except the people under four. Thankfully, I manage to keep my mouth shut and don't drag this exchange out any longer, simply smiling tightly and nodding as Brooks heads out the door.

I close it behind him, but not before taking in the full view of his broad shoulders and the flex of his bare shoulder blades as he jogs down the porch steps and brick path. Thankfully, my dad is invested in the seventh inning of the Rangers game, so I'm spared the teasing I normally expect from him. But Mom is another story.

"Just remember, you're a single woman now. That?" She nods toward the closed door. "You're allowed."

I lift my brows, as if to brush her off, but her words sink in. She has a point. But just because I'm allowed doesn't mean I should.

THREE
BROOKS

The late-night hours that bleed into mornings are rough. Yet there's something about them that I like.

It's so quiet. That's partly the Sweetwater way—quiet and still. Those are two selling points for life in a country-minded small town in Oklahoma. The stench of pig farms is definitely a drawback, but the cattle ranch down the road has a certain touch of something I don't totally hate.

Maybe it all reminds me of Iowa, the place that saved me. Perhaps that's why Sweetwater feels like home. I mean, my *real* hometown never felt that way. I shared a one-bedroom apartment with my drug-dealing, addict mother. I slept on a pull-out sofa I paid for myself and dragged home from a thrift store. No wonder my spine is all fucked up. I spent my formative years sleeping on a weave of rusty springs and layers of sleeping bags.

The full ride to play ball in Iowa wasn't my dream the way playing for San Diego State was the pinnacle for my friend Hunter. That ticket to Iowa was my ticket out of hell. And I soaked up every drop of that gift to make sure I never had to drag my ass back to Inglewood. And I didn't, except for one single flight to sign some paperwork at the coroner's office and pick up the Suburban.

I've been thinking about Inglewood and my mother a lot more lately. And *that* is most certainly the quiet's fault. It's due to nights like this one. My mind wanders to the past as I pace in a circle in my living room while rocking Holly back to sleep. She woke up just after midnight, hungry. She's gotten good at falling asleep right after a feeding, which is the only reason I've been able to function at morning workouts.

Tonight feels different, though. I'm not sure I'll be able to fall back after this round. My mind is racing too much. My thoughts keep coming back to my mom and our shitty life. She used to tell me that things weren't always so bad, that before my father left, we had a house, a porch, and a yard with rose bushes. The only reason I know she wasn't lying is the photo of me sitting in a hard plastic baby pool in the middle of a lush lawn, a man I don't recognize splashing water at me with his cupped palms. I pick up the photo from the open shoebox I pulled out earlier tonight and try to see myself in the tall, slender man's profile, in jeans and a buttoned-up plaid shirt with the sleeves rolled above his elbows. I've tried growing a mustache like his, but even that doesn't make our similarities stand out.

Perhaps it's because I don't want to see the likeness. I don't want to be anything like that coward. He left me with a woman addicted to opioids so he could run from the law. And when the law caught up with him, he refused to be held accountable to anyone, spitting in the face of justice as well as every request I made to visit him while he was serving time.

I quit trying by the time I was a sophomore in high school. I no longer had time for his problems; I had plenty of my own —mostly finding a place to live every few months when my mom managed to get us evicted again and again. I don't know what I would have done in high school without Hunter. I didn't have a car and shit, so I bused my ass to Woodbridge

High every day until he turned sixteen and got a car. The dude never missed a day, once picking me up and taking me to school when he was staying home sick with the flu.

I wish he and I could have played together in college, but his talent is on another level. I'm good, mostly because I work my ass off like my life depends on it. It does. It always has. I'm not even sure I ever really loved this game. It's simply the one thing I am good at that took me away from the chaos, and let me survive. Even now, I find myself pushing the limits so I can be great, not because I want the dream, but because I want to give Holly a life a million times better than mine was.

And that . . . *that* is why I will wake up in the middle of the night to be here for her. Why I took her in that night and never thought of contesting paternity. I still have legal hoops to jump through with my lawyer, and eventually, I'll need to satisfy the state that Holly is in fact mine to formally add my name to her birth certificate. But in my gut, I already know the truth. My heart tells me all I need to know. Holly is mine. Her mom was—*is*—not equipped for the job, so I will be. I'll be her person, her parent, dad, hero, protector. I'll show up for it all, no matter how fucking tired I am. Because my God, that shit's everything to a child. I wish someone had shown up for me.

Holly is fast asleep against my chest, so I ease myself onto the sofa, angling enough to make sure she's comfortable and that if I luck out and doze off, I'll be semi-comfortable as well. I drop the photo of me in the baby pool to the cushion beside me and pull the letter that arrived in Holly's carrier from the box. No matter how many times I read this thing, it never says enough.

> *Dear Brooks,*
>
> *I'm sorry. I wanted to tell you sooner. I tried to, but I couldn't. And I knew Holly deserved to have a shot. We both know that can't be with me. But you can be her universe. You have it in you. Please take care of our baby girl. I'll try to find the courage to fix myself, and maybe then, I can come back to you both.*
> *With love,*
> *Pen*

Pen. I don't even know her last name. We knew each other for less than twelve hours, though we knew *of* each other for most of our college years. Pen worked at the pub about two blocks from the university campus. I saw her there after games when I went out with the team to celebrate. She went to school part-time, on and off, because she was a lot like my mom. She has demons, and she turned to anything to quiet them.

One night, when I was feeling pretty low about myself, she turned to me, and we distracted one another. It wasn't supposed to mean more than what it was. The rules were clear. We weren't each other's types at all. But sex is a powerful drug. Fucking life-altering, it seems.

I got drafted. Pen disappeared from the pub. And that was it. Until Holly showed up at my door with the note.

Pen was right about one thing: I can be Holly's universe. Whether or not I have it in me to keep this hamster wheel moving is another story. But I sure as hell am going to try.

It takes my mind several seconds to sort through the cacophony of sound attacking my ears. It's the loud knock at my door, the third round of knocking, *I think*, that finally pries my eyes open.

"Shit!" The color in the room is my first clue that I've overslept.

I sit up slowly, Holly's body pressed against my sweaty T-shirt, a small pool of her drool crusted in a circle just below the collar. The pounding sounds again.

"Just a second!" I cough to clear the raspiness from my voice. My throat feels like I gargled Jello while I slept.

I get to my feet and run my palm around Holly's back to her butt, and the full diaper makes itself obvious. I pinch the bridge of my nose and squeeze my eyes shut tight, popping them back open in hopes that I'll finally be able to see well enough to make out the time on my phone. I lean over the kitchen counter as Holly breaks into a cry, and that's when I see a dozen notifications from my email inbox on the lock screen. I guess I didn't dream the dinging sound I heard in my sleep. It was my phone. Or, more accurately, my father pinged my email with messages, asking to meet. He's been emailing me for weeks, and I have yet to respond. I only read the first message he sent, the one letting me know he was out of prison and would like to talk.

I very much would not like that.

"Brooks, you said to be here at seven, and it's a little after, so maybe let me take care of Holly so you can get your ass to practice? I had to drop the boys off at preschool so I'm a few minutes late." Lindsey's voice is barely muffled by the door.

I hate to dump a cranky, diaper-bombed baby on her like this, but I guess that's sort of the gig she signed up for, so I drop my phone back on the counter and head to the door. She takes Holly in her arms as soon as I crack the door wide enough, and she shoos me off to get ready for my workout.

"I got her. She's easier to clean up than you are. You . . . you're a mess," she teases. At least, *I think she's teasing?*

"You're a lifesaver," I say, tugging my damp shirt up from the collar as I make my way toward my bedroom. I stop in the doorway when I realize I haven't given Lindsey any directions about Holly's stuff, where the diapers are, whether she's been fed yet—but by the time I crane my neck and open my mouth, she's somehow found the diaper bag and unrolled the pad to change my daughter.

I get caught at the sight for a moment, a little jealous of Lindsey's natural intuition. She begins to hum and glances up, catching me, and her mouth curves up on the edges.

"I promise, I've got this. I've changed a diaper before. I changed four of hers yesterday," she says through a soft giggle.

I sigh out a tired laugh of my own.

"You're right. I'm just . . . I guess all of this is a shock to me. How it's easy for some, I mean." I stretch my right arm up and grasp the door jamb, stretching the kinks out of my body. Lindsey's gaze lingers on me, and I note the slight drop of her sightline to my stomach. Her mouth is still curved into this soft, suggestive grin. Or maybe I'm simply reading the suggestive part. Wishful thinking.

Bad fucking ideas.

"Right, well. I'm gonna . . . ." I jut my thumb over my shoulder toward my shower, and she lifts her brow.

"Yep. Go do that," she says, dropping her attention back to Holly. I back away before I make things weird. *Weirder.*

I wish I had more than two minutes for the shower, but as it is, I don't have time to wait for the water to warm up. That's probably for the best. The cold water does wonders in waking my ass up fully. By the time I'm dressed and heading out the door, I'm running a few minutes ahead of schedule.

I pop out of my room and spot Holly lying on a rainbow-colored play pad, an arch of tiny, twinkling stars stretched over her, from corner to corner of the pad. Lindsey is on the floor next to her with what looks like a textbook flipped open at her side. She's running her fingertips in circles around Holly's belly, and I think . . . no wait, I know my daughter is smiling.

"What is this magical thing?" I carry my sneakers to the couch and sit at the end so I can slip my feet into them one at a time.

"I went through a few of the boys' old things and thought Holly might like this. I have a few more items in the car. I'll bring the swing over tomorrow. I couldn't get it out of the closet without making a mess. The perks of living in what has become your parents' storage room," she says.

I nod and smile.

"Wow, that's really nice of you. Looks like she loves it." I get to my feet and move closer so I can look down at my happy little girl. I'm not sure if Holly is looking at me or the stars right now, but I am sure she's content. More than that, she's happy. And it sort of makes my chest burn that I need to leave her.

My gaze shifts to the textbook next to Lindsey. It's open to a page displaying a series of old Coca-Cola ads.

"What's that about?" I nod toward it.

She flips the cover shut and taps her finger along the title —*Intro to Advertising*.

"I'm thinking about going back to school, finishing my degree. Before I enroll in anything, I figured I should brush up and make sure I still like this stuff."

She flips the book open again, this time on a two-page chart filled with dollar signs. I chuckle.

"Looks like it's all about money, so that's pretty enjoyable, I'd say."

Lindsey smirks on one side of her mouth and shrugs.

"Money is great and all. Don't get me wrong, I like it a lot. But it's not everything. It's a means to an end, if that makes sense." She tilts her head, her eyes centering on mine, and my mouth waters. It's the strangest feeling, like she's been reading my midnight thoughts or something.

I nod softly.

"Yeah, it makes a lot of sense."

Our gazes mingle for a few seconds, long enough for the crackle in the air to become palpable. And before I can stop myself, I say something stupid.

"Maybe you should move in."

The way her eyebrows raise is my first indicator that I've uttered an impulse aloud. The next clue is the way she drops her chin, then fidgets with her book, then her lap, then adjusts her legs, and the way she's sitting on the floor.

"Sorry, that was . . . that's probably a bad idea. I was just thinking about how early I get started, and how my schedule is going to be all over the place. And, I don't know. Maybe if you were here—"

"I have twins, Brooks. You'd be living with a whole damn household." She mashes her lips into a relenting smile, which I'm sure she means as a sign for me to drop the bad idea, but somehow only makes me dig in harder.

"I know. You *and* the boys could be here. Well, not here. I'd get a bigger place, which I was thinking of doing anyhow. I could get a rental near Roddy's house. There are a lot available on his street, and some of the guys with families live in that neighborhood. They're used to contracts with players around here. You and the boys could have your own rooms, and if you needed a hand with something, I'd be around. You could start school, and I wouldn't have to worry about travel games so much. It sort of makes sense."

On the surface, I'm right. And live-in nannies are definitely a thing. I researched them before Hunter hooked me up with Lindsey. There's no reason we couldn't make this a business arrangement. Except there's this nagging feeling that maybe things are good as they are. Like I'm teetering on a slope covered in ice. And I'm hanging on to a damn sled while I'm at it.

"I think it's better we—"

"You know, maybe that's too much—"

We talk over one another and settle into a soft laugh. My cheeks burn, and Lindsey's are a rosy pink. I try to hold her gaze, but neither of us seems able to stick to one another for long. I've ditched the sled at this point and simply heaved myself over the slope into the world's most uncomfortable abyss.

"I'm gonna—"

"Maybe, just—"

We both gesture to the door and freeze when our eyes meet, breaking into a harder laugh this time. It seems to cut the tension, though, and after a few seconds, Holly begins to fuss, taking over Lindsey's attention.

It's difficult to leave like this. I want to jump in and take care of my daughter, to right her wrongs, however trivial they are. This one seems to be chalked up to gas. But for the first time since she showed up in my life, I'm able to step back and breathe. She's in good hands, even if they aren't mine. Which makes the crazy idea of moving Lindsey and her boys in with me circle my mind some more. This time, though, I leave before I say another word.

FOUR
LINDSEY

It's been a while since I stepped foot in a classroom, not counting the preschool that the boys go to. There aren't any fingerpaints or foam blocks in this place. There *are* lots of students four years younger than me with portfolios that put mine to shame. The university's advertising program is part of the business college, and it's hard not to look at everyone in this building and see my ex.

"Ms. Blackwood?" I lift my head and catch the gaze of the kind administrative assistant who checked me in for my meeting this morning. "The dean will be right with you."

"Thank you," I say with a smile that buzzes my lips. I'm so nervous. Her soft nod is comforting, but the moment she leaves me, my pulse races again.

I cross my ankles as I tuck my feet under my chair and shift the leather-bound portfolio propped in my lap. I wore a long dress, aiming for modest, but all of the women who have passed through the lobby while I've been waiting have been dressed in hip clothes. Short skirts, bright power suits, a few baggy overalls with what looks like lingerie underneath. The blend of art-school chic with business elite in this place is mind-boggling. The one thing that's apparent is how little I fit in.

"Ms. Blackwood—"

I leap to my feet, dropping my portfolio in my fit of nerves.

"Here, let me help," the assistant says as she rushes to help me scoop my sketches and writing samples into a neat pile.

"You're going to do great," she says after handing me the notecard I scribbled my questions on. She covers my hand with hers and gives it a much-needed squeeze.

"So far so good, huh?" I joke. We both chuckle as we stand.

I give her a nod and muster the tiny bit of lingering confidence, willing it to flex and give me a boost for the next twenty minutes. Rolling my shoulders back, I step into the dean's office, and Dean William Stratford steps around a massive desk to greet me in the middle of the room.

"Lindsey, it's nice to meet you. You can call me Will." His gray beard clashes with the bright yellow rims of his glasses, and I instantly relax. He falls more on the artsy side of this place.

"Nice to meet you, Will." He gestures to the open chair by his desk, then takes his seat on the other side. I hand my portfolio to him as I sit, and he instantly leafs through my out-of-order materials.

"Things are a little shuffled. I'm sorry. I had a little incident in the lobby. My nerves. I may have tossed everything around the floor on my way in." I pick at my cuticles as he nods and lightly chuckles.

"No need to be nervous. I read your application. Your husband, Brandon, he works in the psychology department, am I right?" He glances over the rims of his glasses, and my sudden, awkward pause must have caught his attention because he clears his throat.

"We're separated," I clarify.

He nods and drops his attention back to my work. The quiet seconds feel as if they stretch on for hours, and sweat builds in my armpits. I don't know why I thought I could do this. I've been out of school for four years, and while that's not a long time in most worlds, in a discipline that depends on technology and being able to adapt, it feels like light years.

"I didn't include it in this portfolio, but I do volunteer my services at my boys' preschool, running their social media for special event days, and—"

I stop my rambling when his gaze lifts again. I swallow hard as he smiles.

"Lindsey, your work is very strong. And you are transferring credits from one of the best programs in the country. You've already been accepted." He closes the cover on my portfolio and folds his hands on top as I quiver in my seat with a sudden sob.

"Oh, I . . . that's wonderful. I'm grateful. Thank you." I reach my hand across the desk, and he takes it in both of his for a soft shake. I really like this man's smile. It ticks down a hair, though.

"You're going to have to take a few prerequisites. Not everything has transferred, and new standards have been put in place, but we should be able to get you into the core classes within a year, maybe two? Assuming you can't attend full time."

My heart sinks. I was hoping to avoid this for lots of reasons, most of all the big-dollar-sign one. Divorce means no more freebies from the school. I never got to take advantage of them in the first place.

I suck in my upper lip.

"I see." I nod and do my best to hold back the tears threatening to fall from my eyes. I was on the verge of a happy cry and suddenly, I feel desolate.

"It can be done, and you can take a lot of the classes

online, and at the community college for a lower cost. They all transfer."

I nod, not really ingesting his words. If things transfer so easily, then why didn't all of my prereqs from a few years ago?

"How many hours do I need?" I quirk a brow.

"Twenty-two, roughly. Of course, you'll be able to take some of those along with your advertising courses, so it won't all be the boring stuff." He chuckles, but it sounds forced. It is.

I let out a heavy sigh, then stand, leaning forward to take my portfolio. Will drops his hand on one end, stopping me briefly, and my head bobs up to meet his eyes. He shakes his head slowly.

"This isn't insurmountable, Lindsey. I mean that. Start slow, and we will support you. You have talent."

I smile, but even I can tell it doesn't reach my eyes.

"Slow and steady wins the race," I say, rattling off the most cliché thing that comes to mind. Slow and steady more likely gets smooshed under a heavy boot on a sidewalk somewhere.

I shake Will's hand one last time, then stop at his assistant's desk on my way out. She validates my parking ticket and hands me an envelope of enrollment forms and financial aid information. It's overwhelming, and I'm growing angry at the dreamer side of my brain that thought I was one of those single moms who could pull off miracles.

I check my phone for the time and see a text from Brandon. He stopped by my parents' an hour early and picked up our boys for his weekend. While I'm relieved that I don't need to see him, I hate the sudden feeling of being alone that fills my chest. Even more, I dislike the sudden uneasiness tickling my nerves as I approach my minivan, where a gray sedan with a dent in the driver's side door is parked a little too close, and the male driver is eying me as I get close.

I grip my key fob in my fist, wishing my van were just a little older so I'd have a real, jagged key to push through my fingers like a weapon. At least with the fob I can press the alarm and heave a decent punch.

My steps stall when the man exits his driver's side door, and a flash of heat washes down my body from head to toe. My stomach rolls as if I'm taking the first drop on a roller coaster. Then, I see it. The yellow envelope, and the stark grimace buried under the ratty, salt-and-pepper mustache on my process server's face. Motherfucker filed before I could.

"Lindsey Blackwood-Berchaund?" I always hated my married name.

"It's just Blackwood now," I say, jutting out an open palm in anticipation for the divorce papers.

"Right, I understand. But for the sake of accuracy, it's legally Blackwood-Berchaund, correct?"

His smugness suits this situation. I huff out a short laugh.

"I couldn't afford to file for divorce yet, so, yeah, I guess paying a few grand to get rid of that barnacle of a last name hasn't been a priority. Legally speaking, of course." I dim my eyes and hope he gets the point. The quick swallow and drop of his Adam's apple are satisfying.

"You've been serv—"

I wave my hand at him before he can finish that dumb sentence.

"Yeah, yeah. I got it. Now, move your car. And try not to hit me. Judging by that dent, you don't have the best driving record."

He doesn't respond other than to roll his eyes and sigh before slipping back into his car and zipping away. Once in my van, I set my portfolio and enrollment papers on the passenger seat, then leaf through the few pages of the divorce petition. I scan the legalese, chuckling when I get to the part that reads like Brandon's attempt to avoid paying me child support. Then I get to the part where he asks for primary custody of our boys, and my chuckles are replaced by a sudden gasp and sob.

"You have to be kidding me?" I read through the few lines again, hoping they read differently this time, but the meaning is the same. He doesn't even know how the boys like their grilled cheese sandwiches, and he wants to be their primary parent. What a joke.

I toss the papers into the passenger seat and fire up my van, pulling away too quickly and rolling over the curb with my right-side front tire. The harsh speedbump jostles me, and I smack my head against the driver's side window.

"Dammit!" I prop an elbow on the door and rub my head as I slowly roll my way toward the four-way stop.

My phone rings through my car speakers, so I glance at the name on the small screen in the center of my dashboard. It's my sister, Renleigh. Normally, I would leap at the chance to unload my very heavy feelings onto her. But for once in my life, I feel ashamed. A part of me knows this feeling isn't warranted or deserved, but it's there. I feel like a failure.

I have one job—to take care of my boys and make sure their lives are better than mine was growing up. My mom may have been gone a lot, but my parents never legally divorced. Renleigh would argue that they probably should have. But she doesn't know what this feels like—the weight a few pieces of paper can carry. The cut they leave in the center of my chest.

How am I going to navigate fighting for my boys when they think their dad is the coolest man in the world? I always thought I'd protect that. Even now, when the temptation to show them who their dad really is fills my soul with rage, I know that's not what's best for them. They're young. He's their dad. And when he *is* around them, he's pretty fun. But there's a whole lot more to parenting than buying the boys video games and feeding them junk food. In fact, those things don't even make the list.

Rather than face my reality head-on while my sister compares my situation to our parents' strange relationship, I press the ignore button and send my sister right to voicemail. And then I drive directly to Brooks's apartment building.

He's not due at the stadium for a few hours, and I planned on running some errands before showing up to take over watching Holly. But I can't handle the monotony of shopping for a new lip gloss and picking up premade salads at the grocery store right now. And I *definitely* don't want to walk into my parents' house where my boys no longer are.

I'm parked outside Brooks's building in minutes, and barely remember taking the stairs that lead to his door. I'm knocking softly within seconds, and the flood of tears rips through my chest and pours down my cheeks about a half second before the shirtless, adorable ballplayer opens the door. I do what any respectable nanny would—I slam my body into his and smoosh my wet cheeks against his pecs as my fingers scrape against the bare skin on his back.

"Uh . . ." His arms slowly fold around me, and the door thuds closed behind me.

"Don't talk. Just stand there and hold me. Just for a minute." I suck in air to steady my breathing, but it's a struggle. Getting a full breath feels impossible, and my vision is blurry.

I must look like a crazy wreck. My God.

Brooks's arms shift, his embrace growing tighter, and his chin rests on the top of my head. The tight hold would normally make me feel claustrophobic, but right now, it seems to be regulating my pulse. The slow drag of his fingertips down my spine matches the long breath that leaves my nostrils and lips, and my lungs deflate.

I let myself close my eyes and breathe in again, focusing on the little things—the way Brooks smells, the smoothness of his skin, the way his chest lines up perfectly with my cheekbone, giving me the ideal resting place. After a few deep breaths, I loosen my hold and move back a few inches so I can lift my gaze and read his eyes. I expect an amused expression;

perplexed at the very least. But all I see in his eyes is a soft tenderness, and as he moves his right palm to the side of my face, literally everything else in the world stops except for the stroke of his thumb along my cheek.

When my gaze locks on his, my chest grows hot. Not with anger, but with something else. And the vibration tormenting my lips is making them numb. I've been married for a few years, but I remember this feeling—the anticipation that comes on the verge of a kiss. I should stop myself from biting my lower lip, but I'm compelled, and the tiny action draws Brooks's eyes to it immediately.

My lips part, and my brain is screaming for me to speak, to utter the words, "We shouldn't." But instead, I close my eyes and Brooks runs his thumb along my cheek one more time before sliding his fingers deeper into my hair. My chin lifts. My mouth opens. And I am drowning in his kiss.

My hands climb his arms, wrapping around his wrists, not to pull him away but to hold him still. He cradles my face as his mouth opens, and his strong lips caress mine. His tongue moves along my lower lip as he sucks it between his, and the gasp leaves my body before it's audible. It's a tiny whimper, and I squeeze my eyes shut tighter at the sound. My cheeks burn with embarrassment. I'm doing something I shouldn't, but so is he. We're both adults, and as long as the line is drawn here, we'll be all right. It's a moment. I was upset. And he was kind. I really needed a kiss like this to remind me what passion feels like. It's been so long.

The sharp notes of Holly's cry hit the air like a hammer to a pane of glass, and just like that, the perfect distraction fizzles into regret and panic. My palms rush to my own face as Brooks covers his mouth with his forearm, dragging it across his bottom lip as if he's trying to erase poison left behind. His eyes are burning, his stare pointed and sharp. He shakes his head, but the movement is frantic, tiny.

"Lindsey, I shouldn't have done—"

"No, it was both of us. I—"

I shake my head and a laugh vibrates from me as I take a step back and stare at the floor.

"My ex had me served today. Right outside the college." I wince, hating that these two moments are now married in my memory. I need this job. More now than ever. What was I thinking?

"Fuck, Lindsey. I'm so sorry. That's really shitty."

Holly's cry grows louder, and we glance in the direction of his bedroom. Only one of us should go in there.

"One second," he says, holding up his palm before rushing into his bedroom to scoop his daughter up from a nap. I linger in the middle of his living room, picking at the edges of my fingernails and replaying the last hour of my life.

"She's probably hungry. She's dry," he says, holding her to his bare chest as he moves toward me. I open my arms and take over holding her while he zips into the kitchen to fix her a bottle of formula.

"I can do that while I hold her. If you have to get ready, I mean." *If you want to go put on a damn shirt, you Greek god of biceps, shoulders and abs.*

"It just takes a second," he says. I avert my eyes, swaying the fussy baby in my arms as I move away from him. He hands me a bottle a minute later, and I position it for Holly to take. She guzzles it immediately, and we both breathe out a soft laugh.

"Girl isn't shy about asking for what she wants," I say, realizing almost instantly the double entendre that sort of implies.

"Lindsey, I didn't mean to . . ."

I squeeze my eyes shut as my back is to him. I don't want to hear him apologize for taking advantage of me. He didn't.

"I know. I was having a moment, and you were being nice. And we're grown-ass adults. This doesn't have to be an issue." I turn around slowly, glancing up at him briefly before recentering my focus on Holly.

"I just don't want you to feel uncomfortable. I swear, that was an aberration. Won't happen again." He crosses his chest with two fingers, blending the scout's honor with the Holy Cross, and it makes me chuckle.

"I'm pretty sure you just prayed for Girl Scout cookies, but I get the point, and it's fine. *We* are fine."

The crackle in the air when our eyes meet begs to differ. Thankfully, Brooks is stuck in a town without a lot of other nanny options, and I have a mountain's worth of personal baggage to sort through to keep me focused on making smart choices.

His mouth quirks up with a slight smirk, and he nods.

"Like nothing happened. Good," he says, his gaze lingering on mine for a tiny extra second before he heads back into his bedroom.

I memorize every flex of muscle on his back before he shuts the door behind him.

That was the best *nothing* I've ever had happen.

FIVE
BROOKS

I get out of my apartment with record speed, but a part of me really wants to stay. My impulsive side. The same damn side of my personality that somehow lands in life-altering scenarios over and over again. And that's why I raced out of there before I gave in to any more urges or whims.

Holly is my priority, even more than baseball at this point. That's the way it's supposed to be when you bring a child into this world—they become number one, and everything else falls to last place.

Baseball is the means to care for her. But it doesn't mean I don't still love it. This game has been my refuge for longer than I can remember.

The neighborhood kids took me in every time we bounced from apartment to apartment in Inglewood, and I was lucky to settle in with a group who liked to throw a ball around. If it weren't for Little League and a sponsorship from the corner market that paid for our team, I'm not sure what trouble I could have fallen into.

As much as I hate the lifestyle my mom lived, high most of the time, I'm not naïve enough to believe that the older I got, I always would have been strong enough to say no. Sometimes dulling the disappointments life throws your way feels way too easy. Bad decisions don't show how hard they are until you're in too deep.

The locker room is busy with the infielders working out today. I'm running late, so I rush through my prep and wrap my own wrists before grabbing my batting gear and heading out to the cages. Jake's already set up at one of the tees, so I drop my bag outside the net and nod when he sees me.

"Work in with you?" I ask.

"Sure." He locks his sights back on the ball and rips through it with the kind of swing I'm trying to build.

I like Jake. He's a bit grumpy, but so am I sometimes. We fit well together. Like misfits. Maybe I'm assuming a lot, but I get the feeling Jake's relationship with his dad isn't all golden gloves and silver sluggers. His old man is out here with him every day, too, and when the PR team pitched him on doing a story about the family legacy of the McKinney father-son duo, Jake looked them in the eyes and laughed.

Jake props another ball on the tee and adjusts the data device on the knob of his bat. He records everything—launch angle, bat speed, exit velocity. I don't buy into that stuff like perhaps I should. I tend to believe it's my performance in the game that matters most. What I do back here is more about the feel. Numbers can lie sometimes. I don't want to make big changes to my swing only to find out none of the tweaks do shit for me when I'm staring down a starting pitcher on the mound.

"You should bring Holly around here more. She's cute. We don't have enough cute things in this place," Jake says through a gravelly laugh as he nods toward Jayden in the cage next to us.

"Fuck you, cowboy. I'm plenty cute," Jayden says, taking a hack at the ball tossed by our new hitting coach, Colby Kessler. She's one of the first female coaches to break into Triple-A ball, and she's a beast with the bat. She's also dangerously hot. Those two facts live separately, but it's damn near impossible to be in the presence of one and not acknowledge the other.

"*Mmm,* jury's out on that. What do you think, Coach? Is Jayden cute?" Jake's teasing our teammate. He can play it off all he wants, but it's pretty fucking obvious Jayden has a thing for Coach Kessler.

"He's more of a pretty boy," Coach answers. Jake and I spit out a hard laugh as Jayden flashes us his middle finger.

"Fuck y'all. You wish you could be pretty like me." He rolls the bat over his wrist, then taps it to the plate before nodding for Coach to toss him another ball. She does, and he takes out his bruised ego on the ball, drilling it to the back of the tunnel where it ricochets off one of the iron posts.

"Okay, okay. You got me. I wanna be pretty like you," I say, holding my hands up to my sides with my bat tucked between my thighs.

"Take some warm-up hacks, Brooks, and I'll get with you next," Coach Kessler says, making it clear the jokes are over.

"You got it," I say, clearing my throat as I make eyes at Jake. We mirror each other's smirks, like schoolboys caught talking about cute girls in the back of the class.

After a while, my hands buzz from the hundreds of swings I've taken with Coach, so I pull my gloves off and tear away the tape on my wrists to let the blood flow. Jake pulls his gloves off and tosses them on his gear bag, then flops down on the bench next to me before spraying water in his mouth from a plastic bottle. He hands it to me, and I take it and spray my whole damn face.

"Okay, we're showering now?" Jake teases.

I spray a shot into my mouth, swish the water around, then spit it out to the side. I hand the bottle back to him, then lean back, squeeze my eyes shut, and pinch the bridge of my nose.

"I'm so damn tired. I should start taking dips in the ice bath before practices and games." It's not my worst idea.

Jake slaps my thigh, and I pop my eyes open.

"You need to get a nanny is what you need to do. I'm not sure how you're pulling this shit off, dude. This life out here takes everything, and being a parent takes everything. That's two hundred percent if my math is right."

Jake gets to his feet and starts to count on his fingers. I chuckle.

"I actually do have a nanny. Just not twenty-four-seven."

"Welp, time to up that contract, buddy. You can't play middle infield if you're yawning when some guy hits a screamer at your face." He scoops up his hitting gear. He's got a bullpen to catch today. All I have left is some cardio. I'm starting in tomorrow's game, so it's a light day for me, other than taking hacks.

"You know the Blackwoods, right?" Jake grew up out here, and I'm pretty sure he played high school ball for Lindsey's dad. I remember Hunter saying something about that. And the way Jake chuckles at my question signals he might know the Blackwoods well.

"You talking about Lindsey Blackwood?" He quirks a brow at me and smirks.

I haven't shared my nanny arrangement with many people. Hunter knows, since it was his idea to connect me with Lindsey. But other than Jake's dad, Roddy, I haven't shared the who and what of my situation. It was hard enough to let the team know why I was running my ass all over Sweetwater to patch together childcare and set up an appointment with a family lawyer. Just because someone leaves a baby with you and says it's yours doesn't make it so, according to the government.

"What about Lindsey?" I decide to feel his direction out before giving away mine.

Jake stands tall and adjusts his bat bag over his shoulder as he pulls his lips in tight.

"Man, what's not to say about Lindsey. I mean, I heard she finally up and left that asshole she married in college. Bradley, or—"

"Brandon," I finish for him.

He pauses and flashes his gaze to me as his lips spread into this annoying grin.

"Oh, so you know Lindsey. I see." He chuckles and waggles a finger at me, like I'm guilty of something. I'm sure I am, I'm just not sure what yet. Other than kissing her, of course. That was definitely off script.

"Hunter introduced us," I add with a shrug. "She needed a gig, and I needed a nanny, so—"

"Ha! Well, shit! You should definitely turn that into a twenty-four-seven job for that woman. And then start walking around in your best cologne all the time and do things like make dinner for the two of you."

I tilt my head. Now I'm smirking.

"You got a little thing for Lindsey Blackwood, Jake?" I tease.

"Dude, there isn't a guy from this town who wasn't in love with that girl at one point. She's a couple years older than me, but damn, what I wouldn't have done to have her give me the time of day back in high school. Her sister scared the shit out of me, but Lindsey . . ." He looks up, his eyes all dreamy-like. "She was this light in a bottle. So sweet, and funny. Smart, too. She had this confidence about her. She was our student body president. Won homecoming queen and all that. When she came back home married and pregnant, every heart in a fifty-mile radius broke."

I let the picture he paints sync with the girl I know. I can definitely see flashes of that woman in there, but the confidence he's describing has definitely taken a beating. Bad people have a way of stripping away spirits, and I get the sense that her ex is one hell of a bad guy.

Jake holds out a fist, so I drop mine on top of his.

"All kidding aside, you should get as much help from Lindsey as you can. Sounds like she needs the steady pay, and you definitely need the support to get through the season."

I meet his gaze and take in his serious expression before nodding.

"You're probably right."

"No *probably* about it, brother." He gives a haphazard salute, then heads toward the pitching tunnels, leaving me with my renewed enthusiasm for moving in a woman I barely know but am dangerously attracted to.

I shuffle that thought to the back of my mind while I finish my workout, but one phone call on my way back to my apartment drags it right back to the front. My agent, Brian, and I have been playing a lot of phone tag the past few days. Truthfully, he's been chasing me down more than I have him. His reaction to my news about being an instant single dad wasn't exactly warm. I get it. I'm a commodity to him. And my stock value got fuzzy the minute Holly showed up. But I'm still driven, and I need him to see that. In fact, I'm more driven than ever now that my little girl's home life depends on my performance on the diamond.

I answer the call and pull over about a block away from home.

"Hey, Brian. Sorry I haven't gotten back to you. It's been busy." I hold my breath for his response.

"Yeah, babies will do that," he says through laughter. I roll my eyes at his attempt to be light. There's a tinge of scorn in his comment.

"Anyway—" I may need him, but one day, I'm going to get called up, and he sure as hell isn't negotiating my contract.

"Right. Well, it's about that. I know we talked about you

maybe joining the team on their away stretch in June, before the All-Star break."

I sit up tall and lean forward, my heart racing as I rest my forearm on my steering wheel. Jake was right—I *do* need Lindsey's help for more than a few hours each day.

"They put the brakes on that," he adds. And just like that, I sink to the back of my seat and slouch as if I'm trying to hide. I *am*.

I fucking blew it.

"Don't get discouraged, my man!" I hate when he calls me that.

"Right," I sigh out. I'm not great at bluffing.

"Brooks, it was insane that they were even talking about pulling you up for a series or two. It's your rookie season. Hell, most guys never make it out of Sweetwater. Sit tight. Your time is coming. Just not this year."

Not this year.

I do the mental math, which puts me right back here a year from now, hoping for the same phone call, with a different result. A year. In Sweetwater. It's not like I have some great life in Cali to get back to during the offseason. Or some fancy facility to keep up my training at. I'd be better off staying here and using the tools in the Mavericks' clubhouse. Maybe giving lessons to some of the high school kids. And giving Holly stability for the first year of her life.

"Okay," I breathe out.

"Start stringing those hits together, slugger. I believe in you. Hey, I gotta run." He ends the call so fast that he cuts off his last word.

Slugger. Beats *My Man*.

SIX

LINDSEY

Brooks messaged me early this morning, about an hour before I was set to head to his place with the boys. Of course, Brandon has yet to drop them off, and Brooks has to get to the field soon, so now I'm stuck pacing my parents' front lawn while I wait for two men to show up and dump news on me.

BROOKS: Can we talk about something?

What was I supposed to say? *No, we can't talk. Not about anything. Not ever.*

I replied: *Sure.*

I'm sure Brooks wants to fire me. He's been quiet ever since our kiss. Which, while I did like it, that man kissed me. *So what if I kissed back!*

Brandon took the boys for an extra weekend to celebrate their fourth birthdays with his family. Their real birthday isn't until Wednesday, but since his parents were in town for something else and rented some penthouse at a hotel with an indoor waterpark, I couldn't exactly put my foot down. Plus, we still don't have a parenting plan nailed down. Mostly because he wants everything, and I would prefer he walk straight off a cliff.

Brooks pulls up first, and my heart kicks at the bones in my chest.

Please don't make that kiss more than it was. Please don't back out on me. I need this job.

"Howdy," I say, lifting a hand as he exits his driver's side door. I instantly feel every bit of my country roots.

I cross my arms over my stomach in an attempt to settle my nerves. Brooks moves to the back seat, and when he unfastens Holly's carrier, I exhale through my trembling lips. He's not firing me today, at least.

"I'm sorry I'm stuck here. My ex was never on time when we were together, so no reason he should start now, I guess." I give him a wry smile, and his eyes droop with what I think is a hint of empathy. I don't want him feeling sorry for me.

"But it's nice to see you, Miss Holly. Why, good morning!" I overexaggerate my smile as I take over the carrier, then squat to rock it on the ground while her tiny lips contort into a smile.

"She's doing that a lot more now," Brooks says. I glance up at him, squinting from the sun behind his head. I can see enough of his face to sense his pride. He's good with her. Better than he gives himself credit for.

"It's because her daddy makes her so happy. Isn't that right?" I tickle Holly's feet gently, and she smiles bigger. I hand her one of the soft toys clipped to the handle of her carrier, then stand back up and meet Brooks's gaze. There's definitely an awkward barrier between us. It's been a week since our kiss, and I don't think we've said more than a few words to one another during shift exchanges for his daughter.

"So . . ." I clasp my hands in front of my body and suck my lips into a tight line.

"Right," he breathes out, laughing lightly. Maybe a little

nervously. Is he nervous because he kissed me? Or is he nervous because he's never let someone go before?

"I really am sorry about this. You having to come here, I mean. It won't happen again."

Not that I can control Brandon's disregard for me and my schedule, but I mean the words as best as I can.

"No need to apologize. Seriously," he says, waving a hand. My shoulders inch down, my muscles relaxing by about ten percent. I exhale through a tiny O I make with my lips.

"Phew," I snicker, wiping my brow in jest. Though there might be some real sweat beading up there.

"But about that . . . me coming here. Or you not being at my place. Or . . . fuck, let me start over."

He drops his gaze and shoves his hands into the pockets of his hoodie. He's wearing compression pants under his black Mavericks' practice shorts, and it's hard to ignore his muscular thighs.

"I'd like to revisit the idea of you moving in with me. I think it might really help me out, I mean. And I wouldn't expect you to work for free. Or pay rent. I did some research, and I think I can swing seventeen-fifty a week plus room and board for you and the boys. We'd need to split groceries and stuff like that, but I'm gonna be in Sweetwater a little longer than I thought, and I just think—"

"Yes!" I blurt out.

Brooks blinks a few times, then laughs nervously through a tempered smile.

"Yeah?" His brow lifts on one side. It's cute. *Too cute.*

"Yes. I love taking care of Holly. And if you are really good with those salary terms, I can't refuse your offer. Brooks, I need to get out of this house. I love my parents, but also . . ." I blow up at the loose hairs tickling my forehead.

He chuckles.

"Yeah, I'm sure it's hard going from running your own

household to being in your childhood bedroom again," he says.

"With two hyper boys of my own. Yeah, it's hard. Which leads to my only question. You have one bedroom?" I squint as I level him with my query. While there's a small part of me that loves the one-bed trope idea, I'm not exactly in a position to see that through. Especially if it would be Brooks, me, and three kids on the same mattress.

"For sure. I hear you. I actually talked to Roddy a few days ago, and there's that place on his street—the one I mentioned before."

"Back when this was a crazy idea?" I joke.

He laughs, glancing down, and a touch of pink hits his cheeks.

"Yeah, that time. Anyhow, it's a two-story, and I know stairs suck—"

"Not when you're a four-year-old boy," I point out.

He points at me and nods.

"Valid point," he says. "It also has horse property in the back."

My eyes light up when I realize he's talking about the old Quinn property. That house was my dream house when I was a kid. I can see with my adult eyes that the place is falling apart in places, but it's got good bones. And it would be really great to have access to the land for the boys. For Holly.

For me.

I could have a horse.

I shake my head when I realize how far ahead I'm dreaming. Who knows how long Brooks will be in town. *But he's in town now . . .*

"I didn't know that place was for sale." I thought it was abandoned, actually.

Brooks shakes his head.

"The owners are renting it. I guess Roddy knows the

investor, some horse guy who plans to retire there one day or something. But he was talking to Roddy about making some money off the place in the meantime, so Roddy put in a word for me. Anyhow, the guy called me last night and said the place is mine if I want it. The rent isn't much more than the apartment I'm in."

My lips twitch at the corners, that urge to smile bigger than I should, hard to hold back.

"So, it's a deal?" He looks at me with one eye squinting, and I swear he's holding his breath. I know he's desperate for the help. I saw the legal paperwork he was working through on the counter in his apartment the other day, and he mentioned his paternity test coming up to prove to the state he's Holly's father. He fell into fatherhood, but damn if he's not putting in the work to do this right.

I hold out my hand to shake on our arrangement, but curl my fingers away when he reaches for me.

Holding up a finger with my other hand, I add one more ask to our deal.

"I still plan to go to school." I hold my breath and meet his gaze with my own, biting down on my lower lip like a bad poker player who just pushed her chips to the center of the table. Maybe I should have waited until we were literally sharing a roof before I threw the school thing out there. It's only that I have spent the last few days building myself back up for it after feeling so dejected after my meeting with the dean. I understand the hill I'm climbing . . . *from the bottom*. I owe it to myself.

"Of course," Brooks says, and I sink onto my heels with relief.

"Thank God!" I grasp his hand in both of mine and begin shaking it profusely. My enthusiasm must tickle him, because he starts to throw his head back with laughter.

"*Ahem.*"

The sour tone that colors the increasingly familiar disdain

in my ex's fake throat-clearing kills the temporary joy in the air, and I drop my hands from Brooks's and twist my body so I'm facing Brandon as he stands at the edge of my parents' lawn.

"You're late." I glare at him with the same hard look he's giving me.

"Someone forgot to pack the boys' clean underwear, so we had to make a stop at Target this morning so they don't show up to preschool commando." He's dangling their backpacks in both fists on either side of his body while his eyelids flutter in that judgmental way I've become numb to.

"Hi, Mom! We're ready! Let's go!" Deacon races past me toward the van. He likes to be the one to pull the sliding door. Riggs stops at my side long enough to throw his arms around me, and the embrace lands more like a punch to the bladder.

"Good morning. Get in the van with your brother," I say, dropping a kiss on what smells like dirty hair. I scrunch my nose as I bring my focus back to Brandon.

"I suppose you didn't make sure they showered since I didn't pack a whole damn bath for them?" I purse my lips, and he responds with his typical fake laugh.

"Who's this? Pool boy?" He glances toward Brooks, then lowers his gaze to the sweet baby playing happily in her carrier by Brooks's feet. My frown picks up into a smirk. It's pretty fucking obvious who Brooks is, and it's not a pool boy. He's wearing Maverick's team gear, *for the love of Pete.*

"We don't have a pool here." I decide giving him a non-answer is a lot more satisfying, but Brandon brushes my snarky comment off and heads right to Brooks to introduce himself.

"Hi, I'm Brandon. I'm their father." He takes Brooks's hand with a firm grip, and I can't help but titter lightly at Brooks's reaction. His mouth curves up on the side closest to me, and he glances my way with a flash of an expression that reads *the fuck?*

"Are you going to be hanging around here?" Brandon continues. "Because I should know anyone who might be around my boys for longer than a short interaction."

"*Our* boys. And are we really doing this?" I step into my ex's personal space enough that he seems compelled to drop his vice grip on Brooks's hand.

"Doing what, Linds?" His fake smile is as gross as the pretend laugh.

"Pointing out new people who might be hanging around our boys all of a sudden?"

I'm, of course, insinuating Caitlyn, his former student who I caught him having an affair with, and who I am *certain* joined them all for the birthday festivities. Not to mention their stay in the penthouse suite.

Brandon rolls his eyes as he peels his glare away from me, gesturing toward Brooks before sauntering toward his Land Rover.

"I'm his freaking nanny, dumbass. Not a cougar," I bite out. Not that I'm that much older than Brooks. Hell, maybe four years at the most. And Brandon's older than me. And Caitlyn just graduated from college. *Grrrr!* I hate that he's made me feel defensive.

"Hey, Brandon," Brooks says all of a sudden. I swallow down the dry knot lodged in my esophagus. I want to reach for his arm and stop him from following my ex to his vehicle, but my feet seem firmly planted in the earth. Probably because a small part of me is hoping Brooks is going to punch my ex in the teeth.

"What, kid?" Brandon's words are purposeful, meant to belittle me and put Brooks in his place. It's because my ex has always been an alpha without the street cred to back it up. He's an academic nerd. He gets off on being smarter than other people and throwing big words into conversations where they don't belong.

"I just thought you should know I'm her father. Right

there," he says, nodding toward Holly. "And you and I might run into each other a lot on account of Lindsey and I being roommates."

Brandon's smug grin droops instantly, and his focus zips to me. I merely waggle my fingers from my folded-arm posture. My turn to grin.

"Oh, and one more thing," Brooks adds, stepping in close enough to put one of his wide palms on Brandon's shoulder. He meets him eye-to-eye, and from my vantage point, the physique comparison is comical. Brandon's skinny pants and fitted dress shirt aren't helping his slim frame. He looks like a well-dressed pile of bones Brooks spit out after eating a whole chicken.

"What's that?" Brandon grits out.

Brooks leans in close, and his mouth curves into a faintly devilish smile.

"I ain't no kid."

His words linger between the two of them for a beat before Brooks pats his hand twice on Brandon's shoulder and marches away. He stops at Holly's carrier, near my feet, and squats to give his daughter his index finger. She wraps her tiny fingers around it and gurgles. Brooks glances up at me cautiously.

"He leave?"

Just then, Brandon rumbles his Land Rover into drive, and pulls away.

"Yeah, he sure did." My smile spreads the farther away his annoying PROF ME license plate gets.

I shift my attention to Brooks when he stands, and he holds out a fist for me to bump. I push my knuckles into his, and our fingers press together for a moment. It feels . . . like more than a fist bump.

"Good riddance," he finally says, his eyes narrowing on mine until the blue is literally all I see. "That guy? He's a dick."

"He is," I agree.

And then he leaves me with this mysterious knowing smile, a look I plan on dissecting and obsessing over—along with that jealous display by my ex—for the rest of the day.

I daresay this day of mine is looking up.

SEVEN
BROOKS

I've never really lived with another person. I mean, yeah . . . I've been living with Holly for nearly two months, but that's a different circumstance. She doesn't talk. She cries or makes a dozen other fascinating, occasionally gross, sounds, but Holly and I don't carry on two-sided conversations. Not yet anyhow.

I'm a quiet guy, and maybe the fact I've spent so much time alone is to blame. When I was in kindergarten, I let myself into the house after school with my own key. I made my own bowl of oatmeal for breakfast in the morning before school, packed my own lunch, and made sure my ass was out the door in time for the bus. I never had a parent around to do those things. Even when my mom was home, she was usually passed out on the couch or in her room.

Today, however, has not been quiet. Lindsey hasn't stopped talking since the moment she hauled her first box into this house. I'm actually shocked her voice isn't hoarse. And what's weird is the way I don't mind. Rather, I keep catching myself smiling and laughing, and my face is starting to hurt.

I also keep staring at her, and that's the part that's going to get me into trouble. I can feel it. I'm not shutting it down, but I feel it—that dangerous pull. And I think she feels it, too.

We both step into the same hallway, each of us holding a box, and our shoulders touch as we pass one another. Lindsey giggles, and I grumble even though I don't mind that she's in my way.

"Sorry," she says. I grabbed the wrong box. This one goes in the boys' room.

She glances over her shoulder and smiles. We decided putting the boys in the room farthest from mine would be best for Holly. I've been lucky getting her to sleep decently, and Deacon and Riggs aren't built for naps. They're like walking alarms.

"I can bring up the rest," I say, tucking the box of towels just inside the hall bathroom, then rushing down the stairs to pull the remaining things from the back of her van. I hook the hangers holding a few dresses and coats on my thumb, then fold the garments in half to make it easier to tuck them under my arm. I scoop up a pillowcase stuffed with bedding along with a plastic caddy filled with hair products, combs and brushes, then tap the button to close up the van before rushing back inside.

It's going to rain today. Any minute, actually. And this house is surrounded by a lot of dirt. We barely beat the mud that's sure to rise up like a moat around the porch. And since the boys have amused themselves by sprinting across the field in the back most of the day, I can't help but project the dirty floors that are in my future once the first few drops fall from the sky. And yet I'm still happy with all of it. The chaos. The mess.

The full house.

"You can just drop that on my mattress!" Lindsey hollers when she spots me halfway up the stairs. She's pacing in the kitchen with Holly, who must have woken up when I was outside. I drop her clothing and hair products off in her room, then fly down the stairs to take over diaper duty while Lindsey finishes making Holly a bottle.

"Hey, we're a pretty good team," she muses.

I laugh softly and wink, "Yeah."

It's probably smart to think of us that way. A team. It's platonic, and friendly. Works within the rules I've mentally set for myself.

I'm good at teams. I don't want to sleep with my teammates. So, maybe that will help me curb this nagging fantasy about sleeping with Lindsey.

"It's ready," she says, and I glance over my shoulder to catch her pulling her sweatshirt over her head. She's wearing a black tank top underneath, and her skin is so smooth. The curve of her shoulders guides my gaze to her collarbones, then lower to the crests of her full breasts. I stop at the hard peaks poking through the tight black fabric.

Shit.

"Thank you," I say, clearing my throat and turning my focus back to my child. I fold up the dirty diaper and snap Holly's onesie back together. I'm going to need to get one of those diaper genie things. I think the grocery store manager is going to ban me from taking entire stacks of plastic bags every time I purchase something, which is how I've been getting by so far. It's the best I've got for now, though, so I stuff the soiled diaper in one of the bags, then twist it and toss it in the trash.

"We managed to get everything inside before the sun set. Are you sure you don't need to go to the stadium tonight?" Lindsey takes over holding Holly and feeding her while I wash my hands. I fish my phone from my sweatpants pocket to check the game status, and when I see the cancelled alert, I exhale and flip the screen to show Lindsey.

"The only time I'm happy about a rainout," I say through a laugh.

I wasn't starting tonight, so showing up was optional. It's why we had to rush this move, though. My next few weekends are taken up by games and travel, and I don't want Lindsey to do all the heavy lifting on her own. I was still carrying this nagging feeling that I should show up for the game regardless, to put in face time. I get more starts than any other infielder, yet I'm still not getting enough to produce the right kind of numbers. If I want to start next season in Texas rather than in minor-league ball, I need to get as many plate appearances as I can.

But if nobody is there, then I'm not missing out. And that means I can give my mind over to the present completely, and right back to the various sins I keep thinking about committing.

"Pizza?" I swirl a flyer around on the kitchen island, some coupon sheet I picked up along with the mailbox key at the post office.

"Pizza!" The boys race between Lindsey, Holly, and me on their way to the stairs. My eyes go to the floor and the shoe-shaped mud prints that dot their path. I snicker.

"I'll buy," Lindsey says, her gaze on the same messy floor. She sets Holly in her carrier, then sighs as she moves toward the sink. Before she can run one of the dish cloths under the water, I graze her wrist with my fingers.

"I'll clean when they sleep. If you do that now, they're just going to run through and do it again." I know that's what I would have done when I was their age. Of course, there was no one around to clean up after me most of the time. I had to tidy up myself unless I wanted to live with dirty floors. Dirty everything, honestly.

Lindsey nods.

"Now see, living with you is going to be good for me. Maybe I'll stop spinning my wheels and making the same dumb decisions over and over again." Her laugh falls out sporadically, then suddenly halts when our eyes meet. "I mean, doing things like cleaning before the boys make another mess. Not making mistakes like you and me—"

I hold up my hand before she says another word, which would only make the weird vibe stronger.

"I got it."

Believe me. I got it.

There's one pizza place in Sweetwater, and thankfully, it's decent. By the time the pies arrive, Lindsey has convinced her boys to take their baths and put on pajamas. They fall asleep about twenty minutes after stuffing down two slices apiece, and I'm pretty exhausted myself, having polished off half a pizza on my own.

I groan as I shovel Deacon onto one arm, then grunt when I lift his brother with the other.

"Are you trying to show off?" Lindsey says through a tired, half-hearted smile.

"By throwing my back out lifting two gremlins? No. But I'd like to make sure these two stay asleep, and I was thinking about watching a movie, so I'm willing to chance it."

"Movie?" Deacon says, cracking open a sleepy eye while rubbing the other with his fist.

"No movies for you. You two have a big day tomorrow." Deacon's mouth contorts into a goofy smile just before his head falls back to my shoulder. His brother missed the whole conversation—*thank God!*

Tomorrow is the boys' birthday. They turn four officially. Lindsey uses that word—*officially*—to spite her ex, who threw the boys a big party at a fancy resort. "That party doesn't get to be the official one," she keeps saying. I tend to agree. Mostly because I don't think her ex deserves any credit. I've had one conversation with him, but it was enough to paint a pretty vivid picture. How a confident, beautiful woman like Lindsey ended up with a narcissistic prick like that blows my mind. I guess his losing her is the universe's way of self-correcting.

I tuck the boys in, and they immediately snuggle beneath their blankets, pulling them over their heads. I smile at the baseball print on the fabric. *Maybe I'll get to coach them a little this summer.*

I shut their door softly and tiptoe into my room, where Holly is asleep in a crib in the corner. There's a small den that branches off my room. I tried to give Lindsey the primary bedroom, but she insisted I take it to share with Holly. She also hinted that it felt awkward to work for me but live in the big room. She has no idea the places I've lived. I could get comfortable in the shed.

But this room, and this house, even though it's old, is nice. It feels right. And it makes my heart happy for Holly to be in a place like this. If I can clear out the old bookshelves and broken roll-top desk that the previous owner left in the den, it will make a nice transition space as she gets older. She's already aged so much. I've only had her for a little more than a month, and she's grown and changed in so many spectacular ways. I feel as though I need to document every single day with her. Every smile. I touch her nose, and she crinkles it without waking.

"There's something about a girl dad." Lindsey's whisper startles me, but I somehow don't jump in place. My pulse picks up, though.

"Girl dad," I repeat, checking the volume on the baby monitor, then turning to face Lindsey. She's leaning inside the doorway, the same black tank top she's worn all day still glued to her body but rolled up just enough at the hem to expose her belly button. She's wearing a giant pair of sweatpants that she's rolled at the top, and her tiny feet peek out in bright white socks.

This is going to be really hard to maintain a friendship. I like this vision too much. A home with a family.

I nod toward the hallway, and she steps back, making enough room for me to exit. I pull the door shut halfway, then lean against the wall opposite her, dropping my hands into the pockets of my sweats and lowering my gaze just enough to catch a quick glimpse of her midriff. *Fucking hell.*

"You're really good at this dad thing, I hope you know," she says, kicking her foot forward and tapping my shin with her toe. I think she's flirting, and while I want to do it back, I have to draw a line.

"I didn't really have a role model for parenting, so thanks," I say, pushing off from the wall and heading back to the living room. It's barely eight o'clock, and it's pouring outside. The heavy darkness makes the world feel small somehow, and it seems later than it is. I'm tired, and I'm sure Lindsey is exhausted. But my mind is too loud for me to hit the sheets just yet. I should be in the stadium right now, charting the pitcher for the next time I face him. I'm kind of glad I'm not, though. I'm glad I'm here.

Lindsey flops down on one end of the sofa, so I take the opposite side, propping my feet on the large ottoman in the center of the room. I flip through a few channels and stop when I land on that movie where Keanu Reeves plays a washed-up quarterback who goes undercover as a surfer.

"I should have married Keanu Reeves," Lindsey jokes.

I chuckle.

"Maybe *I* should marry Keanu Reeves."

"*Hmm*, you two would make a pretty great couple. Can I still be your nanny?" She grabs a piece of crust from one of the pizza boxes I brought into the living room and bites it in half before shifting her gaze to me and lifting a brow.

"Lindsey, of *course*, you would be our nanny." I maintain my serious expression until she nods and looks away.

"Good. I'll plan the wedding."

Our light laughter fades as we settle into watching a young Keanu and Patrick Swayze float on long boards in the ocean. As hard as I try to keep my focus on the screen, though, my gaze keeps being pulled to my left. I catch the small movements of Lindsey's hands in my periphery. She's picking at her fingers and chewing at the inside of her cheek. She was doing that when her ex arrived the other day, too.

I pick up the only throw pillow in this place and toss it toward her knees; she catches it against her body and pulls her lips into a tight smile as she glares at me.

"Something on your mind?" I ask.

Her eyes narrow a bit as she holds the pillow by the seams, her fingers needling the edges as if she's weighing whether or not to throw it back or answer my question. One of those feels safer than the other, at least for me.

"I got the boys one of those enormous Lego sets. At least, I think it's enormous. It's the castle. My parents actually bought it for me to give to them, though, so I feel like a fraud. And it's not like Legos are a waterpark, or a resort, or—"

"They'll love it," I say, stopping her spiral.

Her eyes snap to mine, and I can read the hurt behind them like a headline in the paper. I tilt my head and hold her stare.

"I promise," I add.

Her body sinks a few inches deeper into the cushions as she exhales. She's fighting so hard to keep the glassiness in her eyes from turning into actual tears. I'm not sure how to convince her that no matter what, she's going to be her boys' favorite. I'm not sure what happened between them, but it's obvious who the good person is.

"My mom died when I was in college," I begin. My heart thumps against the wall of my chest, and my palms are sweating, so I tuck them under my thighs. I'm not sure why I'm sharing this, but I am compelled to. Lindsey needs to know my credentials, how I know what an incredible mother looks like, and doesn't.

"I'm so sorry," she says in a soft, raspy tone.

I shake my head and briefly hold up my palm.

"No, it's fine. I mean it. My mom was an addict, and she

was never really there, even when she was. The way I grew up was, well, let's just say it wasn't ideal." I wince at the memory and the confession.

Lindsey shifts in her seat, pulling one leg up and turning to face me, so I do the same. I try to hold her gaze, but it's hard to talk about my parents and look people in the eyes. It's something I've noticed before, like when I spoke to the cops the dozens of times they came to our apartment when I was a kid, or how I talked to the teachers at school, or my coaches. The moment my home life comes up, I shy away. Maybe I'm afraid of people seeing the similarities in our features—me and my parents. I don't want to be anything like them.

"My dad was a dealer. They both were, really. My mom dealt to support her own habit, though, and it's my dad's fault she was hooked. At least, that's the story she told me on the days she was semi-sober. He's been in prison for most of my life. In and out of it, I heard. I'm not sure at this point, actually. I quit keeping tabs on him the day I left for college."

"Brooks, that's . . . that's fucking awful. I'm sorry." She drops her gaze to her lap and kneads her hands together again, so I reach across the sofa and rest my palm over her to make her stop. The touch is a pause button on living and breathing, the air suddenly still, our bodies frozen and pulse stopped. I can't feel mine. I can't feel hers. But I do feel *her*.

I swallow and move away slowly, keeping my gaze safely off to the side. "Sorry. I . . . I don't want you to feel bad for me. That's why I—"

"I get it. I do that a lot. Worry, I guess?" She shrugs, and her movement draws my attention to her body. I flit my gaze up to her eyes before I derail my intentions.

"We all worry. Or we should, at least. Especially when we're parents, so I'm learning." I give her a lopsided smile as a breathy laugh slips out. "You're a great mom. Even better than you are at nannying." She quivers with a silent laugh, and her lips tinge up on the corners. She's beautiful when she smiles. "They're going to like the Legos. I promise."

Lindsey sucks in her bottom lip, the glossiness still there in her eyes, but I can tell it's for a different reason.

"Thank you," she mouths, before closing the distance between us and throwing her arms around me and sinking into my chest. My arms close around her naturally, without thought, and by the time I realize that I'm holding her and dropping a soft kiss to the top of her head, it's too late to do anything but let it ride.

And I do. For the rest of the movie, and well into the hours after she falls asleep in my lap.

EIGHT
LINDSEY

It's a good dream, despite the fact it's only a dream. I'm willing to appreciate it for what it is. I rub my eyes until I'm awake enough to understand my surroundings, and it takes me a few more seconds to recognize the couch, this living room, and the strange absence of ghosts from my past.

I'm in the Quinn home. My boys are safe. I *feel* safe.

I sit up at that realization and glance around the dark space. Brooks was here when I fell asleep. On him.

Oh jeez.

I bury my face in my palms and sigh. At least I wasn't drinking wine. When I think about how I literally threw myself into him, though—*gah!* I may as well have been drunk. I drop my hands into my lap and gather up the throw blanket he must have put over me. I bring it to my chest and press my nose into the faux fur, breathing it in. It smells like Brooks—a mix of linen dryer sheets and musky body wash. I shouldn't pay such close attention to the way he smells.

I push the blanket from my legs, then stand, stretching my arms above my head while I squint to read the time on the microwave oven across the kitchen. It's too dark to be eight in the morning, so that must be a three I'm looking at. My mouth contorts with a sudden yawn. Definitely three a.m.

The faint light from upstairs catches my eye, so I cautiously take the steps until I spot movement in Brooks's room. I pause just outside his doorway and hold my breath so I don't disturb him. He's holding Holly against his chest, rubbing circles on her back as he hums softly, his eyes closed. I bet he has a nice singing voice. His lashes flutter as he rotates and sways, and when his gaze catches mine, a soft smile tugs at the corners of his mouth.

"Hush, little baby, don't say a word. Daddy's gonna buy you a mockingbird . . ."

His whispered song is sweet, and it pushes my smile deeper into my cheeks. I was right. He can sing. At least enough for it to leave a mark. He lays his daughter back in her crib before treading toward me with light steps.

"I'm sorry if she woke you. She needed a change," he says in a hushed tone as he pulls the door mostly shut.

"I don't think I heard her. I woke up from a dream." I run my fingers through my tangled hair and scratch at my head. Brooks reaches forward and helps by tucking one of my locks behind my ear. His fingertips linger near my cheek, and his tongue peeks out of his lips. The sight sends a rush of dopamine deep into my chest, making my heart flutter.

"What was your dream?" he says, his knuckles grazing my jawline as his hand falls away. The touch is faint enough to be accidental, but the way his gaze slides to my throat sends a different message.

"Well, at first, I was in my old house, and my ex was there. He was telling me I wouldn't want to join him for his conference in the city because I wouldn't know anyone, and I'd be bored."

Brooks's gaze lifts to mine as he rests a shoulder blade against the door frame. His head tilts.

"He say that to you a lot?"

I lift one shoulder and pull my mouth into a crooked, brief smile.

"When we first got married, never. Then I had the boys, and it made sense that I stayed home. I didn't really have anyone to leave the kids with for a getaway. Still, it's nice to be asked. To be *wooed*." A bashful laugh slips from my lips.

"She likes to be *wooed*." He says it with a smirk, amused but also as if he's taking notes.

"All women like to be wooed, Brooks. Every single one of us." I step forward and tap a finger on the center of his chest before walking toward my room, hoping he'll follow while knowing he shouldn't.

He does.

It's dangerous territory we're in, but it feels good to be in the vicinity of affection. It's been so long since someone looked at me like they wanted me for more than a grocery trip and babysitting. And yeah, technically, the whole reason I'm living in this house is for babysitting. But right now, that's not how Brooks is treating me. And I'm going to let myself indulge just a little.

"So, what else happened in your dream? After your ex told you not to bother joining him in the city?" Brooks hovers near my doorway while I move toward my bed. My room is barely unpacked—stacks of clothing on the floor, a blanket thrown over my mattress because I never got around to putting on sheets today. It's still a million times homier than the spare room in my parents' house.

"Well," I say, looking up at the ceiling as I spin then flop down on the foot of my bed. "I went to the city anyway, and when I got there, I saw my husband having dinner with one of his former students. A very beautiful former student."

I drop my gaze to his, and he blinks a few times.

"That part wasn't in the dream, was it?"

I suck my lips into a tight straight line and slowly shake my head.

"He's an idiot," he says.

I breathe out a short laugh and exhale before falling back on my palms and kicking my feet back and forth.

"Mostly, yeah. I mean, he has a PhD, but I think he cheated to get it. I mean, once a cheater . . ."

We both laugh quietly at my terrible joke.

"But"—I straighten my neck and widen my eyes on his—"My dream did get better."

"How so?" he asks while slowly working his way across my room toward me. I scoot to my right, making room for him to sit next to me, and the way my body hums with nervous energy should be a warning sign. If it is, I choose to ignore it.

"You showed up, for starters," I say, biting the tip of my tongue as it peeks out of my nervous smile. I fight my urge to glance to my left, but I can feel Brooks's eyes on me.

"Did I kick your ex's ass?"

I shake my head, my smile itching to grow. I give in to a sideways glance instead.

"You gave me a job, moved me into my dream house, then put me to sleep while I wallowed in self-pity." I pull my knees up and hug them as he holds my stare, letting his head fall to the same side so we match.

Neither of us blinks for several seconds, until the itch to laugh is too great and we both give in. I lean into his side, and he pushes his weight back into me. I could stay like this—bare arm against arm—until it leads to something more, but this is enough, and I'm not drunk, so I know better.

"You do know that's what really happened, right? I mean, except for the wallowing in self-pity part."

I roll my eyes and utter, "I know. There was a little wallowing, though."

He shakes his head.

"Being human is not wallowing. And wanting your kids to feel your love is far from self-pity. I know your feelings are about more than resorts versus Legos."

The gentle nudge of his elbow at my side is followed by another, and his second poke finds my ticklish spot.

"She likes to be wooed, *and* she's ticklish," he says, wiggling his fingers between us as if he's about to pin me with tickles. More temptation. *Sigh.*

I narrow my gaze on him.

"Are you scouting me like one of your opponents?"

He rocks back with a short laugh then gets to his feet, shaking his head as he pushes his palms into his pockets.

"We're on the same team. So no, Lindsey. I'm merely taking notes on what you like."

His upper lip twitches, the movement so small that I wouldn't notice if I wasn't staring at his face. It makes his right eye flinch just a hair. And the quiet second or two that follows feels like a slip in time, lasting for minutes rather than the tiny breath it does.

"You know, if . . ." He stops himself, biting the inside of his cheek.

My lips buzz, and I have to suck the top one in to scratch the itch. It keeps me from asking—*if what?*

If I didn't work for him. If he wasn't mere weeks into learning he was a father. If this house wasn't full of kids, and I wasn't looking at what I fear is about to become a messy divorce.

Another time. Different versions of us.

"Nevermind," he mumbles.

He walks to the corner of my room and pulls out the comforter, folded along with a few towels, from my laundry basket. He turns to me and nods his head for me to scoot back in my bed. I do, hugging one pillow to my chest while resting my head on the other before he fluffs out the floral bedspread that I stole from my parents' house. The blanket's weight is soothing, and I pull in the edges so I'm cocooned.

"Get some sleep. I have to be up in a few hours, so I'll try to be quiet when I leave for workouts. Maybe Holly will sleep in."

I close my eyes and pull my blanket under my chin, embracing the darkness behind my eyelids.

"It's not Holly who's going to wake me. Those boys haven't slept past six since birth. But don't worry, my eyes are programmed to pop open at five-fifty-five every day. It's like magic," I say, feeling the pull of slumber take me under.

"A constant five a.m. sounds like a curse to me, but I love that you see it as a blessing." He chuckles. "Good night, Lindsey. I hope you get to finish your dream. And I hope whoever he is in there, he woos you."

I hope you do, too, Brooks.

NINE
BROOKS

Somehow, Lindsey and I have managed to fall into a comfortable friendship, and it only took a week of living together to get past the thick tension that filled the room whenever we were alone together.

Of course, Holly has been waking up a lot at night, and Lindsey's boys have been running to her bedroom in the middle of the night to sleep with her because they're scared, so our alone time has been drastically limited. Those few moments when I'm not at the ballpark, and Lindsey's not at the table taking her online classes, have been filled with unpacking boxes and figuring out the many quirks of this place. Like after dinner last night, when we tag-teamed locating which light switch kept causing a full-house power outage every time we touched it. It's the downstairs bathroom light. Roddy and his son, Jake, are coming over later to take a look at it with me.

It's all been a lot—finishing the legal process for Holly, getting established with a pediatrician, moving, house repairs, parenting, and stressing out over this new blended-family situation I chose. Oh, and baseball. Yeah, the thing I need to be great at if I want to give my daughter the best life I can. I need to get the rest of my shit in order so I can focus again.

Despite my scattered brain and chaos-ridden life, I'm somehow getting it done on the field. I made some highlight reels after my game last night—first with my diving stop that I turned for a double play to get out of bases loaded, then almost hitting for the cycle. I was one triple away. I swear they're harder to hit than homers. I need to really bear down on my speed work. I can be faster on the bases. Every skill I dominate gives me an edge. Play hard this season, get to Texas next year. That's the plan.

But first, I need to get this paperwork approved, make my custody official, and order a certified copy of Holly's updated birth certificate. Until I have every single dot dotted and T crossed, I simply don't feel settled. Even if I hadn't grown up the way I did, I would still feel scared about losing her. But the stakes seem escalated when I try to calm my worries and chase sleep at night. It has been elusive and rare. It's going to catch up with me, for sure. But not today.

"Lindsey?" I have tried to knot this tie around my neck a dozen times. I give up.

I saunter out of my bathroom and head downstairs, where she is camped out at the table with a dozen books open around her laptop. She's trying to knock out three college courses online so she can enroll in the university's advertising school and finish her degree. I wish I could help her, but she needs to complete three of my worst subjects—biology, algebra, and some course that surveys the world's religions. I only hope she's better with a tie than I am with parts of the cell.

She pushes her reading glasses up on top of her head, and they get buried in the hair she's tied into these crazy-looking buns on either side of her crown. She's cute in her glasses— and with the hair knots, to be honest—something I have kept to myself because things are going well. We've found a groove, the kind that throwing out words like "cute" can mess up.

"Come here," she says, twisting in the kitchen chair and uncrossing her legs. I don't know how she sits like that on a wooden chair. I can barely sit cross legged on the floor.

I step in front of her as she stands on her toes to reach the tie I've butchered around my neck. She unfurls my attempt at a Windsor knot, and her mouth is bunched with her concentration. That's another cute thing I keep to myself.

"So first, you need to make this side twice as long," she explains, tugging one end of my tie lower along my chest. I drop my chin to watch her work, and her fingers thread through the gray silk, wrapping one strip of fabric around the other until suddenly she's pushing a perfect knot toward my throat.

"Now you try," she says, reaching to undo her work.

I flatten my hands over hers and stare directly into her eyes.

"If you untie this thing, I'll scream like Riggs and Deacon do when you force feed them broccoli."

Our stare-off lasts about three seconds before she relaxes her hands under mine and we both let go.

"Fine," she says, blowing up at the loose hairs in her face, then dropping her reading glasses back down the bridge of her nose. "But if you don't practice, you're never going to learn."

She sort of sings that last part, and it makes me chuckle. I bet her mom talked to her and her sister a lot like that, at least when she was around. I'd take a part-time mom like hers over the addict I was stuck with.

"Are you sure you don't want me to come with you? I can help with Holly," she says while I grab a protein drink from the fridge and shake it. I'm too nervous to eat anything, but I have a game tonight. I'm going to need to pack away some energy.

"I can handle it. Plus, if she gets fussy, I want to show off that I know what to do." I shrug and gulp down the rest of my shake before tossing the empty bottle in the trash.

"Unless, of course, she has one of those epic meltdowns that leaves you utterly helpless." She laughs for a second, then snaps her mouth shut and draws a line across her lips when she realizes the effect of her words probably missed the humorous target.

"You're going to be fine. You have everything ready. And this part is basically the formality. You're her dad. You have the DNA to show it. And you've been doing great. I mean, look at the nanny you went out and found for her?"

She breathes on her nails, then rubs them on the center of her T-shirt before heading back to her seat. I roll my eyes, but her confidence does calm my nerves some. I wish I could help with her anxiety in return.

Her ex picked up the boys for the day, for some behind-the-scenes thing for the monster truck rally out at the fairgrounds. Lindsey said things like that are completely out of character for the guy, which I can tell, even from only meeting him once. He doesn't strike me as the type who's into motors, or sports, or outdooring. *Academic* is the word Lindsey uses to describe him, but from where I come from, the guy's basically a snob.

She threw herself into her studies the moment the boys left this morning. She does this thing when she begins to daydream, though, where she hooks a strand of hair around her index finger, then wraps it around her first knuckle until it nearly cuts off her circulation. I'm pretty sure she does that when she's stressing over her boys being gone. *Gone with her ex.*

"I think we might get the castle done this weekend," I say, to pull her out of her own head.

She lifts her gaze to take in the scattered Legos on the other end of the table, the drawbridge nearly complete. That was last night's big moment. Deacon figured it out on his own after dinner. A faint smile plays at her lips before her eyes shift to me.

"They really like their birthday gift, don't they?"

I nod.

"So do I," I tease. I've put my fair share of blocks in place. And maybe have a little envy that Deacon got to do the drawbridge.

Our shared gaze drifts into that too long territory, so when I feel the shift in the air and inside my chest, I drop my chin and feel my tie against my button down, then drop my hands to my pockets to make sure I have everything.

"What am I missing?" I ask.

"Uh . . ."

I look up and follow the direction of Lindsey's finger, which is pointing to my sleeping daughter nestled in her carrier.

"Right," I breathe out.

"Don't worry. That's just a sign you're legit. We parents lose our minds sometimes."

I take her pep talk to heart, then stride across the room and grab the handle. Just as I make my way to the door, though, there's a harried knock that startles me and wakes my napping baby.

"Shit," I mutter.

"I'll get it," Lindsey says, leaping from the chair while I raise the carrier to my chest so I can soothe Holly back to sleep before she really gets going. My face close to hers, I make the popping sound with my lips that seems to be her favorite thing lately. I'm so into this tiny world that I'm not paying close attention to Lindsey's interaction at the door until I hear a strange male voice say my name.

"Son," he says when I meet his stare.

The man standing in the doorway is a ghost. A shell of the man from my memories and in the photos in that box. The Jared Callahan I knew was a smoker who swore a lot, with muscles and a tattoo of a naked woman on his forearm. His hair was shaggy, always a bit dirty, and his mustache grown too long. This man's cheeks sink in, and his face is clean shaven, his hair buzzed and balding at his widow's peak. The tattoo is there, though. It's been covered some with other things, but if I tilt my head and look just right, it's a perfect match. It's an answer key barely disguised under time served.

"What are you doing here?" I shift the carrier in my hand, moving the baby seat to my side, away from the doorway.

I glance at Lindsey, hoping she'll see the seriousness in my eyes as my jaw tightens.

"I've been looking for you for a year. I got out last spring, served the last year on parole. They just approved my move last month, and I've been trying to get the courage to come see you."

I swallow hard, then bite, "Why?"

My father flinches, his eyes blinking rapidly. His nervous system was misfiring before his last run-in with the law, when I was in junior high. You push too much poison into your body, and it reacts. It's inevitable.

"Well, I was hoping—"

"I'm busy. You shouldn't have hoped," I say, cutting him off.

Lindsey has slowly made her way toward me, and when she reaches my side, she takes over holding Holly's carrier. My father's gaze darts to his grandchild, and his eyes widen as his mouth forms an O.

"Is that—"

"She's mine," Lindsey says, as if on instinct. My pulse races, my veins teeming with energy. If I need to throw him out of this house, I will. I'll carry him to the street and leave him for the dogs, or the teenage drag racers that I hear run their engines around here sometimes.

"Is this your wife?" he asks.

My mouth remains a hard line. I won't give him anything. Lindsey, however, chuckles politely.

"No, nothing like that. We're roommates. I'm living here with my kids. Brooks was just helping me to the car." Lindsey waves her hand as if this unwanted, unexpected visit isn't hitting me like an ax in the center of my chest. She's intent on building a story for him. What she doesn't know is that this man doesn't deserve a story. Or another minute of our time.

My dad's gaze drops to Lindsey's bare feet. She follows his sightline and curls her toes under.

"I was about to put on my shoes. I'm always running late," she says, laughing in a self-deprecating way.

"We have to go. I have . . . work," I say, catching myself. I'm sure he's figured out I got a contract to play ball. He's not here to see his son, the accountant.

I grasp the door and lean toward the man, who, though we are the same height, is half my weight.

"I'm sorry I bothered you. Maybe if you have time later this week, or—"

"Probably not." I shut the door before he can utter another word, then rest my fist on the wood before letting my forehead fall against my hand.

My entire body is vibrating. I tried to visit him when he got locked up, and he had zero interest. I played baseball as a kid, hoping maybe I'd get his attention, that he'd come home and get straight. Other kids had dads in the dugout coaching them. Their moms were in the stands, waiting with orange slices and cold-water bottles. They wore shirts with their sons' numbers. Nobody wore my number to anything.

I rode home with friends. I was invited to stay at their homes after games because their parents knew I didn't have anyone to go home to. I didn't get it when I was a kid, but looking back now as an adult, I see how they all took pity on me. I don't resent them for it, either. I love every family that was kinder to me than my own. Hell, Hunter damn near saved me when we were in high school.

"Come on. You don't want to be late," Lindsey says as her palm lands on the center of my back.

"I need a minute. I don't think I should drive right now," I say, my eyes closed and my forehead still pressed against the door.

"I know. I'm driving," she says.

I open my eyes and twist just enough to glance down at her feet. She put on shoes. She skipped the socks, but the sneakers are tied. My lip tugs up on one side, and I lift my gaze to her.

"So, that's my dad."

"Yeah, I pieced that together. Sorry I lied about Holly. I had a feeling you didn't want him to know."

I bring my palm to her shoulder and cup the curve of her arm.

"You read the room perfectly. I don't ever want him to know he has a grandchild. He would just ruin that relationship. It's better for Holly if she never knows he exists."

Lindsey's eyes hold on to mine for a moment, and the way they grow heavy, along with the downturn of her mouth, sends a wave of shame and guilt into my chest. I know how my words sound. But when you've lived through hell the way I have, you lose faith in second chances. Redemption is a fairytale.

"You should ride in the back seat, so you can watch her sleep." Lindsey pats the center of my chest, covering the wild thump of my angry heart. "You want to have a cool head in the courtroom, even if this is just a formality."

I drop my gaze a tick and nod. She's right.

I take Holly and her carrier from her and follow her out the door to her van. She presses the automatic door button on her key fob so I can load Holly in while she starts the van and cranks the air. The summer heat is beginning its brutal reign.

Once Holly's seat is locked in place, I slide into the one next to her. My gaze lands on Lindsey's in the rearview mirror.

"Hey, Linds?"

She arches a brow in the reflection.

"You're a great fuckin' nanny."

Her lips pull into a tight smile, and she drops her sunglasses down over her eyes before nodding.

"Damn right I am."

She backs out of our driveway, and I give my focus over to the one thing that matters most in this world—Holly. But I save one percent for someone else, sparing a few glances back to the mirror every few miles. I shouldn't have called her a nanny. She's a friend. Probably my best one at this point.

TEN

LINDSEY

Brooks's custody petition was approved, the court handed over the unofficial copy of Holly's birth certificate, and he hasn't stopped staring at it. I'd tease him, but he seems so relieved and happy, I don't want to ruin his euphoria. His father's drop-by the other day really shook him. But once the judge signed off, his world seemed to center again.

"I'm thinking of framing it," he says, craning his neck to keep the certificate in his view as he rounds the kitchen table in search of his compression sleeves. He left them on the back of the recliner in the living room before we left for his appointment, so I snagged them when we got home and have been holding them out for him to take for the past several minutes. He simply hasn't been able to pull his attention from Holly or her birth certificate long enough to notice them in my hand.

I clear my throat after he glances my way without clocking the fact I have what he's looking for. Finally, he pops his gaze up, and it sinks in. He laughs out a short "thanks" before snagging the sleeves and heading right back to the table to stare at the document. I'm not one hundred percent certain where my boys' birth certificates are, yet he's framing his daughter's.

"You should wait for the real thing to come in from Iowa. It will be embossed and everything." I waggle my brows, but Brooks waves a hand my direction.

"*Pssh*, I don't need the embossed one in a frame. This one is the first with my name on it. Right there. It's special." He drags the paper closer with the tip of his finger, then taps the line listing him as the father.

Of all the times Brooks has seemed attractive to me—which are many—he's never seemed sexier than this moment. The pride that stretches his grin well into his cheeks and the gleam in his eyes over something so simple sit in my heart. Brandon likes playtime with the boys, and it was always my favorite part of our marriage, watching him swing the boys around in the back yard or play wrestle with them on the living room floor covered in couch cushions. But those scenes were rare, and they were always brief. The last rays of sun if he got home from the college in time, or before bed on the days he stayed to work late.

Grading. Office hours. Faculty meetings and enrollment studies. There were so many things that kept him at the office late, and now, I can't help but assume they were all bullshit. He didn't come home when he could because his dick was too hungry for someone else. He passed up tickle time and tag so he could cheat on me.

Brooks disappears up the stairs just as my phone dings with a text. My stomach fills with dread at the sound. I hate messages now because they're almost always from Brandon. And they're usually curt and tinged with his special brand of superiority.

I carry my phone to the kitchen chair, where my books are still piled up from my morning study session. I close my eyes and draw in a deep breath.

Please be from my sister. My mom. A coupon for my favorite online clothing app.

I pop my eyes open and see my ex's name, and my chest tightens.

> BRANDON: We're heading back. The boys
> had a great day. I would really like to do more
> things with them. We'll talk.

My shoulders sag, and the polarization of his words mentally knocks me around. On the surface, Brandon wanting to do more with our sons is a wonderful thing. I should be thrilled about it. Healthy co-parenting looks like this on the surface, or so says the book I'm reading on the subject. Yet I can't help but feel the weight of skepticism. His words feel like he has an ulterior motive. Like he wants to show off how much fun he can have with them and win their favor. And all of it is against me.

I shake my head to rid myself of those sour thoughts. I have to keep my resentment separate from his relationship with our boys. So what if he never seemed to have time to do things with us as a family before. He's putting in the effort now, and isn't that more important? That the boys know they are equally loved despite their parents' separation?

I type back.

> ME: I'm glad. Talk to you soon.

Bile creeps up my esophagus, so I set my phone screen-down on the table and walk away for a few minutes. I unroll the yoga mat I stole from my mom when I moved, and sit in the center, stretching my arms up and closing my eyes while I focus on my breathing. I used to be good at this. I could do all the poses and clear my mind at the drop of a namaste. It's going to take more than a few deep breaths and a good stretch to get my head right now, though. Regardless, I give it a whirl, stretching forward until my fingertips reach the edge of the mat. My phone vibrates on the table, though, and my eyes pop open as my jaw tightens.

"I'm heading out. But I was thinking . . ." Brooks speeds down the stairs in his pre-game clothes. I've learned all too quickly that I like the way a man looks in baseball shorts and compression pants, and shirts. I like the way *Brooks* looks in these things. And in dark blue. And with hair that's a little too long for his hat.

I pull my legs in and hold my ankles as he passes me, then picks my phone up from the table. I'm about to protest—I don't really want to see what else my ex has to say—when Brooks hands my device to me, and I realize the ding wasn't from Brandon; it was from Brooks.

"I get free tickets for every game. And Louisville is a good team, so it should be a good game tonight. And if you and the boys are bored, maybe—"

I hold his expectant gaze, then look at his text, which includes a link for three tickets. My mouth ticks up on the side on reflex.

"I bet they would like that," I say.

"Yeah?" He threads his hands together behind his neck and squints one eye at me as if he's not sure.

"Uh, the boys think you are *way* cooler than I am. I know they'll want to go." I press the download button for the tickets and save them to my phone.

"I mean, I *am* pretty cool," he teases, exaggeratingly lifting a brow as he reaches toward me to help me to my feet. His grasp feels warm, and his grip practically engulfs my hand, and when he doesn't let go right away, even after I'm standing, my belly warms.

Shit. Not again.

I break our hold and quickly bend at my waist to snag the yoga mat I barely used. I turn my back to Brooks to tuck the mat into the hallway closet, where I decided it shall live, and by the time I come back to him, he's busy tucking a few energy bars into his gear bag. I'm not sure whether he's running away from our spontaneous electricity like I am, but he rushes out the door with a quick, "All right, see you at the game," and suddenly, other than the five-month-old who is fast asleep in the playpen behind the sofa, I'm all alone.

That's been the hardest part since Brandon and I split. It's the moments when I'm all by myself that my mind grows loud and my thoughts work against me. I feel like a failure, not as a mom, but as a woman. Like I chose wrong, married wrong, couldn't keep our relationship intact, and am getting exactly what I deserve—solitude. I know my mind is a liar, but it's also so very noisy.

I stand in the center of this big, empty house filled with very few of my things, and unravel all the decisions that landed me here. Am I better off? Are the boys? I know what the experts would say. I've read all their books in the two months since I moved out of the house I literally built with my ex. I get the impact of my decisions—showing my boys what a woman is worth, my independence and loyalty, and how to coexist with an ex-spouse in a healthy way.

But why do I feel as if this is all falling on my shoulders? Why does Brandon get to keep the house that I decorated? That I cleaned for three years, and that I rocked our boys to sleep in late at night. I won't walk away with nothing in the end; Brandon, for as much of a jerk as he is, has said a few times that he intends to push for an even split of our assets. I won't have to battle for money. But time? That's another story. And time with the boys, as wild as they are, is priceless.

I'm not sure how long I've been standing in place and staring at the empty wall by the front door to my temporary home when Deacon and Riggs barrel through and rush past me. It may have only been seconds, but I think it's veered closer to several minutes.

"Mom, Deacon says I can't keep the truck dad bought us here. He says it's a toy for Dad's house." Riggs pulls out a chair at the kitchen table and promptly flops into it on his knees before plunking a hefty toy monster truck on the tabletop.

I shake my head and pinch the bridge of my nose, rehashing my son's tattle in my head. I'm not quite sure who he's telling on, his brother or Brandon.

"I'm sorry, but huh?" I pull out a second chair for Deacon, who hoists his small backpack onto the table before holding his hands out toward his brother. Riggs proceeds to push the truck across the wood toward his brother. I snag it midway before it scuffs the table or falls to the floor with a bang that might wake Holly.

"This is not a ramp," I say, carrying the toy across the room to the entertainment center. I set it on one of the high shelves, much to the boys' protests.

"Ask your question again, about the toy and Dad's house." I pull out my chair and collect my books into a pile before my children build things out of them.

"Riggs wasn't supposed to bring the truck in here. Dad specifically said to leave it in the SUV so he could take it home to be a toy for *his* house. But Riggs brought it in anyway. Now Dad's gonna take it away." Deacon folds his arms over his chest and pushes his lip out in an incredibly forced pout. I'm tempted to do the same, because *WTF!*

I let my head fall back for a beat, laughing lightly at this incredulous situation. First, he cheats on me. Then, he thinks he can set the rules.

"Dad also said for me to give you this," Deacon says. I right my head and anticipate whatever gift my son is pulling out of his backpack. I prepare myself for a poisonous snake. Instead, I get a booklet stamped with the Oklahoma State seal.

My brow pinches as I pull the book close enough to read the title: *Helping Children Cope with Divorce.*

"He said you need to read it and then the two of you need

to take a class together next week. He said if you don't, he'll have to tell the judge."

I'm sure Deacon isn't getting the wording exactly right, but also, there's some truth at the root of his message. I'm sure Brandon's words weren't too far off. And the fact he's saying things about court and a judge to our boys so early makes my skin itch.

"You know what?" I begin. "No. Just . . . no."

I glance between the two boys, then toward the truck. I push my tongue into my cheek, ignoring the very confused stares on my twins' faces while I calm the fire brewing in my belly. Another soft laugh bubbles from deep in my chest, and I hear how it sounds when it hits the air—like the kind of laugh a woman who steals dalmatians for coats would make. I will not let this divorce turn me into the bad guy. But I won't be a pushover either. That's not who I am. Never has been.

"You guys want to go to a baseball game tonight?" I flash my gaze to Deacon first, and he kicks his feet under the table as he shifts his stare to his brother.

"Do we get hot dogs?" Riggs asks.

I pivot my head and meet his gaze next, my grin inching up as I nod.

"And popcorn," I add.

"Yes!" Riggs throws his hands in the air, and Deacon sprints from his chair, rushing to his brother and wrapping his arms around him as if I just told them we're moving to Disneyland.

"Why don't you boys go wash up and change while I feed Holly, and make sure you grab sweatshirts. The stadium gets cool at night." I march across the room toward the truck while my boys slip from their chairs and skip toward the stairs.

I position the truck in the middle of the floor and take a photo of it with the stairs, and the rest of the house blurred behind it. I save the image, then place the truck next to my small purse before waking Holly for her afternoon bottle and to check her for a diaper change. I'm eager to fire off a text, or maybe even call my ex so he's forced to listen to my words through the speakers in his SUV. Nice and loud. And possibly in front of his young girlfriend, whose perfume I can clearly smell on our twin boys' clothing. But I'll hold it in for something better. I'll wait for the weekend, after we take this truck —the toy that's supposed to stay at Brandon's house; a perk for being with dad—and photograph the shit out of it in every fun place we go for the next several days.

Holly coos as I lift her, and I swear there's a sisterhood smirk on her lips. It's probably just gas. Both fitting reactions to a cheating ex who has no idea the hornet's nest he's kicked with this shit.

ELEVEN
BROOKS

A lot of the guys are in the clubhouse already when I walk in, all watching the TV. Hunter got the start today, his first full start for Texas, and went six innings with only a hit. By the time I get here, he's facing his last batter, and when he sends the guy down swinging, there's an eruption of pride in the room.

I feel bad I didn't know about his start, but I wouldn't have been able to make it here in time regardless.

"How'd it go today?" Jake taps my shoulder with his glove as he passes behind me on his way to his locker. He rolled in late too.

I pull my phone from my pocket and slide over on the bench closer to him.

"Check this out," I say, showing him the pic I took of the birth certificate.

He takes my phone in his palm and chuckles.

"Man, I love how excited you are about a document. I thought I was going to get to see a pic of your kid sitting up or some shit, but nope." He hands the phone back to me and I stare at the line with my name for another second before tucking it in my locker and removing the clean jersey from the hanger.

"Believe me, I can bore you for hours with footage of Holly sleeping. You give me the word." I'm a little tempted to retrieve my phone and watch some myself.

"I'm good, dude," Jake says with a chuckle. "But I'm happy for you."

I meet his gaze and nod, the smile on my face feeling permanent ever since I left the courthouse with the paper in my hand. It's the renewal I need, a reminder of what all of this is about. I was determined when it was just me, but I would have been content to spend a few years in the minors, building up my baseball cred, then slipping into a coaching gig somewhere and calling that a good life.

But now? I want more—*for her.*

My late-round, one-hundred-fifty-thousand signing bonus is only the start, but I don't want to have to touch that until Holly's eighteen and getting into Harvard or Yale. Because yeah, my girl is going to be brilliant. And she's going to have the world at her fingertips without the pressure and fear of living in poverty.

My life has been one big gamble. My college grades were all right, but I got an easy pass simply because I could hit a fastball out of the park. I don't even know what the details of my business degree qualify me to do. My guess is telemarketing or selling season tickets to Hawkeye basketball back in Iowa. I've never really had a dream other than this game— playing it or coaching it.

I slip out of my shorts and put on gray mids before slipping my arms through the sleeves of my jersey. I'm not sure I'll ever get over the thrill of seeing my name stitched on the back of something.

"You're hitting lead-off tonight, Callahan," Coach says as he pops his head into the clubhouse. I hold my thumb up in response.

"Awesome. I'm feelin' it tonight, Coach," I say, my voice vibrating a bit and giving me away. I hope he can't tell how fast my heart is racing all of a sudden.

I wait until Coach leaves the locker room, then shift my gaze to Jake as my jaw drops. I haven't hit higher than the six hole since I got here.

"Time to show up, son!" Jake says, holding his fist out. I pound my knuckles into his, then stand to indulge in one more glance at Holly's sleeping face on my phone screen. I kiss it, then close my locker door.

It's show time.

I didn't expect Lindsey and the boys to get here so early. After my first round of batting practice, though, I hear a whistle followed by my name, and when I glance over my shoulder to spot the random fan, I am met with my own personal fan club. I'm not sure where Lindsey found a Mavericks onesie, but when she holds my daughter up and waves her tiny hand at me, my eyes tear up.

My teammates still haven't stopped giving me shit for it, but I don't care. The older guys get it, the ones with kids of their own. The young players might understand one day, if they're lucky. And I am lucky.

When Holly first showed up at my door—in my life—it felt like the end of everything. I was scared, afraid I'd somehow fuck things up the way my parents had. But it didn't take long for those fears to morph into sheer determination. Those first few nights, when I wasn't sure I'd ever sleep—if *Holly* would ever sleep—were intense. And I wasn't my best self to anyone I came in contact with. I was a real dick to Hunter when he got called up. I felt like he won the lottery while I was being buried.

But I was wrong. If ever there was a winner in this life, it's me. Holly taught me that.

I pop my head out of the dugout and scan the seats for her tiny head. I spot her clutched in Lindsey's lap and the two of them wave at me, though really Lindsey's doing the work for both of them.

"Let's go, Brooks!" Deacon and Riggs shout. It's the fifth time they've screamed my name, and I haven't yet stepped up to the plate. But I'm finally about to, and it feels good to have people cheering my name.

I carry my bat to the on-deck circle and rub on some pine tar while the Louisville pitcher warms up. Alberto Tovar has a great slider, but his bread-and-butter is his fastball. Funny thing, though—so is mine. And I love to hit that first pitch.

I time up my swing, watching his release point for clues. I did the work before BP, watching his video again. He doesn't show the slider right away, so if I can jump on his ninety-seven-mile-per-hour strike right out of the gate, I might just surprise him. I steady my breathing, drawing in a slow stream of air through my nose before holding it hostage in my lungs. My pulse thumps against my eardrums, rattling my helmet. I'm used to feeling my nerves, but I'm also good at subduing them.

I move closer to the plate as the catcher throws down to second, and pause just outside the batter's box, resting my bat against my thigh while I adjust the Velcro on my gloves one last time. I keep to my routine—the same set of habits every at bat. That's my secret. And that's how I'm going to win today.

"Now hitting, number seventeen, Brooks . . . Callahan."

I smirk when the announcer calls my name. Hearing that never gets old. The slight pause, and the little lilt in his tone when he utters my last name. It's perfect. I used to practice this moment as a kid. I'd go to the Little League field by the Inglewood Baptist Church all by myself and hit crushed water bottles at the fence because I didn't have enough balls to sustain my imagination. Now, I simply need to complete living out that fantasy and send the ball over the fence. Or at the very least, to it.

I dig my back foot into the hard clay, twisting my toe into the dirt until it's set, then shift my weight back and steady myself with my front leg. One more deep breath, and I'm ready. I hear the whistles behind me, the chants from the few local diehards who come to every game, and the high-pitched hollering from Lindsey's boys. But it all quickly fades into a hum in the background, and all I see is the ball in Tovar's hand.

I catch his grip on the way into his glove, and his wind-up is fast. Two seams spin toward me, no curve to them at all, and I . . . just . . . know.

The ball flies from my bat with a *crack*, soaring over the second-baseman's head and into the right-field gap. I press the gas as I round first and dive headfirst into two, and by the time I stand, my heart is pounding in my ears twice as loudly as before.

I pump a fist toward the dugout, then shout, "Let's go!" before clapping my gloved hands together. I spare a quick glance toward Lindsey, Holly and the boys, and catch the twins high fiving in celebration. Lindsey is holding Holly at her chest, making sure she can see, not that my baby girl has a clue what's going on. Still, maybe there's a chance she sees this. Maybe she's watching me do my thing. Tonight, I intend on her watching me be great.

Jayden hits behind me, a deep fly ball that gets me to third before Roddy steps in and brings me home with a double of his own.

"Hell, yeah!" his son, Jake, shouts as I jog back to the dugout. He is pretty burned that his dad is getting more time than he is behind the plate, but he's not letting that get in his way of celebrating me. That's a class act.

I leap toward him outside the dugout, and we bump shoulders in the air. When I look up at the seats, Deacon and Riggs attempt the same thing. It's a lot less graceful, and a bit more painful looking, but it doesn't seem to slow them down at all. They're rushing up the steps a second later, chasing down a foul ball.

I laugh and shake my head when my gaze reaches Lindsey again. She rolls her eyes, seemingly calling out her wild boys, and I duck into the dugout, earning myself a swift slap on the ass from Coach as I pass.

I end the night going four for four, two singles and two doubles, and I have to stick around at the field for a while after to talk to the local reporter who covers our games along with the rep from the radio services. He gets a few soundbites from me, then I head down to the outfield gates that lead to the clubhouse.

Deacon rushes into my side first, then Riggs piles on, the two of them clinging to me as I slow walk my way toward Lindsey. Holly's out like a light, her sweet face resting against Lindsey's chest. I run the back of my finger along her pink cheek. The night air is giving her a bit of a chill, but Lindsey has her wrapped in a soft yellow blanket.

"You were amazing, Brooks!"

"Yeah, can you teach us? I wanna hit like you!"

The twins take turns tugging on my arms until I crouch low enough to meet their eyes. I tap a finger on Deacon's bicep when he flexes to show me how hard he's been working. He's four, so the muscle isn't real, but I play it up really well, and soon, he and his brother are doing pushups on the side-walk in an attempt to out-train one another.

I stand back up and shake my head, ready for Lindsey to make one of her usual cracks about her hyperactive boys. But there's something different in her eyes. I'm not completely sure, but perhaps she's a little starstruck.

"Well, lay it on me. How did I do?" I run the back of my arm along my brow, then rest my hands on my hips in case she musters up her usual snarkiness. She bites her bottom lip, though, cutting off a bashful smile.

"Wow."

Her right shoulder hikes up in step with her one-word review, and her lip is tucked between her teeth again. My body warms under her adoring gaze, and the heat in my cheeks is actually me blushing from her attention.

Well, damn.

"Coach put me in the two-hole, and I really wanted to step up," I say, feeling the need to explain things to her.

She blinks slowly as her smile grows, her bottom lip slipping free of the grip her teeth have on it. For the first time since I met her, she's the one off her game. And I did that to her.

"I took a video for you. I know the team has lots of footage, but when my dad coached, sometimes he liked it when we got a record of things from our point of view. Here . . ."

She leans to the side and pulls her phone from the back pocket of her jeans, then hands it to me. I scroll to her videos, then play the most recent one of my last at bat. It's not the greatest view, actually, through the safety netting, but the thought was sweet, so I stick with it as I take the first pitch then back out of the box.

"Is that your daddy? Who's that?" Her voice carries through the phone speaker.

My eyes flit up to her as my breath hitches.

"Watch. You don't want to miss it," she says, and I return my focus to the small screen just as she flips the camera's view to Holly's face.

"Go, Daddy! Right, Holly?" Lindsey bounces softly with my daughter held to her chest, and Holly's eyes fight to stay open. Then I hear the crack from my bat and the cheering crowd, and Holly's eyes widen with a yawn that I swear turns into a smile.

"That's right! That's your daddy. He did so good, didn't he? Yay!" Lindsey waves Holly's tiny hand to the camera, and for a few seconds, she giggles. My heart melts on the spot.

"Can I watch that again?"

"*Mmm hmm,*" she says with a nod and a smile.

My eyes are misty, and I don't care who sees me falling apart. I can't believe Lindsey caught this moment for me. She steps in close, and we watch the video play through again. Even the battle cries her twins are blaring from the edge of the warning track—where they aren't supposed to be—can't pull me out of this moment. I watch all the way to the end, until the video cuts out, then send the video to myself and hand Lindsey her phone.

I can't blink when our eyes meet. I don't know how to thank her enough for something so small, yet so huge.

"Linds, that was . . ." I pause with my mouth hung open. My lips shift into a smile as I shake my head. "I can't thank you enough."

We're face-to-face, smiling like fools at one another. The only thing I can think of doing to show her how much I appreciate her is to kiss her, but that is not an option. If I were to break this very thin wall we've built between right and wrong, I wouldn't want to mix up the reasons at all. If I kiss this woman, I want it to be abundantly clear why—because I simply can't help myself. And I'm getting dangerously close to not being able to hold back.

TWELVE
LINDSEY

Is this what life would be like?

I could kick myself for letting that thought float through my mind, even for a blip. Because once I entertain it, it's all I can think about. And the hard answer is, yes, in another life. Not this one.

I wait with Holly and the boys while Brooks changes after his game, and feel like one of the wives I saw out there. I'm sure a lot of them know our situation. Holly is a bit of a celebrity in that clubhouse, and it's not like my family doesn't have a name around this town. But in the moment, walking to our vehicles together, it feels so normal. *It feels good.*

When we get home, Brooks puts Holly to bed while I bathe the twins and tuck them in for the night. Now, here we are, just the two of us sitting on a dark front porch, sipping wine that I normally drink with my sister while we listen to the chirping crickets and wait for shooting stars. I know this place isn't permanent. I understand that all of this is temporary, a convenient arrangement that works for both of us. But I can't stop wishing for a way it could be real.

"Thanks again . . . for the video," Brooks says, breaking

what's becoming a weighted silence. I don't think I'm alone in feeling . . . *something.*

I roll my head along the head rest of the wooden rocker I've claimed as my own. Brooks seems content on the porch swing, though I'm not entirely sure about those bolts holding the chains to the beam.

"Of course," I say, taking a small sip from my wine glass and holding his gaze. Wine nights on the porch were a common thing when my sister lived nearby. Now that she's gone, I haven't cracked open a bottle in ages. I don't think I can handle much more than this glass, so I'm taking it slow.

Brooks has barely touched his. I think he abstains from things like alcohol because of his family history. I probably shouldn't have offered him the glass, but I was craving the comfort of sitting outdoors with someone I care about and waxing poetic about life. Of course, life is the last thing I should talk to him about. Doesn't mean I'm not going to, though.

"You called me Linds," I say, the two sips I've had making me braver than I should be.

His brow pinches.

"Earlier, at the ballpark. When I showed you the video and you thanked me. You called me Linds."

His gaze drifts to the side as his mouth pulls in on one side.

"Yeah, I guess I did." His focus returns to me. "Should I not have?"

I shake my head slowly, then realize the mixed message that sends, so I start nodding. I abruptly stop when I realize that response feels wrong, too, and we laugh softly. The crickets pause their chirping, which fuels my smile to stretch bigger before I verbalize my honest response.

"What I mean is, it's fine. I liked it."

There's a flicker in his eyes in reaction to my words, and a lump forms instantly in my throat. I swallow, suddenly aware of the vibrato in my own breath. I think I'm shaking.

"I wish I had met you earlier in life," I confess.

He takes a deep breath, shifting in the swing so he's slightly turned to his side and facing me. I haven't stopped rocking since I sat in this chair, and I've picked up speed in the last ten seconds. His gaze lingers, his lips on the cusp of a smile, the curve so faint it makes my tummy feel uneasy in the most exciting way.

"Maybe we were supposed to meet now," he finally says.

He slides to the end of the swing seat, moving his feet to the ground so he can lean toward my chair. His palm rests on the ornamental finial on the end of the armrest, and his forearm flexes as he forces my rocking to a stop. I want to look away from him, but I can't seem to.

"I can't," I croak, shaking my head. "*We* can't. Not now. It could only have worked in the before, when I could have been reckless."

I'm definitely quivering, and I'm certain Brooks can tell. Maybe it's the wine making me emotional, or perhaps my ex still makes me feel small. His words, which he passed through our sons like a toxic game of telephone, still sting. I can't seem to shed my worry that he's going to eventually take me to court. That he's going to throw my new living arrangement in my face—I didn't exactly run it by him before doing it. I worry my boys won't be with me—*that they won't want to.*

My throat closes up from my internal emotional assault, so I excuse myself before I start to cry.

"I'm sorry," I say, clutching my wine glass and heading inside, away from temptation. When I don't hear the door close behind me right away, I know he's followed me. And when I stop in front of the kitchen sink to pour the remnants of my wine glass down the drain, I'm not surprised when I feel the warmth of his body close in on me from behind.

"I'm here now, Lindsey," he says, sweeping my hair over one shoulder before dropping a soft kiss on the nape of my neck. "I'm here, and I want you. I want to make you feel like the beautiful woman you are. To give you all the pleasure you've been denied. Even if it's just for tonight. We can go back to the rules tomorrow. Tonight, maybe we deserve to break them."

My knees literally get weak, and I cling to the edge of the sink while Brooks's lips graze my shoulder, pausing to kiss my skin while his hands snake around my waist and clutch my hips.

"Tell me to stop," he says, and I know he doesn't mean it. He has to know I won't.

I spin so I'm facing him, and run my palms up the center of his chest. His body is so warm, and his pectorals are hard from the disciplined work he puts in. My fingers trail higher, along his neck and into his messy hair that's still damp from his post-game shower.

"I'm not this girl," I say, ignoring my better judgement and letting my eyes rake over his squared jaw, the broadness of his shoulders, the fit of his white T-shirt.

"What kind of girl," he asks, moving his hands to the sides of my bare midriff, his thumbs teasing my bare skin before playfully hooking the belt loops on my jeans.

My gaze makes its way to his, and the blue in his eyes is as clear as spring water ice. It nearly renders me speechless.

"The kind of girl who chases hot ballplayers and tries to land *the big one*," I say in a soft tone.

He inches closer, and my arms fold against his chest, my hands gripping fistfuls of his T-shirt as I lift my chin to maintain eye contact.

"I'm not the big one, so you're fine." He closes his eyes and kisses my brow. My cheekbone. My jawline. He hovers over my mouth for a few delicious seconds, a whispered laugh leaving his lips when I finally let out a breathy cry.

"You're wrong," I say, sliding my hands up along his jaw

before lifting on my toes. "You are the big one. In every single dangerous way. But I don't care. At least, not tonight."

His mouth drops to mine in the very next breath, and there is absolutely nothing subtle about his kiss. About anything, really.

As he sucks my bottom lip between his teeth, he bends his knees and scoops me into his arms, wrapping my legs around him as he pivots to march toward the stairs. He takes them two at a time, not even needing to look as he climbs and kisses at the same time. He makes a beeline into my room, not wanting to disturb Holly, I presume, and pushes the door shut behind him with one hand while I slide down his body and squirm out of his grip of his other. Our lips part, and I can feel the burn on mine from his rough kiss and the scratch of his stubble.

"Tell me to leave your room, and I will," he says, slowly gathering his shirt from behind his neck, then pulling it over his head before discarding it on my floor.

I shake my head and toe my shoes off one at a time. I take cautious steps backward, toward my bed, and let myself enjoy the attention of his heated stare. I peel my socks off, then whisk my own T-shirt up over my head, feeling every bit of the cool air kiss my nipples under my flimsy white cotton bra. Brooks licks his lips as his steps sync with mine. And when the backs of my legs hit the foot of my bed, I halt at the realization that this is it. The moment of truth.

Falling for a single dad wasn't part of my plan. Of course, being a single, divorced mom wasn't either. Maybe it's time I start saying yes to whatever the universe seems to think I need. Right now, I need Brooks Callahan to fuck me senseless.

Brooks reaches into the front of his joggers and grips himself as his gaze washes over my breasts, then dips to my navel. He lifts his chin slightly, a tiny nod encouraging me to strip for him. I haven't done something like this in years, not since Brandon and I first started dating. Once we got pregnant, the seduction dances ground to a halt. I'm not sure I have what it takes to please him. But I'm willing to try.

I hook my thumbs into the waistband of my leggings and wriggle them down my hips, stepping out of them before kicking them toward my T-shirt. My eyes trail down the center of Brooks's chest, then lower to where his hand is now wrapped around his now exposed cock, and I'm instantly wet.

I shiver from a rush of cool air, and Brooks steps toward me, gliding his free hand up my arm and to my shoulder, stopping at my bra strap. He hooks his index finger underneath and slowly drags it down my arm, stroking himself while he strips me of my last remaining garments. It's the hottest fucking thing I've ever experienced, and the ideas running through my head would make the old Lindsey blush. That Lindsey was all talk. She lived vicariously through her sister, and she faked most of the orgasms she had with her ex.

But this Lindsey? The one who's on the verge of coming, *right now*, just from the heat of Brooks's gaze . . . is willing to experiment. I drop to my knees and wrap my hand over his on his cock, then tug his pants down enough to give me the full view of him. His hand moves to the back of my head as my mouth inches toward his tip, and when I taste the precum on the crest of his dick, his head falls back with a breathy groan.

His fingers flex as his palm stretches along my skull, and he gently guides my head into him so his cock fills my mouth and nearly touches the back of my throat. I will myself not to gag, instead pulling back as my lips close tightly around his shaft. Brooks shudders under my power, and as I gaze up at him through my lashes, he looks drunk from what I'm doing to him.

I take him in my mouth again, slowly picking up my rhythm until his breathing becomes heavy and his cock flexes against my lips. He pulls out and lifts my chin, cupping it in his palm and forcing me to stare up into his eyes. I feel safe with him. But what's more is I feel alive. I feel like a young, hungry woman again.

"My turn," he says, urging me to stand.

He quickly works the other strap of my bra down my arm, then unhooks the clasp between my breasts so the garment drops to the floor between us. He traces the curves of my breasts with the back of his hand, letting his knuckles graze over the aching peaks before he pulls one of them into a vice between his thumb and index finger. The sweet pressure sends a rush of morphine-like tingles through my core and between my legs. Brooks seems fully aware of what he's doing to me as he cups my pussy the very next second, his fingers gliding against the wet cotton strip between my legs.

"So fucking wet," he says, his voice husky and almost a growl.

I can tell my pussy is swollen with need, and each pass of his finger over my sensitive skin threatens to make me come undone. But it's too soon. It's not enough. I want all of him. I want him inside me, filling me.

I wrap my hand around his cock, still wet from my saliva, and stroke him a few times before lowering myself onto the bed. I scoot back and part my legs, bending my knees and begging him to finish me with my wanting stare.

He catches the tip of his tongue between his teeth as his eyes narrow on mine, and I'm hoping he's asking for permission to not use a condom with me.

"I'm on birth control, and for added measure, the timing for this is pretty much perfect. If we're ever going to fuck, this is the night," I say, my brazen proposition seeming to amuse him as a sinister smile takes over his mouth.

"Then we're going to fuck, Linds. And it's going to happen more than once tonight, because when I have a good game, I like to celebrate."

He slips his pants and boxers from his lower legs, then wraps his hands around my ankles, dragging me to the edge of the bed with my knees parted and my center pulsing with need. He drops to his knees, and I brace myself for his tongue. I wish I was wearing something sexier, but this is what giving in to spontaneous bad decisions begets. Besides, Brooks seems perfectly fine with my mismatched set of basic lingerie.

His eyes are fixed on mine at first, until his fingertips walk along my inner thigh. When he reaches the strip of material barely covering me, he drags it to the side and covers my swollen clit with his mouth. He sucks hard at first, flicking my pussy with his tongue before lapping me up with flat, wide strokes. My hips buck, but his heavy palm rests on my abdomen, pinning me down and forcing me to take every pass of pleasure as he brings me near the edge.

I fold my arms over my face, muting my whimpers by covering my mouth as my orgasm threatens to climax with the next pass of Brooks's tongue. But just when I mentally give in to the fact I'm going to come this way, he stops.

"What?" I breathe out, the ache in my chest deep with need.

I lift my arm at the feel of his absence, but before I can protest, he's urging me to lift my hips so he can slide a pillow under my ass, making our bodies better aligned. His focus is singular, and the second I come to rest on the pillow, he tugs my panties to the side and thrusts his cock inside of me.

My head falls back, and I cup my mouth with both hands to hold in the scream of pleasure I'm desperate to let out. Brooks is thick, and even if I had a sex life with my ex for the last year of our marriage, I wouldn't have been prepared for his size.

He slides out slowly, pressing his thumb against my clit and rubbing circles. The pulses take over almost immediately, and when he slides into me again, the first wave takes over my body. My knees fall apart wider, and my gaze is glued to his as he rocks his hips, driving his cock into me while my entire nervous system shudders in response. The orgasm takes my breath away, but the vision of Brooks staring at me with such hunger, such intent to make sure I am satisfied, fills my lungs again. And I'm no sooner over one orgasm before a second one builds.

"Come with me," I say, moving my hands to my breasts and pinching my nipples while Brooks watches.

His hands dig into my hips, pulling me into him with every thrust so his cock sinks deeper into me. The rush of pleasure winds up again, and the intensity in Brooks's stare signals he's close, too.

I roll my hips as he pulls me toward him, my body pushing onto his in new ways that seem to carry him into bliss. He grunts as his cock flexes inside me, filling me with warmth until he finally pulls out and paints my abdomen with the last drops of cum to spill from his tip. I run my fingertips through his arousal, massaging it into my skin until I'm sticky and coated with him.

While I would understand if he gathered his things and escaped to his own room to shower and sleep, he doesn't seem in a hurry to run away. Instead, he peels back my comforter, coaxes me to crawl underneath, and covers me with it—then he slides in and holds me against his chest.

My room smells of sex and bad decisions, but my heart is steady and my lungs fill completely. I'm caught in an odd paradox of delayed regret and a realized fantasy, and before I can talk myself out of making things worse by staying right where I am, I close my eyes and let the weight of the day carry me to sleep.

Anything that happens next is for future Lindsey to sort out. Present Lindsey thinks things are *jusssst fine.*

THIRTEEN
BROOKS

There are good ideas, and there are bad ideas. Then there is the irresistible pull of a beautiful, naked woman wanting to be touched. Lindsey is all three.

I should leave this room. The sun will be up soon and I'm pushing it already. Holly has never slept this long straight through, but I can't seem to pull myself from the warmth of this space next to her body. I think it's the view. She rolls on her back, stretching her arms toward the headboard while her head rolls to the side and her hazy-eyed gaze lands on me.

"Hi," she whispers, biting her bottom lip to really sell the coy smile on her lips. She knows the blanket has slipped off her body. She knows *exactly* the effect it's having on me, too. I can see it in her eyes.

"I should go," I say, clearly not moving.

She sucks in her lips and hums, "*Mmm hmm.*"

She knows I'm not going to.

My eyes scan the length of her body, following the tendrils of hair that seem strategically draped over her shoulder and onto her breast. I glide my hand across her chest, taking the ribbon of hair between two fingers, then slowly drag it away from her nipple. A tiny gasp parts her lips, and her back arches slightly.

Well, fuck.

I study her face for clues as my fingertips trace slow circles around her breast, each pass coming closer to the hard nipple I'm straining not to bite. When my thumb finally grazes the pink skin, she hisses, closing her eyes tight as her back arches even more and she squeezes her thighs together. My cock flexes in response.

"Somebody is getting very wet," I say, scooting close to taste a nipple. I press my tongue against the one closest to me as I look up at her through my lashes. She's shading her eyes with both hands and biting her lip, and the look of anticipation on her face is so fucking adorable I almost want to pin her in this moment forever.

I breathe out a soft laugh that puckers her skin even more, then smile, letting my bottom lip tickle the hard bud before I turn all my attention to it, drawing it into my mouth and sucking hard as my tongue swirls against the tip.

"Fuck me," she whimpers, still careful to keep her voice low. These walls are thin, and the twins could come knocking on her door any minute. Holly could start to cry. But so far, we seem to be caught in a pause in time. And I plan on milking every last second of it.

I continue to punish her nipple with my mouth as my right palm glides along her ribcage, then her hip, until finally centering just below her belly button. I nip at the hard peak of her breast before glancing up at her while my hand inches lower, until I slide my fingers against her soaking wet pussy. I bite the tip of my tongue as I smile at her, but she's frozen on the edge with her expression—lips parted, eyes locked on me, body teeming with anticipation. She's quivering, and it's absolutely delicious.

"You want to come this morning, Lindsey?"

She gives me a tiny nod.

I suck her nipple one more time, then sink one finger inside her while my thumb presses against her swollen clit.

"Shit," she says, grabbing the closest pillow and covering her face to dull her moans.

I glide my finger in and out a few times before adding a second, and her hips buck in response. She's so ready to come undone, and I want so badly to drag this out for her, to tease her endlessly and watch her fall apart on me over and over again. But the room is now a golden glow, and we're down to minutes of alone time.

I slide my finger out, and she pulls the pillow from her face so I can see her puppy-dog eyes begging me not to stop.

I chuckle softly and get on my knees.

"I'd fuck you, baby, but there simply isn't time. So you're going to need to come on my mouth, okay?" I say, situating myself between her legs, then dropping my chin to the mattress between them.

My tongue flattens against her pussy, and I work it up and down in languid strokes at first, pausing to suck her swollen skin into my mouth while my tongue flicks against the most sensitive part. Her hands suddenly dive into my hair, and she holds my head in place as my tongue continues to work her. I slip a finger inside her when I feel her body begin to writhe, and when her pussy tightens and begins to pulse, I am relentless. She squeezes her thighs around me, squirming as my finger fucks her and my mouth drinks her in. I don't stop until she's completely limp and her legs fall open at my sides. Even as I pull away, I leave her with the promise that I'll be back, kissing her sweet cunt one last time before wiping my chin and standing at the foot of the bed.

"I'll save my turn. It will be that much sweeter," I say.

It's clear to me once with her will never be enough.

Her cheeks blush, and she closes her legs, drawing her knees up to her body as she bites a fingernail on one hand. It's hard to pull myself away, and I let my gaze linger on her longer than I should. Holly's cry breaks the quiet of the house before I'm able to get my pants on, and about ten seconds later, there's a thunder of child-like knocks on the other side of Lindsey's door.

Lindsey leaps from her bed, her sheets clutched around her body haphazardly, like she's a zombie on the run.

"One second. Mom's getting dressed," she hollers.

"Holly needs something. I'll go wake up Brooks," Deacon says.

"I'm in here, buddy. I'll get her," I say, my brain clearly malfunctioning. My fuck-up becomes obvious to me the moment the words spill out, but the hard glare Lindsey shoots my way sets it in stone.

"Sorry," I mouth.

She rolls her eyes.

"Why is Brooks helping you get dressed, Mommy?" Riggs asks.

I start hopping around the room, pulling my pants up while also wrangling my T-shirt right-side up.

"Uh, because Mommy is putting on a fancy dress. I have a—"

"A party," I say when Lindsey looks at me for help.

"Party!" The boys start chanting in unison. I slap my palm on my forehead, seeing my fuck-up . . . again.

"Not that kind of party," Lindsey says, her voice harried as she bellows over her shoulder while rifling through her closet.

"What kind of party?" Riggs asks.

"Your boys are goddamn persistent," I whisper, finally getting my shirt on the right way.

"I taught them to be curious. What can I say? Now, here, help me get this up." Lindsey has stepped into a tight blue silk gown with a slit on one side. The back is mostly lace, and there's a zipper, which is a pretty solid cover for my story.

"Remember that church I told you I got in trouble at when I was younger?" Lindsey says.

"Yeahhhh," one of the twins drawls. I can't tell which one, but we're dressed now, so Lindsey opens the door, and the boys come rushing in.

"Oooooh, pretty dress, Mommy," Riggs says, immediately leaping onto his mom's bed. He begins jumping, and I blink rapidly, trying to erase the fact that I just ate his mom out on those sheets.

"What's at the church?" Deacon says, still locked in on the original lie.

"They want to say sorry for punishing me. It turns out that none of it was my fault when I was a kid," Lindsey says.

I cup my mouth to hide the laugh I'm dying to let out.

"Really? Not even the fire in the trash can?" Deacon adds.

I shift my gaze to Lindsey, who left out that little item when her parents were tattling on her. I'm actually surprised her dad didn't mention it. He seemed to get a kick out of embarrassing his daughter.

"Yep. Not even the fire," Lindsey says, giving me a hard stare. "Anyhow, they're going to formally shake my hand in apology, and they asked me to dress up. So, what do you think?"

She spins slowly with her hands out, and the boys jump to hold onto her arms.

"You're so pretty!" Deacon shouts.

So far, neither of them has asked to join her for this made-up handshaking ceremony, and before they do, I need to get myself out of this room.

"Is your zipper good now?" I say, clearing my throat.

"Yes, thank you," Lindsey says, pulling her arms free from her twins before walking me to her door.

I'm one step away from total freedom when Riggs calls me back inside.

"Why are your underwear on the floor?"

I spin on my heels, and Lindsey does the same, just in time

to see one of her boys lift my boxer briefs in the air over their head.

My jaw goes slack. I rarely got in trouble when I was a kid. Other than my parents snapping at me for irrational reasons like being too loud while they were getting high, I was never in trouble. Perfect attendance at school. Quiet in the classroom. Never late.

This is my equivalent of being hauled to the principal's office, it seems. And at the helm, a four-year-old boy swinging my underwear around his head like a helicopter propeller.

"They're mine," Lindsey says, snagging them from her son and promptly tossing them in her dirty clothes hamper in her closet.

"You have boys' underwear?" Deacon has a future in law.

"Well, if you must know . . . I stole them from your dad. When we were in the same house together. I didn't have any clean pajamas, and so I took a pair of his underwear. I really like sleeping in them, so I simply never gave them back. And that's that." She claps her hands together in such a way that the boys seem to understand that this case, at least as far as they are concerned, is now closed.

I leave the room without my underwear. And now Lindsey is going to have to keep them forever and probably wear them from time to time.

I got out of the house relatively unscathed for a guy caught red-handed. I even managed to get Holly fed and changed before I had to leave for the ballpark. And according to Lindsey, she is currently driving all the kids to her parents' house so they can watch them for an hour while she drives around the block and pretends to be getting an apology for setting a fire in the church when she was nine.

I'd love to hear her parents' reactions to this, but that means they would have to know the real story, and I'm not sure how much Lindsey is going to share with them about that. I get the feeling she's not ready to make what happened between us anything more than a secret for now. I'm bummed a little, but I also understand. Our lives are complicated, each in their own way. And Lindsey's divorce isn't official yet, so according to the state of Oklahoma, she's one step away from wearing a scarlet letter. You'd think Brandon would be the one worrying about that. Laws turn a blind eye to men sometimes.

Most times.

I imagine Lindsey's words in my head, and it makes me smile. My memories then drift to the soft curve of her hips, and the way they felt under my hands while I held her off the bed just enough to drive my cock inside her.

"You awake, Brooks?" Jayden snaps his fingers at me, and I shake myself from my daydream before reaching into the bucket of balls and setting another one up for him on the tee.

"Yeah, sorry. Had a late night," I say through a yawn. It's not a total lie. And having a baby is a good built-in excuse to be tired.

"I bet. I don't know how you do it, man. My mom was always tired when my brother and I were growing up. She was a single mom and all that," he says, lining up his bat and narrowing his focus to the ball before taking a solid hack.

"Do you talk to your dad?" I ask, setting up another ball.

Jayden eyes me skeptically, so I fill him in a bit on my situation.

"I'm curious because mine just got out of prison, is all. I barely knew the man from the time I was ten on. And my single mom was basically useless, so . . ." I shrug, and Jayden's gaze drops to his feet for a beat.

"Sorry, dude. I didn't know. But hey, the dead-beat-dad club has some pretty cool members." He holds his fist out, and we bump knuckles. "My dad took off. He might be in prison. Who knows. But my mom is a saint. Sorry about yours. If you ever want a home-cooked meal and she's in town . . ."

He makes the chef's kiss motion, and I nod and laugh.

"Sounds good. I'm still banking on getting a meal at the Blackwoods' one of these days."

Jayden takes a swing, then rests his bat on his shoulder and tilts his head as he glares at me.

"What?" I shrug.

"You mean Lindsey hasn't cooked for y'all yet?" Jayden says it as if it's something Lindsey is famous for and has done for everyone but me. I shift my weight on the bucket I'm sitting on.

"We haven't exactly had time for a family dinner. I'm busy, and when I'm home, that's her time off. And she's finishing her degree, so—"

"Listen, all I'm saying is you need to drop the hint that you heard she makes shepherd's pie and southern cornbread. Leave it at that and see if she takes the hint." Jayden fishes out his own ball, sets it on the tee, and knocks it to the back of the cage.

"Have *you* had her shepherd's pie?" I lean forward and rest my elbow on my leg as I stare at him.

"Dude, I think you're the only one who hasn't, brother." He snickers, then picks up another ball and takes one final hack before flipping the bat and pulling off his gloves.

I put in my hitting rounds for the next thirty minutes, and my hands are buzzing from my heavy swings. Despite the chaos I left in my wake, when I left the house today, things seemed clearer than they have for years. Lindsey's going to need time, and I'm aware what happened between us can't be a regular thing right away. But also, there was more to it than just two adults needing a release. I felt it. I *know* she did, too. There was too much passion in our kiss. We said words with our bodies that neither of us has the courage to utter aloud.

And if I need to ease her into the idea that we can do this, I'm willing.

I'm the last one in the hitting tunnels, so I spend my time cleaning up the place, resetting the stools, and wiping down the machines to make sure they're fresh for the guys hitting tomorrow. We travel this weekend, a road trip to the wondrous Ozarks for a series against the Royal Round Fish of Sutherlin County. I don't know what a round fish is, but my guess is it's a bit . . . well . . . *round.*

I'm making my way back to the clubhouse, my gear bag slung over one shoulder, when a car door opens from a beat-up, boxy sedan parked in the handicapped spot closest to the front entrance. I squint when the sun reflects off the chrome siding on the door, but the second the door slams shut, I wish I hadn't looked this way.

"Hi, son."

My father holds up his open palm before stepping up on the sidewalk and making his way to me. I survey the immediate area, not for help but to make sure nobody is catching this moment I'd rather not live through.

"Why are you here?" I drop my bag by my feet, in case I need my hands. When I was a kid, he used to push me around sometimes. The odds of that are unlikely now, mostly because of the sheer physical calculations of my body compared to his. Still, the reaction is ingrained in me. I feel better having all my tools at my disposal. If I need to block a punch, I know I can.

"I figured maybe stopping by your work would be a better way to see if we could talk. I understand how my showing up at your home felt like a violation." He rocks back and forth on his feet as he talks, and his eyes struggle to remain fixed on me. I'm pretty sure he's tweaking. I'm sure he was the other day, too. That's how he exists, and there ain't no amount of prison that's going to cure him of that.

"Yeah, well, it's a violation here, too. It says so on the sign," I say, pointing over my shoulder to the no-trespassing sign affixed to the gate I just walked through. Technically, the front door is open to the public. But I'm willing to run back to the practice facilities if it means he'll leave me alone.

Instead of getting defensive, my father coughs out a laugh. The hacking takes over quickly, though, and he has to hold out a finger while he covers his mouth and clears his throat of some nasty sounding shit.

"All I want is a cup of coffee with you. Ten minutes over some eggs, maybe. Come on. What do you say?" He steps toward me and holds out his hand. His nails are trimmed low, and his fingers are covered in tiny cuts that look to be infected. I'm not sure whether it's from razor blades or what, but I doubt it's from his work in the scrap yard. That kind of work leaves real, actual bruises. My dad's hands look sketchy as fuck. And they're shaking.

"Fine. Friday morning, seven a.m. at Earl's. If you're a minute late, I'm leaving. And I can only give you twenty minutes. Then I have to get on a bus and leave for a game." I nod at his hand, refusing to shake it, and instead I spit on the ground. My gaze hits his, and I make sure the expression on my face means business. He seems to get the message.

"I'll be early. And this is my treat. Breakfast, I mean. And the company," he says through an awkward chuckle.

"Whatever."

I turn my back on him and walk toward the back entrance, and don't let the weight of the moment hit me until I'm alone in the showers. There, I will the hot water to spray down the drain everything having to do with this new memory.

FOURTEEN
LINDSEY

It's so much easier to be bold in the dark of night, under the auspices of a starry night and a few sips of wine.

It's been three nights since the one Brooks and I spent together, and between his schedule and my record-setting stress, bedtime has been early and done alone.

I'm sure he thinks I'm giving him the cold shoulder. *Maybe I am.* I don't mean to, but I'm freaked out. Not only because the boys basically caught us red-handed and will one day unravel our ridiculous cover story, but also because my parents clearly know something is going on. I had to explain showing up at their house in an old cocktail dress at eight in the morning, and despite my best attempts at telling them it's a long, crazy story, their quizzical expressions definitely verged on the judgmental side.

My mom did say I was allowed, then pointed at Brooks. She didn't specify exactly what I was allowed to do.

Brooks and I haven't talked about what happened or how it changes things. Rather, how it *can't* change things. We still need to have that conversation, but for now, I'd rather live off the leftover high from our amazing night, than run whenever I see him.

Totally practical to pull off for a year.

Not that I don't want more. Because I do. And not just the intimacy, but more . . . period. Sex has a way of tricking the brain into believing anything is possible, and in the moment— or rather, *moments*—with Brooks, I did. I convinced myself we could live a double life. Have our own secret world at night, after the kids went to bed, then go back to business as usual during the day. Eventually, when my divorce is final and custody settled, Brooks and I could go public. Then I spent a full day with my thoughts.

Now, I realize I am anxious for him to come. I want to see him. To be with him. All of us together. A family. And I don't want to wait. I want it now. And *now* is the only time I'm certain that can't happen.

So, I've been running. When he enters the kitchen, I leave. When he's in the room with the boys and me, my headphones are on and my books are open. And well before it's time for bed, I disappear.

It's exhausting and depressing.

I'm in the clear for the weekend, at least. The Mavericks are on the road, and Brooks left early this morning. He was moody, too, which made it easy to play moody right back. I should probably have asked him what was going on, but I was so relieved that he didn't want to hash out our situation that I let him stew in the kitchen after giving Holly a morning bottle without a single questioning eyebrow. He didn't even say goodbye when he left. He just kissed his daughter's forehead and walked out the door, never glancing my way.

It's probably his way of dealing with the tension I've created between us. The guy has had a lot of shit happen in his life, and he has every right to be gun-shy about letting people in. That makes me feel even worse about how I've behaved. If I were an adult, I'd suck it up and have the hard talk about my reality.

I'm not truly divorced. My ex is using anything he can to

make me look like the bad guy so he can keep the boys in Oklahoma City. And Brooks makes a pretty damning checkmate.

Not that Brandon doesn't have plenty of skeletons of his own. Hell, he has the boys today, and I'm sure he's having his girl-toy Caitlyn watch them while he meets me for our first co-parenting class. I dropped Holly off with my parents so I could get here early, and so far, I'm the only co-parent in the classroom without her other half.

Typical.

Brandon was even late to our wedding because he booked an early tee time with his college buddies. He's not even good at golf.

I keep checking my phone for updates from him, but he's stopped putting messages to me in writing. His texting consists of time stamps for when he'll arrive for pick-up and drop-off dates, and that's about it. I think he's paranoid that I'll screenshot his words and use them against him in court, so instead, he no longer types any. He's probably right. I would. I *have.* Mostly the ones from the past, before we separated, when he promised to be home by morning only to turn around and message Caitlyn the room number for the hotel room he's waiting in. He didn't realize I could see those because he doesn't understand how cloud IDs work. I definitely crossed an ethical line by logging in as him, but I had to know if my suspicions were justified. Seeing the text messages led to spending five hundred bucks on a private investigator, which led to the photos that showed me exactly who she was.

It was my choice to leave. I knew I needed my family's support. At first, Brandon played the part of the repentant husband who had made a grave mistake. He actually begged me to stay, and I almost gave in. But when I asked him to call her and end it right then, he flinched. He wouldn't take the phone. And I felt like the biggest fool in the world.

My mom and dad paid for my legal counsel so I could file

a response to his divorce petition, challenging the custody portion. I don't have the funds to fight him on my own, and they don't have the funds to pour the same amount into it that I'm sure he will. His parents have money to burn. And his mom never liked me. I could tell. I'm sure she has a notebook somewhere of every parenting misstep she thinks I ever made. I have a note for her—don't raise a man who cheats on his wife.

I'm going to need to bluff my way through most of this. And if that means flashing a few texts in front of him so he knows what cards I have, then that's what I'm going to do. We'll both know I can't use those in court. But he'll know I could send them to the folks in charge of tenure decisions at the university. And that sounds like something I'd do.

"Okay, let's get started," the instructor says, flipping up the doorstop on the community center door with her foot. It's nearly closed when Brandon slides his hand in and makes it inside.

"You must be Mr. Berchaund?" the instructor says as he weaves through the rows of seats until he finds the one next to me.

"Yes, sorry. I'm leading a summer session for PhD candidates at the university, and I had students with questions after class. I won't be late again." He's trying to impress the instructor, and probably the rest of the class. Nobody responds, not even a nod. My smile veers into smug territory.

"Here's your workbook," I say, sliding over the extra I picked up for him. I had a feeling he'd be late.

"Parking was a bitch, huh?" He chuckles, but I merely meet his eyes for a moment and blink.

"Come on. We're supposed to be showing how we can work together. At least melt the ice a little," he whispers.

My brow draws in, and I continue to stare at him while he flips through the pages of the workbook, reading ahead while the instructor illuminates the first slide of what I dread will be a very long presentation.

I think I hate him.

I shake my head as that thought floats through my mind. There was a time when I thought I loved this man, when I willingly gave up my career to support his. I'm so glad to have my boys, but how in the world did I ever have sex with their dad?

"Lindsey? Did you have an example?"

I snap my focus forward and instantly bead up with flop sweats. My gaze darts to the screen at the front of the room, and I manically read through the question being posed.

Would I make this same parenting decision if we were still married, or am I allowing my anger, pain, or resentment to affect my judgment?

"This has come up for us," Brandon says, answering for me.

My brow dents and my head swivels until he's all I see.

"Explain." The instructor leans her weight on the back of an empty chair as she narrows her attention on my ex.

"Well, my wife—I mean ex-wife," he begins. The instructor holds up a palm, stopping him.

"She has a name. Use her name." My lips draw into a faint, smug grin that I try to keep to myself. I'm sure it's obvious to Brandon, though.

"Okay, you're right. *Lindsey* was looking for a job, and she decided to take on nannying. Only, she chose to live on premises."

I roll my eyes at his choice of words. Also, I'm not sure how the fuck any of this applies to her question for us. He just wants to put the fact I moved in with another man out there for public consumption, to make me look bad. And, well, I didn't exactly notify him first, which I now know was a mistake as far as custody sharing is concerned.

"Okay, and you're saying that if you were still married, would she have made the decision to work as a live-in nanny?

I'm not sure I'm following." Our instructor squints as she stares at Brandon, and he scratches at the back of his neck under her scrutiny. It's one of his tells. He does it to buy himself an extra second or two to think, plus it makes him seem affable. I'm not sure why, but it has always worked. With me. With his parents and mine. It's his superpower. One doesn't win college debate tournaments without knowing a thing or two about swaying opinions.

"What I mean is, would she make a decision about something on the level of where our children sleep without consulting me if we were still married? I'm not sure she would have."

I catch a few people in the classroom nodding in agreement with him, and I audibly huff out a single laugh. I can't believe any of this.

"Lindsey? What do you think?" The instructor shifts her body so she's solely focused on me.

"I'm sorry, but I'm not even sure I understand this question. Would I have taken a job to support myself and the boys if Brandon hadn't slept with one of his PhD students? I mean . . . probably not."

The gasps that fill the room are accompanied by a few snickers, which does feel good. Any classmates he thinks he won over with that little performance of his have likely abandoned him.

"Lindsey, that's not productive," the instructor says, admonishing me.

I laugh again, a little louder this time. But I quickly snap my mouth shut when I realize I'm the only one amused by this. I scan the room for anyone else to commiserate with, but by now, I've made this space so goddamn uncomfortable that everyone is looking down at their books and pretending to read.

"Sorry," I croak, twisting my lips, then flipping through my book simply to have something else to look at.

"It's not the best example, but let's explore this more," the instructor says. She leaves her seat and returns to the front of the room. Meanwhile, I boil where I'm at, and don't retain a single word for the rest of the class.

I can tell that Brandon wants to talk to me when the session ends, probably about spending more time with our boys—or his ultimate goal, having them live with him closer to the city. And if I had actually learned anything about good co-parenting in this class, I'd probably stick around and hear him out. But I'm hurt, and rather angry. So I tuck my workbook into my tote bag the minute our instructor tells us what to read for next week's class, then make a beeline out the door, straight to my van. I'm out of the lot first and in my driveway in less than fifteen minutes.

I should head to my parents' house to pick up Holly, but I'm too worked up. I don't want to drive angry when I have kids in the van. I just need a few minutes to sit by myself. I used to believe in the power of meditation. It got me through honors classes in high school. Maybe I need to revisit that practice.

I consider pulling out my yoga mat as soon as I get inside, and I'm nearly to the front door when I realize something is off. The door is actually open. Not fully, but a crack. The door jamb is bent near the lock, too, as if someone pried it back with a crowbar. My heart races.

"Hello?" I say, my voice loud enough to carry into the foyer without me stepping foot inside. I hold my breath and listen for clues, praying whoever did this is not still inside. I pull my phone out and dial nine-one-one, then hold my phone to my ear while I take one more step toward the house.

"Nine-one-one, what is your emergency?"

"I think there's been a break-in at my house. I'm going to get back in my van and leave, but can someone check it out to make sure whoever did this is gone?"

"Yes, ma'am. I want you to get in your car right now but

stay on the line with me. Can you put the phone on speaker when you're in your car?"

"Yes," I say, backing up rapidly. I run once I'm in front of the garage, and practically toss my purse, phone, and self into the driver's side seat of my van. I crank the engine and back out of the driveway while giving the operator the address. I head straight to my parents' house, rushing inside while I'm still on the phone. I hold on through it all, the operator alerting me when the officers arrive, and when they give the all-clear. They snap a few photos and send them to me, and I nearly fall over taking in the view of papers thrown all over the house, books torn in pieces, glass shards on the kitchen floor, and holes punched in several of the walls.

"I can't stay there tonight," I say, both to the operator and to my parents.

"Mom's making a bed up," my dad says, his stutter from his stroke nearly gone thanks to months of vocal therapy.

I end the call and mentally prepare myself for the detective's visit within the hour. Holly is fast asleep, something I wish I were. The only thing left to do is to call Brooks. And he's on a field somewhere in the Ozarks, probably in the third or fourth inning of a game.

I dial him anyhow, and when I get his voicemail, I try to keep my voice from quavering.

"Hey. It's uh . . . it's me. I don't want you to worry, but there was a break-in at the house. I'm fine. Holly is fi—"

"This voicemail is now full." A beep sounds in my ear, followed by dead silence. I dial Brooks again, and the call simply goes nowhere once the rings fade.

"Shit," I mutter, my mom the only one close enough to hear me. I flit my gaze to her, and we give each other a shared look that basically says the same thing I uttered. *Shit.*

That message cut off at the worst possible time. At some point tonight, Brooks is going to freak the fuck out. And he's going to be in Lake of the Ozarks when he does.

FIFTEEN
BROOKS

Things are weird. Sex makes things weird. I knew it would, but I did it anyway. And now that I know what it's like to be with Lindsey, to taste her and feel her naked body next to mine, I don't think I can stop. I don't *want* to stop.

But it's not up to me.

And Lindsey hasn't said a goddamn word about *us*, or what happened, or . . . *us* since I left for my workouts three mornings ago. Of course, since my dad showed up again, I haven't exactly been in the frame of mind to have the kind of conversation that Lindsey and I deserve. I've been distracted, but more than that, I've been angry.

Lindsey's avoiding me, and this morning, it reached new levels. That's probably for the best because I don't know what's liable to come out of my mouth right now.

I'm meeting my dad at Earl's in ten minutes, a concession I made and instantly wanted to take back. I think that's what bothers me most—I'm still weak around him after all this time. It's different than when I was a kid, though. I'm not giving in because I'm afraid of what he'll do to me. I'm giving in because he looks so fucking pathetic and unwell that I feel obligated to give him my time.

But that's the thing. It's *my* time. And he had zero hand in anything I've done to get where I am.

I rinse out Holly's bottle, prop it on the drying stand by the sink, then kiss my daughter's head before heading out the door to my own damn doom. Maybe kissing her will be a good omen for me. I kind of doubt it, though. My father isn't just a dark cloud; he's a black hole that sucks me in then forgets I exist.

I purposely didn't aim to get to Earl's early. I said this man could have twenty minutes, and he's not getting a single second beyond that. But as he promised, he seems to have arrived early. His thinning hair pokes up around his ears, and the collar on the button-down shirt he's wearing is crooked, half of it flipped the wrong way. He keeps running his hand over his head, probably trying to flatten the various cowlicks.

The clock in my SUV flips to the top of the hour, so I kill the engine and head inside. My dad scurries out of his chair when he spots me, and he rocks back and forth on his feet as I approach. He doesn't hold out a hand or make a move to hug me. That's good. I think I'd have to turn around if he did that.

"I wasn't sure what you'd want, but I figured coffee probably, so I ordered you a cup of that. I got it black, but she's bringing over the sugar and cream." My dad's gaze can't seem to settle on any one thing as he nervously scans the inside of Earl's.

"Ah, there she is," he says, holding up a hand as Daisy approaches.

"Here you go, hon," she says, offering me a sympathetic smile as she tucks the small tray of sugars and cup of cream next to the steaming mug in front of me.

"Thanks, Daisy," I say, holding her gaze for a beat in an effort to convey just how miserable this is making me. I get the sense she understands.

"You ready to order?" She pulls a pen from behind her ear, and my dad flips over the simple laminated menu. Earl's isn't really a breakfast joint; it's a bar. I figured it would be pretty low-key this morning, which is why I picked it.

"What's good here?" My dad pulls a pair of reading glasses from his pocket and struggles to unfold them, then slips them on his face. I don't remember glasses when I was young. He's becoming an old man. I'm not even sure how old he is. I just know he was always older than Mom, and much older than me.

And he was terrifying.

"We'll both have the eggs and toast," I say, pulling a twenty from my wallet and sliding it on the table.

"No, no. I said my treat," my dad says, pushing the money toward me.

I flatten my hand on the half closest to me, and he stops.

"I don't have a lot of time. Just let me pay. And the eggs are good." I'm making that last part up. I've only ever had a beer here, and maybe some shelled peanuts. I'm not a big party guy, so when the team went out to celebrate before Holly came, I rarely stayed long. Now, I have other people in my life to celebrate good games with.

"Thank you," my dad says under his breath. He pulls his glasses off and tucks them in the breast pocket of his shirt.

"Sure." I pour a little creamer into my coffee, then stir it with a spoon before testing the temperature with a cautious sip. It's strong. That's good. I'm going to need it.

"So, you have a game today, huh?"

I take another sip and eye my father over the rim of the mug.

"Yeah, it's a series. That's how it works." I'm being short with him, and my lungs squeeze with guilt. I hate that I feel guilty, though, because he doesn't deserve me being nice. I really should talk to someone about my complicated feelings. I don't want my relationship with either of my parents to color my relationship with Holly.

"Right, yeah. I remember. You know, I taught you how to

throw a ball." He smiles tentatively, while my mouth remains a hard line.

"*Hmm*," I drone. I don't remember that, but I suppose it's possible. I don't remember much about those early years, before I was five. By the time I was in school, though, he was in full-on criminal mode.

My dad leans into the table and pulls his hands together, fidgeting.

"That girl seems nice. She's really not your wife, huh?" he pries.

I'm tempted to remain silent, but I don't want him making assumptions about Lindsey. I'd rather stick with the story she created.

"She's a friend. She and her kids needed a place to stay. It works out," I say, leaving it at that. My father's stare lingers, though, and there's something sinister about the curl of his lip. I'm not sure he's buying the story we sold him.

I pull my phone from my pocket and check the time, deflating when I see I've only been sitting here for six minutes.

"You know, I thought about you a lot when I was in." His gaze squares on mine suddenly, and it makes me wonder if he's rehearsed this part.

"Oh, yeah?" I draw in a deep breath, knowing I should stop there, but fuck it. "You think about those times I tried to visit or call, and you denied me?"

I hold his stare until he looks away, wanting him to feel uncomfortable. Yet when he does, I squirm in my seat. What the fuck is this?

"I wasn't in a good place," he says.

"No shit! You were in prison. For selling drugs. And being involved in a murder or two." He needs to know I've read the reports. It's not like I had a mom who protected me from the worst. Hell, she threw the paperwork on the coffee table when it arrived. It was right there for me to weed through.

"I know I haven't been a good man . . . a good father."

I huff with a short laugh.

Daisy brings out our plates, but I'm too sick to eat anything, so I push mine toward my father. He tilts his head and looks at me with a disappointed expression. He used to get that look in his eyes before slapping me when I was young. I can practically feel the sting on my cheek.

"Anything else?" Daisy says, glancing between us.

"We're good, Daise. Thanks." I give her a tired, tight smile.

"You bet." She pats my shoulder, then moves on to take the order of a man at the end of the bar. He's the only other person in this joint at this hour.

"They say breakfast is the most important meal of the day, you know." My father nudges the plate toward me a few inches. I shake my head.

"I'm not hungry. Let's just get this over with. What is it you want?" I lean back in my chair, gripping my thighs with my hands. I'm wearing dress slacks and the same shirt I wore to court. The team rules require players to dress nicely for road trips, just like they do in the majors. I'm miserable, though. Wearing this makes me feel even more like a banker, which I'm pretty sure is what this impromptu visit is really about.

"I don't want anything. Except, maybe, to spend a little time with my son."

I laugh again, and just like that, his fragile fist grows stronger, coming down on the table with enough of a bang that it shakes the silverware and draws Daisy's gaze from across the bar. I tuck my tongue inside my cheek and lean to the side, waving Daisy off. She doesn't deserve this shit going down in her bar. My bad for bringing it here.

"I'm sorry," he says. I don't laugh this time, though I want to. And that's our story at play again, the same after all these years. He blows up, and I react by learning my lesson.

"I really am working on that. My anger. It's something I

spent time on in prison. They had me seeing one of those therapists. The person was always changing, though. Not a lot of tenure in the prison health system." He shakes with a gurgling laugh that makes me wonder if he's sick. He's probably dying of lots of things, all brought on by his lifestyle. I'm sure none of them will kill him quickly.

"Maybe we can do this again in ten years. When you get better at controlling your temper." I brace myself for another outburst, but he laughs instead, pointing a finger at me before taking a slice of toast and biting off a corner.

"You're funny. You get that from me," he says, chewing with his mouth full. His toast is dry, and crumbs stick to his cracking lips.

"Yeah, that's what Mom always told me about you. 'Your father, he's a riot.'" My dry tone makes the point, and my father's smile immediately drops to a straight line. He tosses the half-eaten piece of toast back to the plate, then rubs his hands together while his elbows rest on the table.

"Come on, son. All I need is one chance to prove it to you. Maybe a little boost to help get me back on my feet, too. You know, I could help you out a little, huh? I'm sure you're busy. You probably have a lot of places to go. I could house sit for you while you're gone. I could watch after that roommate of yours, help with her kids. Or . . . hey, maybe hire me as your driver. I was always good at driving, and—"

"I can't do this," I say, standing and pulling another forty bucks from my wallet. I press the bills on the table in front of my father, between the two plates of food, then look up at him through my lashes. That's what I was waiting for—the grift. He knows I'm doing all right for myself, despite the hand I was dealt. He's come to collect.

"My home is off-limits to you. My roommate does not need your help. I do not need your help. And I'm not giving you a penny more than this." I tap my index finger on Andrew Jackson's face.

I glance at Daisy when I stand, and she pulls her attention up from the coffee she's pouring for the other diner long enough to meet my gaze and shake her head in sympathy. I'm glad she's the only one to witness this moment. She doesn't make me feel ashamed.

"You'll change your mind one day, maybe regret this," he says as I walk away.

I hold up a hand as he continues with his new tactics.

"I won't live forever. I'm an old man, and you and I won't have many shots at fixing this," he says.

I pause at the door. I should leave without another word, but I just can't let him have the final say.

"Then, maybe you shouldn't have broken us to shit, Dad. That's on you." I hit him with a hard glare and hold in the other vitriol I'd love to spew. My disdain is obvious, and I don't need to practice forgiveness today. Besides, he'll somehow work me into paying for it. That's what he does.

I march through the exit and head straight to my SUV. I fire the engine up remotely, so it's ready to go when I climb in. I focus on the interior of Earl's one last time before I pull away, though, and catch my father folding the bills I left on the table, including the one meant to pay the bill. He stands and pushes them into his front pocket. My gut twists.

I'll stop in again when I get back from this road trip to cover the bill. My dad's about to dine and dash; I'm sure of it. I'm just not going to stick around to be his getaway driver.

I expect to play like shit today, given the mood I was in when I got on the bus. And my rage only got hotter the closer we got to the Ozark stadium. But instead of letting it tear me down and riddle my glove with errors, I channel it into strength. I hit my first homerun as a Maverick by taking the first pitch I see—four-twenty, over the bleachers, and into a swamp behind the right field wall. Then, in the sixth inning, I hit my second.

I should be living it up, celebrating my great game in the hotel bar with the guys. But instead, all I want to do is crawl into bed and turn off the lights, maybe flip through a few videos of Holly on my phone.

I'm the only one in the elevator as I head up, so I pull my phone from my gear bag to check my messages. My voicemail says it's full, and there are twenty-two missed calls in my notifications. All my dad.

I play the first voicemail, which is from him, and his message starts politely, carrying on the same rehabbed personality he tried to sell me on this morning. But about thirty seconds in, he loses it. My gut says he probably took a hit of something and the drugs just hit his system, because in a single breath, he goes from apologizing to a lunatic raging about what a fuck-up I am.

"How dare you judge me, you little shit. I'm this way because of you, I hope you know that. You weren't planned. Your bitch of a mother, ha! She tricked me, got knocked up before I could leave her. But *ohhh,* you're too good for me now!"

I stop the message there, not needing to hear the rest. I scroll my finger down the line, selecting every message he left, and then I select the option to delete them all at once. I'm about ready to press YES when my phone prompts me, asking if I'm sure, and something makes me second-guess my action.

Scrolling through the list of messages one more time, I eyeball the incoming number, noting the California area code from my dad's phone. Then, at the very end, is a call from Lindsey. I uncheck that box and delete the others before pressing play on her voicemail. I hold my phone to my ear as the elevator opens, and make it three steps into the fifth-floor lobby when her words make me halt.

"Hey. It's uh . . . it's me. I don't want you to worry, but there was a break-in at the house. I'm fine. Holly is fi—"

I hold my phone out in front of me and check the screen to see if the message accidentally paused. It didn't. That's all there is.

I spin on my heels and press the elevator call button with my knuckle before dragging the message back to the start so I can listen again. This time, I pay attention to her tone. She sounds out of breath. Maybe a little panicked. *Someone broke in.*

Was she there when it happened? Was Holly? Are the boys still at their dad's?

I call Lindsey's phone, but it goes right to voicemail, so I dial again and get the same result.

"Come on, Linds. Come on," I chant, calling nonstop as I head back to the main floor.

The coaching staff is walking into the main lobby as the elevator doors open, so I rush to Coach Kessler since she's lingering behind the others. I don't want this getting out. I've seen things like break-ins for athletes get overblown by social media, and while I'm not in the majors yet, a lot of reporters are paying attention to my story. Word got out that I'm the single dad in the clubhouse. All I need is to fuel a breaking news story that brings a media circus to our house back home.

"Hey, what's up, Brooks?" Coach Kessler's eyes dim, and she tilts her head to the side, urging me to follow her to a quiet corner by the front desk.

"Someone broke into my place. I don't know the exact details yet, but I'm kind of freaked out. If I need to talk to authorities, what do I do? I don't want to leave, but—"

"Brooks, we won by eleven today, and we had shit on the mound," she says, leveling me with a hard stare to really make her point. It was a bullpen day, and when you're a minor league team scraping together innings, it can get kind of rough. The fact we handled the Ozark team easily says more about them than it does us.

"What I'm saying is, if you need to go, go. That's what we have a PR team for. We'll manage it."

I consider her advice, but I'm still uneasy leaving in the middle of a series. I know it's in our contract, contingencies for emergencies, but in many ways, pro ball at this level isn't so different from my high school days. If I'm not here, someone else is going to get my innings. And if they perform, I'm shit out of luck. And I just got the two-hole.

"Brooks," she says, snapping me out of my spiral. I meet her eyes. "You hit two dingers. You're good."

I exhale and smile for a heartbeat before the stress takes over my jaw again, and all I can do is gnash my molars. I hear her, though, so I nod and head out the lobby doors to the curb while attempting to get Lindsey to pick up. I order a rideshare between my calls, and within ten minutes, I'm on my way to the tiniest airport in Missouri, where a charter plane is waiting to fly me three hundred miles west. How my shit is going to get back to me, I have no clue. All I know is I can't get Lindsey on the phone, and someone fucked with my family.

SIXTEEN
LINDSEY

"We got a good print."

I talked with the sheriff's investigators for three hours, and they said a lot of things. But it's that five-word sentence that stuck with me. They said it as if it's good news. A person I don't know, likely a large male, was in the house I call home. Uninvited. Alone. And they have proof.

Hooray.

My neck is killing me from sitting at the kitchen table while I met with the officers. And my eyes are so heavy. My mom has been a saint with Holly. I should probably split my pay with her this week since she did as much nannying as I did, if not more.

The sun is down, it's somehow only nine o'clock, but I feel as if it's the wee hours of the morning and I'm just rolling in from a bender. I stand behind my mom as she bids the officers goodnight, then collapse into her arms the moment she closes the door.

"You can put your guard down now. Holly's asleep. Dad's asleep. Maybe it's your turn to go to sleep."

We both chuckle in our embrace.

"I should check my phone," I say, straightening my spine

when I realize how long it's been sitting on the charger. Basically, the entire time the police were here.

"I got it," my mom says, grabbing it from the breakfast nook. She taps the screen, and her facial features fall.

"Did he call?" I cross the small room and take my phone in my palms.

Forty-two missed calls. Zero messages. The last call came through . . . *two minutes ago!*

I tap the last incoming call from Brooks and instantly hear his phone ringing. I race to the front door and fling it open before he's even able to bring his arm up to fully knock. I throw my arms around his neck and begin to bawl from relief and exhaustion.

"Hey . . ." His arms fold around me, and his chin closes in on the side of my face.

"Holly's asleep. I came here because I didn't want to be alone with her at the house. I'm so sorry I didn't pick up your call. The detectives were here, and my phone was charging, and—"

Brooks's hands move to my shoulders, and he steps back a few inches to look me in the eyes. He studies me while I run my arm over my runny nose, then push the butt of my palm into each puffy eye.

"I freaked out when I couldn't reach you. I'm not angry. I'm scared. I *was* scared. Now, I'm just so sorry, Linds. I should have been here." He pulls me back against his chest, and my hands claw at the center of his T-shirt, balling it into my fists as I press my tear-soaked face against him.

"She's a little over-tired," my mom explains.

"I get it," he says.

"I fixed up the spare room. Lindsey and Renleigh's old room. There's more space in there now, so why don't you both head upstairs and try to get some rest? I put Holly in my room since it's quiet. If she wakes up tonight, I'll get her." My mom squints with a kind but slightly guilty smile. "I owe my daughters plenty of favors."

"Thanks, Mom," I croak, slipping from Brooks's arms to give my mom one more hug and a kiss on the cheek.

"Come on," I say to Brooks, nodding toward the stairs. "It'll be like high school, when I used to kick Ren out of the room so I could sneak a boy in."

"Hush your mouth, Lindsey Blackwood!" my mom chastises. She winks at me as I pass, though.

Brooks and I peek into my mom's room where Holly is out like a light. My mom created a sleep-space for her with rolled-up quilts. I don't rush Brooks as he hovers in the doorway. He needs to see his daughter breathe. I get it. I've done that with the boys.

When he's finally satisfied, we cross the hallway and step into the spare room.

"Your mom didn't even flinch that we're sharing a bed," Brooks says as he shuts my childhood door behind him. The Nirvana poster Ren hung on the back of the door is still there, and I snicker when I see it.

"She had us figured out before I did, I'm pretty sure," I say, too tired to mind my words before I utter them.

Brooks's gaze traps mine, and heat creeps up the back of my neck. So much for avoiding a talk about *us*. Nothing like being the victim of a class four felony to make one loose with their lips.

Brooks glances at the poster on the door, pointing at the somehow still vivid blue eyes on the print of Kurt Cobain. I'm pretty sure it was Nirvana's third wave of resurgence when my sister bought that poster. Kurt really held up.

"I feel a little inadequate. Not gonna lie," he jokes.

"Why? Because he was a celebrated rock legend and you're playing triple-A ball in a shit town in Oklahoma?" I quirk a brow as Brooks stares at me with his mouth agape. He shakes with a silent laugh, then steps into me, wrapping his arms around me and taking me down on the bed with him. We quickly settle into a comfortable position, his chest on my back. Spooning. That's something Brandon quit doing when the boys came along. He always said my body didn't fit against his the same. My hips were too wide.

What a dick.

"Did you really sneak boys in here under your mom and dad's noses?" His voice is like velvet against my ear, and I close my eyes easily to the sound.

"I mean, it's not like she was actually here when I did the sneaking," I explain. "Dad's really who I pulled one over on. And frankly, it wasn't very hard."

Brooks chuckles, and his body vibrates against my back. His warmth relaxes me, and for the first time since I saw the pried-open door, my pulse isn't drumming in my ear.

"My dad was always so exhausted after spending the day out on the field coaching. I could usually count on him being out like a light in his chair by eight-thirty, the nightly sports news humming like a lullaby. All I had to do was set Ren up with a tablet and some ice cream, and I was covered for a good hour of make-out time."

Brooks vibrates with another silent laugh, but it fades after a few seconds, leaving the two of us alone, spooning, in a room I can only describe as nineties shabby chic.

"My mom's not great at decorating. I think it was better how my sister and I had it," I joke. My eyes scan the wall, taking in the weird shelf with potpourri and random books I don't think my mom's ever read.

"I got pretty scared," Brooks says softly.

My hands move to hold on to his right one, where it rests at the center of my ribs. His left arm is bent under my head in such a way that his fingertips are able to brush the hair on top of my head.

"I didn't mean to scare you. The voicemail cut off, and I had a feeling my message wouldn't sound right. I was going to text you, but next thing I knew, the detectives were here, and my phone died, and—"

"I was afraid someone hurt Holly. Or that they hurt . . ." He swallows, then rests his forehead on the back of my skull. He's talking about me. He doesn't have to say it.

"Holly is safe. She was with my parents. And I was at my class. The one where I get to hear all the ways I'm a shitty parent . . . and a shitty wife, apparently."

Brandon's smug comments filter through my mind, sending a rush of adrenaline and anger through my belly. I need to bottle the feelings up again, but no matter how hard I try, the pain still sinks into my diaphragm like a fat silver bullet.

"You're not a shitty parent, Linds," Brooks says.

My thumbs graze over his knuckles. I want to be tender with him. I want to be his. "Thanks," I say, my voice cracking in spite of my efforts to hold in the pain.

"Hey," he says, the same way he said it when I crashed into his body at the front door. His arms have somehow become such a safe place for me.

I shift in the bed until I face him, and he moves both of his hands, finger-combing my hair from my face, then cradling my cheeks as he runs his thumbs under my exhausted eyes.

"You're an amazing mom," he reiterates.

I blink slowly, fighting to keep my eyes open. Staring into his blue is too soothing to stop.

"I'd venture to guess you're a pretty great wife, too. Today, when I thought . . ." He stops shy of finishing again, but this time, I really want to hear him say it.

"When you thought what?" I prompt.

His mouth tugs up on one side into a guilty but faint smile.

"When I heard your voicemail, all I could think was I needed to get back here to protect my family. My daughter, of course. But also . . . to protect *you*. And not because you're my friend. Because you're not just my friend, Linds. You're not just the nanny. You're . . ." He sucks in his lips and shakes with a single, silent laugh.

"What am I, Brooks?" My hands crawl up his chest again, grasping at the dry-fit fabric of his post-game shirt. He literally got on a plane immediately after his game and flew home for us. For Holly.

For me.

"You're mine, Lindsey. You're fucking mine."

SEVENTEEN

BROOKS

That felt good to say. Lindsey is scared, and not only because of the break-in at our house. I see it in her eyes as she's staring back at me, though I can't tell whether she wants to cry or utter, "Okay," then climb on top of me. Maybe both.

I move my hand to her chin, my thumb caressing the soft skin below her bottom lip. It's not quite pouting, but it is trembling. I move the pad of my thumb to it as my gaze narrows to this minuscule piece of her body. One square inch of perfection among so many more. I love this fucking lip.

"We both know it's too late to pretend we aren't in this," I say.

A slow exhale leaves her nostrils, and I drag my thumb across her lip one more time before moving to her jawline. My gaze follows each touch of my hand, following along as I trace her beauty with my fingertips, moving from her jaw to her neck, then up the side of her head where my fingers thread into her hair. I settle my gaze on her eyes.

"I thought of you as family. *My* family. You, Holly, the boys. When I heard your message, something took over my chest, like this tight vice that threatened my lungs." I move my fist to the center of my chest, covering her hands that have clung to my shirt for the last several minutes.

"This is a bad idea," she finally utters.

A short, breathy laugh escapes through my nose and my mouth twitches into a faint smile.

"I know. But here we are." I swallow the fear threatening to derail me from spilling my guts. "I can't keep moving forward like there's nothing here. This thing between us got complicated the minute I saw you in the damn diaper aisle at the market. And then fate made sure I had to look at you every day."

Her gaze dips to my mouth, and I lick my bottom lip, wanting to kiss her.

"It wasn't fate, Brooks. You're the one who made sure we saw each other every day. You offered me a job. I work for you. That's the arrangement, and I can't—"

I move closer to her, resting my head against hers, moving my hand back to the side of her face as I close my eyes and breathe her in.

"I can't jeopardize my custody. My divorce isn't final, and Brandon is being—"

"So, we'll be careful. We'll keep it a secret. Just ours." I dust a kiss on the tip of her nose, and her chin tips up slightly as her lips part.

"Nobody can know," she whispers.

I shake my head slowly and pull back enough to meet her eyes.

"I will guard this secret with my life until you say so. I promise. I promise *you*, Lindsey. I need you like I fucking need air."

My pulse is racing. I never thought I would be able to hand the power over to anyone, but I sense I have to right now. If I don't try, I'll never be whole. It's Lindsey, or it's no one for me. That's how deep I am.

"Say it again," she says.

My brow dents. *Which part does she mean?*

"Tell me I'm yours."

I roll on top of her, caging her under my body, guarding her head with my arms. I drop my forehead to hers and close my eyes.

"You're mine," I say in a low growl.

Her hands snake up my chest until the coolness of her fingers slides up my jawline, and she lifts her chin just enough to press her lips to mine. I bite her bottom lip, holding it between my teeth and gently letting it go, grazing her skin.

"You are fucking mine," I say in a low whisper before diving in for a hungrier kiss.

Lindsey matches my intensity, opening wide as my tongue explores her mouth. She moans against me, her hands working my T-shirt up my body. I help her pull it over my head, tossing it to the floor, then we frantically remove hers. I push the cups of her white, lace-trimmed bra up over her breasts, exposing them. The craving to hold her hard nipples hostage with my teeth is strong, and lean in so I can feast. I suck her nipple hard, sawing gently at the tip with my teeth and igniting a fire that makes her squirm beneath me.

I sweep a hand under her hip and align our bodies so I can push my hard cock against her while I flick her nipple with my tongue. She arches her back at first, then lifts her hips to increase the friction between us.

"I need to fuck you," I say against her lips, and she nods with a faint whimper.

I get up from the bed to push my joggers and boxers down my legs and kick them away. Lindsey shimmies her leggings and panties down her hips, and I take over, pulling them from her legs and throwing them on top of my discarded clothing. She removes her bra completely while I crawl my way up her body, kissing the inside of her thigh until I'm inches away from her beautiful pussy. I glide along her center with my tongue, and her hands immediately sink into my hair.

I chuckle and lick again. She reacts by lifting her lips, trying to get more.

"Not tonight, baby. We need to fuck," I say, satisfying her with one more stroke from my tongue before continuing my ascent up her body.

I press a kiss at the top of the tiny landing strip that adorns her pussy, then to her navel, and the skin above her ribs. I spend a full minute suckling each nipple, making her peaks hard and raw.

I balance on my forearms above her as her legs part, then I grip my cock and guide it along the soaking wet skin between her legs. I coat myself with her, drawing with the tip of my dick until her breathing shifts and I can tell she wants to come.

"Not yet, baby," I say, thrusting into her. Her hand flies to her mouth, muting her cry, and our eyes lock as I slowly pull out of her.

"Again?"

She nods, her mouth still covered, eyes hazed with need.

I rock my hips into her again, driving my cock in deeper, pushing her body toward the headboard. She moves her free hand to the wood above her and braces herself before nodding.

I lean to my left so I can grab her ass with my right hand, sliding out of her almost completely before diving back in. She grunts, then hums with pleasure, so I repeat my stroke, this time waiting only a fraction of a second before pummeling into her again. Her hand slides away from her mouth after a moment, and her gaze fixes on mine, her mouth open and panting as I fuck her hard.

I'm leaving a mark, claiming her. As much as I want to take my time, cherish her intoxicating curves with my mouth, and bring her to the brink on my cock before pausing to draw this out for the rest of the night, I can't. I'm rabid for her orgasm, hungry for my own. We're both manic. Maybe it's the lingering fear that this could all disappear, or perhaps we simply know the kind of fire we're playing with and don't want the flames to burn us up. Whatever it is, my cravings won't be satiated until I fill her completely and she falls apart with me inside of her.

A tiny cry leaves her mouth, so I let go of her hip to cover her mouth with my hand while she wraps her fingers around my wrist to hold on. I pump into her and she wraps he legs around my waist, holding me to her, forcing me to stay inside, even as the first wave rocks through her core. Her eyes fight to stay open as she hums her sweet song against my palm. I can't hold on any longer, and my cock spills into her as my orgasm strips me of my breath. I shudder with each final push, leaving every last drop inside her sweet pussy before pulling out and collapsing on her tits. I taste her nipple while the final waves carry her back to earth, then tilt my head to gaze up into her eyes as she pushes my sweat-damp hair from my forehead.

"Mine," I say, gliding my palm up her side and covering her breast completely.

She moves her hand over mine and holds my gaze with her sleep-heavy eyes.

"Yours," she says. "So very much yours."

EIGHTEEN

LINDSEY

I'm still not quite used to the security system Brooks had installed. It's been two weeks, and I've set the alarm off every day except for one. Normally, I can get to the panel in time to shut it off before the screeching starts. Not today, though.

An arm full of groceries, two hangry boys, and Holly in her carrier all make it hard to be nimble. The auto-call to the sheriff's department has probably already gone through, so I punch in the code once my hands are free, then dial the non-emergency line to wave off the troops.

"I felt safer without the loud alarms," Deacon says, his hands over his ears. He may be a wild boy, but he's never been fond of loud sounds.

"I know, sweetheart. But I promise the alarm system is a good thing. I'll get better at using it," I say, holding up a finger as soon as the operator answers my call.

"Payne County Sheriff's Office. How may I direct your call?"

I recognize the voice on the other line, which is a bit mortifying. It's bad enough to set off a false alarm, but to have someone you knew during your awkward teenage years in charge of it is the cherry on top.

Jade Zildesky was the prom queen my grad year. And she was a genius. She had a full ride to Texas Tech, but like me, she left school early to raise kids. She got divorced last year, or so I heard through the very loud Sweetwater grapevine.

"Hi, umm . . . I had a false alarm. Is there a chance you can cancel the alert before a squad car shows up?"

"Lindsey Blackwood?"

Fuck. She recognizes my voice.

"Hey, Jade. Yep!" I let out a breathy chuckle as I start to pace around the kitchen table. "Can you help a girl out?"

I bite my nail while she tells me to hold on, and after nearly a minute, she pops back onto the line to let me know the alert was canceled.

"Bless you," I say.

"No sweat! Hey, I didn't realize you were back in town? Weren't you living out in those fancy homes on the county island?"

I sure was. Felt kind of smug about it, too. Until I found out my ex snuck his girlfriend over when I wasn't home.

"Yeah, Brandon is still there. I'm . . . here."

There's a long, quiet pause while Jade likely pieces together the clues, and eventually she says, "Got it."

"It gets easier, just so you know," she follows up.

I plop down in one of the kitchen chairs while I rock Holly's carrier with my toe. She's getting heavy in that thing. I think it's time to move her into something bigger. It all happens so fast.

"That's good to hear. Because it's pretty damn hard right now," I say through a soft laugh.

"I'm sorry," Jade says.

I straighten my spine and shake my head.

"I mean, not because of the ex. Believe me, there was *nothing* hard about that." I realize after a pregnant pause that she probably thinks I was making a dick joke, so I laugh. She joins me, then says she understands that part, too.

We make plans to get together sometime, an idea that will probably never come to fruition but feels nice to say, then I end the call and unpack the ingredients for shepherd's pie. Apparently, this town has been talking about my cooking skills, and Brooks has been listening. I'm actually in the mood to make something good from scratch, and it's been a while since I've pulled my grandmother's cornbread recipe out of the tin. Of course, now I need to find the tin.

I start my search for the recipe once the groceries are all tucked away. I want everything ready so I can cook later. I'm half buried in a cabinet under the sink when I hear the front door swing open along with the three beeps from the alarm. My heart skips, and I crack the back of my skull on the edge of the sink as I sit up.

"Ohh, that must have hurt," Brooks says, shutting the door and punching in the code in seconds before darting into the kitchen to inspect the back of my head.

"I think I'm fine," I say. Meanwhile, he cradles my head as if it's a priceless Fabergé egg.

I swivel my neck to meet his eyes, and when his gaze hits mine, it's quickly followed by his perfect smile.

"Hi." He leans into me, but I flinch, moving back and banging my head on the cabinet's edge.

"Ohh, you need to leave this room. He helps me to my feet.

"The boys are washing their hands. We can't . . ." I shake my head, and he grimaces but nods.

I hate the rules, too. It would be so much easier if we could just act like a couple all the time. But there are too many things at risk, and too many people with opinions I don't want to hear.

"Fair warning. The boys have decided they want to play tee ball in the fall. And they would like you to coach," I say to him on my way back to the chair I pulled out from the table earlier. I sit down and begin pulling my things together for my mediation meeting with Brandon. We've completed two sessions of co-parenting class, in which I learned how challenging it's going to be to co-parent with a narcissist. This afternoon, we hash out our differences in the parenting plan each of us submitted. The distance between Brandon and me in our ideas is canyon-esque.

"Really? The boys want me to coach?" Brooks says, taking a seat across the table from me. He stacks my notebooks neatly, then hands them to me to tuck into the leather satchel I now refer to as my divorce bag.

I nod, but bite my tongue because there's a second part to their plan that he's going to dislike perhaps as much as I did. He tilts his head and reduces his smile to a straight line.

"They'd like Brandon to coach, too. With you. Which is—"

"Fucking awesome!" he responds.

I eye him skeptically.

"No, seriously. This is perfect. He'll get comfortable with me out on the field, because we're dudes, and sports is like neutral territory. And then he'll grow comfortable with the idea of us cohabitating, and eventually, we can pretend our relationship was just a natural progression, and then—"

I hold up a hand, chuckling so hard it takes me a minute to speak.

"I'm sorry, but that was, A, a pretty misogynistic fantasy, assuming just because you both are dudes that sports will save the day. B, Brandon has zero athletic ability. At least, not on your level. He'll resent you for making him look stupid. And finally, C, there is no way he is ever going to buy the idea that we weren't hooking up all along."

Brooks chews at the inside of his cheek, but a slight smirk takes hold.

"Hooking up," he says with a snort laugh.

"Gah!" I wave a hand at him before grabbing my satchel along with my phone and keys. "You're impossible."

His hand grazes my ass as I pass, and I swat it but giggle because dammit, I like the dangerous flirting. We're going to get caught; I'm sure of it. But we haven't yet. And the rush makes every stolen moment so much hotter.

The boys rush into the room a second later, diving onto the couch and pretending to slide into second base the way they saw Brooks do it a few weeks ago. They're dying to go to another game. Maybe this weekend, if I can swing it.

"Hey, I have an idea!" Brooks raises his hands up to get the boys' attention, then glances at me and winks on my way to the door. "How about we build a baseball diamond in the living room out of pillows?"

"Yeah!" The boys start pulling apart the couch as I leave, and it's hard not to stay. As it is, I'm going to have to be vague about who I left them with. Kind of like Brandon was during our parenting class.

Mediation is about thirty minutes away in one of the county's satellite offices. It was the closest thing to a neutral location we could settle on, and it was mostly smack in the middle of both our homes. I pull into the parking lot next to Brandon's Land Rover, and the sight of my six-year-old base-level minivan next to his year-old premium ride speaks volumes. Unfortunately, I'm the only one listening and seeing.

I shrug my bag over my shoulder and beep the fob for my van as I trek across the gravel lot and into the portable building used for traffic court and divorce hearings. The next time I show up here, it will be the actual end of us, and truthfully, I can't wait.

I check in at the makeshift front desk, and the administrator makes a copy of my driver's license before waving me to the back of the building. I spot Brandon first through the slender window, then his lawyer comes into view, followed by the last-minute attorney I was able to cobble payment for, together with my parents' help. It looks as though they're still waiting on the mediator, so I let myself in and do my best to avoid making eye contact with anyone but my lawyer.

"Thank you for coming," I say to the man whose name I don't quite recall. He stands and straightens his tie, then shakes my hand before pulling a chair out for me to sit down. He's already more chivalrous than my ex. I somehow keep that thought internal, and preen a little for that.

I pull my bag to my lap and flip through the folder I tucked in there before I left, searching for the torn paper I scribbled the attorney's name on. *Jeff Peters!*

I pull a notebook out next, then tuck my bag next to my chair just as the mediator enters the room. It's a woman, which probably shouldn't mean anything, but means a lot to me. Brandon leaps to his feet first, reaching across the table to shake the tall blonde woman's hand. Brandon may be a professor, but I swear, sometimes he acts more like a salesman.

"Good to meet you," the woman says, offering a pleasant smile. She doesn't look overly impressed, however, and that gives me a dose of hope.

"I'm Meg Redmon." She turns to me, and I take her hand.

"Lindsey. Nice to meet you." I clear my throat when I hear how raspy it sounds.

"You tired?" Brandon says, and I glance at him, wondering why he's trying to come off friendly.

"I'm fine," I say. My response is curt, I realize as we all sit, so I tack on, "Thank you for asking."

It all feels so fake. Every word we say in here. Because it is. I hate this.

"I've gotten up to speed on your case, and I commend you both for putting in the work. I hope you got a lot out of the parenting class," Meg says.

"Oh, absolutely!"

"Meh."

Brandon and I speak over one another, and only one of us

is honest. My attorney twists in his chair, the wheeled feet knocking into mine. I think that was his hint that I need to reset my attitude.

"We get that a lot," Meg says with a chuckle, and I give my attorney a sideways glance and a half smile.

"It wasn't all bad," I say.

He blinks at me as Meg responds with, "That's good."

"It looks like all we have left to agree on is the parenting schedule. Am I right?" Meg pulls out both of our forms, two pages that paint very different pictures.

"That's correct," I say, pulling my hands together and resting them on top of my notebook as I scoot in close. I feel underdressed all of a sudden. I wore jeans and a floral blouse with my sneakers, which, for me, is rather dressy. Brandon is in a business suit, and our lawyers look like, well, lawyers. At least Meg is wearing a dress. It's long-sleeved and drapes to the floor, though, so definitely not casual.

I swallow the dry lump my stress is forming before bobbing my head up to meet Meg's gaze. Her soft smile sets me at ease. I'm sure it isn't intentional, but I use it to get myself on track.

"I understand you have a proposal to make, Mr. Berchaund?" Meg turns her focus to Brandon, and he twists his chair enough to cross his leg over his knee. I used to watch him talk to his students this way when I waited to ride home with him from school. It was before we had the boys, and he was just an assistant professor. It always caught me off guard, the way he'd lean back a bit and fold his hands behind his neck, almost peering down at the female students across from him. I could see everything in his office from the lobby. I wonder, though, what happened when he became fulltime and got a new office in the back, without a window to the lobby, and blinds that shut out the world outside.

I shake my head, ridding myself of the vision of him picking up Caitlyn this way. I have a strong feeling my gut isn't far off, but I don't need to fuel my dislike for the man more than I already do. I can wait until later, when I'm at home and able to throw things in the back yard.

"I'd like to try fifty-fifty. At least until the boys start kindergarten. Maybe we can re-evaluate then." His gaze lands on me, and I feel small under his scrutiny. I glance to my attorney, and he clears his throat.

"It's proven that it's better for the kids to have a primary residence at this age, and typically that's with the mom," Jeff says.

I swivel my seat to look back at Brandon, and he's smirking but biting the tip of his tongue.

"Yeah, but I thought, you know, since you have a roommate and all, that maybe we should let the boys get used to things and have a place to go to that they're used to. I'm still in the house, and their room is the same. It just makes sense, don't you think, Linds?"

Linds. He doesn't get to all me that.

"Don't do that," I say.

My attorney clears his throat, but I press on.

"Do what?" Brandon leans forward, resting his hands on the table as his posture straightens. It's smug. Like him.

"Don't pretend you're any better than me," I say. "Are you telling us you live in that house all alone?"

I quirk a brow and hold his stare, and he mocks me, exaggerating his tight smirk and forcing a pulled-in brow. After a few awkward, quiet seconds, he scoots back from the table and switches his crossed leg.

"All I'm asking for is a few months, through the fall. And then in January, we can evaluate how the boys are doing and see where we're at." He's baiting me, and I know if I don't agree, it's going to look like I'm being difficult, but I also know that when he has the boys, he won't be doing things with them. He hasn't done as much as take them to a park since the monster truck day trip, which I found out he only did because

Caitlyn's father owns one of the racing teams. *I may have done some social media sleuthing.*

"The boys want to play tee ball. They'd like you to coach," I say, leaving out the other half of the boys' plan. If Brandon agrees, I'll cross that bridge, but I have a feeling he won't want any part of hitting practice and baseball pants.

"I have a full course load, and my office hours are late. I can't commit to that," he says, his voice softer now. His cracks are showing. He's not going to give up any of his priorities for our boys, and his priorities are to spend long hours at the college and to galivant about at faculty parties with Caitlyn. I give this proposal two months before he begs me to take the lead.

"They'll be so disappointed," I say, biding my time for a few seconds before raising a finger with my next idea. "Can you at least get them to practices? I'll get them on a team, and if I need to pick them up when you're working, I'd be happy to do that. They really want to try this. It means a lot to them."

I hold his gaze, and the anger brewing behind his pupils is intense.

"This is *their* idea, huh?" he says.

"Yes. It is." I'm not lying about this, so I'm able to say it with certainty and not look away. Brandon studies me silently for a beat, likely deciding whether I'm telling the truth. I'm sure he's pieced together that Brooks is a ballplayer, but the boys' grandfather is a storied high school baseball coach, for Pete's sake. It's entirely possible their newfound interest in the game came from him. It probably didn't, but it *could* have, and that's the difference.

"Fine. I'll take them to practices, though I won't need your help. I don't want anything cutting into my time with them even more. I'll already be losing hours with tee ball."

Our attorneys exchange glances, and I hope everyone in this room is bearing witness to my ex's perspective. He doesn't care that this is an activity our boys want. It's not something he's interested in, so therefore it doesn't count and he shouldn't be punished. What a piece of work.

"And we re-evaluate in November, before the holidays," I say, finding my spine all of a sudden.

Brandon holds my gaze hostage, and I feel as if there's something whirling in his head that he's not saying. I just can't figure out what it is.

"I agree," he finally says.

"Excellent," Meg interjects.

She pulls out a new form, and we spend the next few minutes filling out each of our parts with our lawyers. I balk a little at the fact that his lawyer is the one who will file the plan with the court, but that's my paranoia feeding into my mind. There are witnesses in here. And by the time I tell the boys their father said okay to them playing tee ball, there's no way he'll be able to take that back. None of this is easy, and I hate feeling like I'm fighting for territory rather than my children. It's hard not to let my emotions get in the mix, but I swore when I walked away from my marriage that I would put the boys first. And if what's best for them is spending more time with their father, I will find the strength to support it.

So help me, God.

NINETEEN

BROOKS

It's a big game for me. If I perform in the next two series, there's a slim chance Texas will call me up for a game or two. They've blown their season, so now's the time when everything is on the table. They're going to evaluate everyone, top to bottom, and maybe make some moves. It's my last big chance before the winter meetings to show I'm the right man to slide into short.

My glove is good, but it's my bat that's going to get me there. I need to keep hitting bombs. Driving in runs. And getting fans excited. I hate that my experience for them is as much on the table as my skills on the field, but this game is a business. Everything is for sale. Including personality.

"Hey, Callahan. PR has that interview set up and is waiting for you in the media room. Lots of fancy lights. Try not to sweat," Adler says, laying a hand on my shoulder with a little extra weight and a chuckle.

Adler's a toxic piece of shit, and the reason he got sent down from Texas was to work on his attitude. So far, all he's worked on is everyone's nerves. I made the mistake a few months back of getting drunk with him and told him things I wish I hadn't—about Holly, about how she showed up on my doorstep, and that at first I was afraid to keep her. It was an honest moment, and I went through the same emotions most people would in my situation. It's just that I went on to share my truth with the one guy who likes to hang things over people's heads for sport.

I begged Daisy—Roddy's . . . *girl? I'm not sure what the fuck is up with them*—to watch Holly for the night so I could get my head straight, then I barreled into the woods with the guys and got shitfaced. It was the only time I felt like my parents, and after I threw up most of my insides the next morning, I made a promise never to act like them again. And I made a commitment to giving Holly everything.

All Adler remembers, though, is the scared kid who suddenly had a baby and was thinking about running away from his problems. And now he's jealous because I'm having the season he's being paid to have, and the media is paying attention to me. My gut says after this season, Adler gets released. They won't even bother to designate him for assignment—who the hell would pick him up? He's hitting one seventeen.

"Hey, thanks for being such a great stage assistant and coming to get me," I say, pushing buttons I know are a bit raw for him.

"Fuck off," he says as I leave him alone in the clubhouse. I smirk as I make my way down the hall.

Adler got one thing right: the lights are a bit much in here. It's not a very big room. We don't hold a big media briefing after games in Sweetwater. The only reason this room exists is because of the year the team got the hall-of-famer Jose Contreras back from injury, and he was doing his rehab pitching in Sweetwater. Every sports media outlet in existence wanted a piece of his story, so the team owner gave up his office. Now, it's my stage.

"Brooks! Hey, man. Thanks for taking the time," the reporter says. His name is Ted, but I forget the last name. He's with *The Athletic*, a monthly that's still trying to exist in print. It gets a lot of readers, mostly online, and everything I say to him will shape his story. Since I'm trying to sell Texas on the whole package, I crank my smile up a notch.

"No problem, Ted. Thanks for coming out." There's a glimmer in his eyes when I say his name, and I lock that away as one chip in my favor.

"Take a seat," he says, gesturing to the stool set up amid the bevy of lights

"Interrogation or interrogation?" I joke.

He chuckles, then hands me the mic to clip on the edge of my collar. I try to hide it as best I can, but I'm wearing a Mavericks undershirt and my uniform pants for the game tonight. I'm heading right out of this room to the field.

"It's fine. People are sort of used to seeing the equipment on the video podcast."

I nod and settle into the seat, doing my best to get comfortable on a stool half the size of my ass. I stretch out my legs and fold my hands in my lap.

"Let's just talk for a bit, until you're comfortable. Then we can get into it, yeah?"

I nod. "Sounds good."

"Sweet, sweet." Ted seems nervous, which oddly makes me feel less so. The only interviews I've really done were in college, for the campus paper, and a few for the local Sweetwater rag. This is a big step up for me.

"You cover a lot of baseball? I was checking out some of your stories, and I saw that piece you did on Jarvis when he retired from the Falcons. That was a great look into his mindset at the end of a great career. Really nice work." I did my research.

"Wow, thanks." He grabs at the back of his neck, his cheeks glowing red and not from the lights like mine probably are. "Uh . . . yeah. That piece was a one-off for me. I grew up in Atlanta, and Jarvis was the man, you know? But other than that one, mostly it's always been baseball. I love this game. Grew up pretending to be one of you guys one day. The whole *bottom of the ninth, two outs* kind of thing."

I chuckle and hum, "Yeah." It's a universal core memory we're sharing.

"How about you, Brooks? Was it always baseball?" He sits back and glances at his camera lens, and I'm instantly aware that our conversation is now for real.

I glance up and mash my lips with my thought.

"Was it always baseball . . . uhm, yes and no," I say, dropping my gaze back to his. I'm not supposed to stare directly into the camera, but I swear that lens is ten times bigger than it was a second ago. It's hard to ignore.

"What do you mean by that?" His urging is easy for him, so I bury the bullshit from my childhood that drove me to the sandlot as a form of escape.

"I guess I was like any kid, figuring out what I was good at, what I was bad at. I always liked field day and running at school. I liked to compete. And one day, some neighborhood kids back in Inglewood were throwing a ball around one of the streets, and I jumped in and joined the game."

"Cool, cool. So, it was like actual sandlot ball, then? Wow, I'm jealous," he says.

I laugh lightly and settle into the memory, at least the good parts.

"Yeah, it was Inglewood, so you either rode a BMX bike around and jumped wheelies off of plywood propped up on bricks or you played stick ball in the street. It wasn't really a stick, though. This guy, Dennis, he was four years older than me, had a really nice bat. He played for one of those travel ball teams, and when he wasn't playing in a tournament, he set up a game for us in the street. The first time I swung that bat . . . *man.*"

I close my eyes for a beat, the visual still ingrained in my mind of the ball sailing across the intersection and busting the beer sign hung on the open door of the bodega.

"You remember what kind of bat it was?" he asks.

My eyes peel open, and my smile slowly spreads.

"Easton Echo," I say, practically singing the words like a love song.

"I know that bat. My family couldn't afford it when I was a kid, but I got to swing one once or twice. Black and gold, right?"

I point at him and laugh.

"That's the one."

I sink into the stool, my shoulders relaxing as I get more comfortable with our talk. Ted feels his way into the subject of Holly next, which I was prepared for, and we manage to navigate it without prying into her privacy too much or diving too deep into how she landed with me.

"It seems like parenting is as important as baseball to you, at least when you talk about your daughter, and making sure you're there for her," he says.

"It's more important. Being Holly's dad is number one. Everything else is second place. I'll say this, though. I'm a better player, a better teammate out there on the field since Holly showed up. She gives me purpose. I put in the work because I want to make her proud."

I worked out that answer during my drive here this morning, and I'm glad I got to say it. If Holly ever sees this interview, because lord knows things live forever on the Internet, I want her to know that she has always been my reason. My inspiration. My best self.

"Now, your relationship with your own father hasn't always been so easy." His sudden shift in topic throws me, and I'm not sure how to respond.

"Your dad, he was in prison for most of your life, but he's out now, am I right?" he follows up.

I rock back and draw in a deep breath, blinking my gaze

down to my lap. I'm not sure why this is coming up, but I have a feeling either Adler gave Ted a tip or my father's been talking to anyone who will listen.

"I guess so. We don't really talk. When I was a kid, I was definitely not his priority. Pretty much everything else came first, so . . . yeah. That's *that*." I snap my mouth shut, and my short response seems to send the message I intend.

"That's not how you're parenting, though. Holly . . . she's number one," he says, his gaze meeting mine, and his eyes are weighed down at the corners with what I perceive as a touch of apology.

"Number one," I reiterate.

"Let's talk baseball," he segues.

"Now we're talking," I say, rubbing my hands together. We spend the next ten minutes rehashing my highlights over the last two years, as well as the last two weeks. It's a cake walk compared to the first half of the interview, but I don't relax again until the mic is off and I'm heading out the tunnel to the field.

"How'd that go?" Adler says when I pass him in the dugout.

"Fuck off," I say, and his chuckle tells me he is the one to thank for the deep research that landed in Ted's lap.

I was careful not to clue Ted in that Holly's at the game. I didn't want him knowing about Lindsey, either. And I'm damn glad I kept my mouth shut around Adler about my fan section for the night. The only ones who realize I have family at the game are Roddy and Jayden, and only because the two of them are peppered with chirps from Deacon and Riggs for every foul ball that doesn't clear the net.

"Look how many we got!" Deacon says, holding the front

of his hoodie out to show off his collection of baseballs as if they're Easter eggs.

"Nice, dude! Maybe we can use them for tee ball when the season starts. For practice," I say, ruffling his hair.

"Yeah!" Riggs cheers, snagging one of the balls from his brother's shirt and dropping it to the ground so he can kick it all the way to the parking lot.

"You were great tonight," Lindsey says, her subtle smirk making me wish we're alone so I could kiss it.

"Yeah?" I fish for more.

"You know you were good. Four RBIs and a solo home-run? Come on. Just don't get yourself dealt to one of those faraway franchises like Seattle or Boston."

"Linds, if Boston picks me up, I'm going and you're coming with. We're all going. Hell, I'll even move Brandon there just to keep the custody intact. If Boston calls, you go."

She chuckles and nods, then leans her body into my side. Holly is fast asleep in the carrier, and my forearm is tiring from hauling her. I'm not sure how Lindsey does it on her own. She might be stronger than me.

"Hey, so I've been thinking," I say, my heart rate picking up as I venture into my question. I've been wanting to ask Lindsey to come on a road trip with me for a while, and Brandon has the boys next weekend, so this would be the perfect chance.

"Why am I nervous that you were thinking?" Lindsey teases.

I laugh, and my nerves show in the vibration. We get to her van, and I slide the door open so the boys can pile in before I lock Holly's seat into place. I close the door but keep Lindsey outside for a moment so I can talk to her without her two little spies eavesdropping.

"On Thursday, we leave for Arkansas," I begin.

"Uh huh," Lindsey says, her head tilting as she gives me side eyes.

"And the boys will be at their dad's."

"Yeahhh," she says.

I really thought she'd get it by now.

My head falls back as I let out a light groan, then I drop my chin and meet her gaze.

"Come with me."

She blinks a few times.

"To Arkansas?"

"No, to the gas station. Yes, to Arkansas," I tease.

She twists her lips, and I can sense her reluctance.

"Come on. It's not that far of a drive, and I always get my own room. The story can be you're watching Holly while I'm on the road."

"But I already watch Holly . . . at home."

I bend my knees and groan, glancing to the side.

"Yes, I know. But maybe if it works out well, you can come along for more games. And I'll sell it to the guys that I'm nervous about leaving you and Holly alone since the break-in. Which isn't much of a tall tale, to be honest. I don't like leaving you guys.

"If it makes you feel better, we can get adjoining rooms. And according to everyone else, you'll be there for Holly. Except at night, you'll be there . . ." I feel dumb having to finish this.

"For you?" The way she says it, with a touch of snarky sass, makes me want to sink my head into my shoulders. I look off to the side again, my stomach quickly knotting.

"You know what? You're probably right. It was a crazy idea. Just forget—"

"I'll come," she says.

My gaze flies back to her, and I temper my smile as I'm well aware of the audience pressed against the windows inside the van.

"Yeah, we'll try it. I think we should get adjoining rooms, though. And if Brandon asks any questions, you'd better get one of those assholes on your team to vouch for this story. But yeah, Brooks. I'll come to Arkansas with you."

I bite my lower lip.

"You know I want to fucking kiss you so hard right now, right?"

"I know," she says, smirking as she rounds the front of her van and opens the driver's side door.

"What are you guys talking about? What's funny? Why is Brooks so happy?" Her boys pepper her with questions, and she looks to me to fix the mess I made. She doesn't seem upset, though. Instead, it's like she's challenging me.

"We had a bet that if I hit a home run, I could bring home donuts for second dinner. And guess what?" I say, earning me a killer eyeroll from Lindsey.

"You hit one!" Riggs shouts.

"Yep! I'll pick them up on my way home. You guys get ready for bed, okay?"

I shift my gaze to Lindsey, and she mouths, "I'm going to kill you." She doesn't mean it, though; I've seen her with a chocolate long john. She's happy about the donuts, too.

"See you in twenty minutes," I say, pushing Lindsey's door shut, then waving goodbye.

I wait for my family—*my family*—to pull out of the lot before I head to the players' section where my SUV is parked. I press the remote start to get the engine going and start my seat warmer. That shit feels amazing on a sore back. A man pops up from the driver's side undercarriage when I start the truck, and I stop with the length of the vehicle between us, feeling my pocket for my phone. I've never wanted one of those pocketknife keychains until right this moment.

"Can I help you?" I say, my senses pinging every clue around me. I smell weed in the air, and there are enough lights out here that I'm sure the security camera is picking this up. I'm okay. This is okay.

"Hey, man. Sorry, I was just sitting by your ride and

waiting for you to come out. Name's Marcus. I'm a big fan." The guy is clearly a bit out of it. He sways on his feet as he attempts to walk toward me. I hold up a palm to stop him.

"Whoa, that's good, man. We're good. Nice to meet you, Marcus." I shift my feet, guarding my stance so I'm ready for anything.

"This truck of yours, your mom give that to you?"

My gaze narrows on a dime.

"Marcus, I think you need to leave." I pull out my phone, no longer caring if he sees me call the cops.

"Oh, hey. No, no. It's not like that. Just, I recognized it is all. Your mom and me, well, I knew her. I sold her this SUV. You were in college, I think. Maybe high school."

I was in college, but Marcus doesn't need to know shit about me.

"You ever think about selling it?" he says.

"Marcus, I'm calling the cops in about three seconds."

"Yeah, I hear ya. It's just, I really liked this car, ya know? And I'd buy it back. If you were selling it. Maybe get yourself a fancy new ride with that signing bonus."

"I'm dialing now," I blurt out, pressing the red button on my phone. I put it on speaker so he can hear the ring.

"Fuck, dude. Fine. I'll go. Shit," he mutters, hiking up his jeans that sag well below the band of his red boxer shorts. His face is neatly shaven, but his body is skinny, and as he wanders into the darkness on the other side of the security fence, I catch the flare of a lighter flame and the glowing end of a smoke. Probably a joint.

"Nine-one-one, what's—"

"I'm sorry. That was an accidental dial. Thank you." I end the call, but stick around the bright parking lot for a few minutes until I can't see Marcus and his joint glowing in the distance. He walked in the opposite direction from where I'm going, but I'd be a whole lot happier if he never showed up at all.

He's a junkie. Probably dealt with my mom. Or paid off some debts by giving her this SUV. And he's right, I should sell it. There's no sentimental value in it whatsoever. It was more of a trophy for my survival. But now, it's dangerous, especially if Marcus wants it back. Hell, maybe I'll trade the guy at the donut shop for it. A dozen long johns for one big pain in my ass.

TWENTY

LINDSEY

I'm still not convinced this is a good idea. In fact, I'm sure it's not. But I feel young and excited, like I've been given a second chance to experience a great love story, so I'm going to stuff those worries deep down while I'm away with Brooks. I deserve to enjoy this.

The boys are excited for their weekend with their dad, which helps. He's taking them camping, which . . . I don't think Brandon knows much about. But he's going with our old neighbors, who have three boys of their own. I suspect the reason Deacon and Riggs like going to their father's so much is ninety-nine-point-nine percent due to seeing their friends down the street. Two weekends ago, the neighbors were gone, and the boys were miserable.

Brandon rented a fifth wheel, so it's not like they'll be roughing it. It has running water, and a full working kitchen. I doubt they'll actually fish, which is one of the things the boys want to do, but I can take them when they come back. I'm better at it anyhow.

This weekend, I'm just the nanny. Well, not *just* the nanny. I'm also Brooks's dirty little secret, and I haven't stopped thinking about it for the entire drive to Little Rock. Brooks had to ride with the team, but I've trailed along, keeping pace with the charter bus for most of the way. I maybe should have held back a few miles to avoid walking into the hotel with the team, but I've already parked near the bus and have been spotted by several of his teammates.

I flip open Holly's stroller, then secure her carrier to it. She's still asleep from the long car ride, but I'm sure she'll wake soon. And she'll be hungry.

I'm loading her things into the space at the bottom of her stroller when a shadow looms over me. I glance up, expecting Brooks, but it's Roddy getting in his baby fix.

"Nice of you to bring her for this trip, Linds. Too bad the boys couldn't come along," he says, tucking Holly's blanket around her feet.

"Maybe they can make the next one," I say, standing and stretching my back from the long drive. "If this goes well, Brooks would like to make it a thing. So he has more time with her . . . ya know."

"Yeah, I bet," Roddy says. His gaze lingers on mine, and I can't say for sure, but I think he knows me being here isn't strictly to be Holly's nanny.

"Hey, how was your drive?" Brooks says, stepping in before the tension between Roddy and me boils to my breaking point, and I confess everything right here in a Marriott parking lot.

"Same as yours, only my experience was probably more like your bus driver's," I say, rubbing my lower back.

"You should give her a massage," Roddy says, a little under his breath but not enough so I can't hear it. He winks at me, then walks toward the bus to unload his catching gear.

"Shit," I mutter.

"Yeah, Roddy might be on to us. But honestly, Linds? Nobody really cares. If I tell them you're here to take care of Holly, that's the story they'll tow. And Roddy wouldn't say shit to anyone. You know, he said he never liked your ex."

I stare at Roddy's back while he yanks his catcher's bag from the belly of the bus.

"Yeah, I think he and Daisy wanted me to get with their son, Jake. But I babysat that boy when he was ten, and I just never saw him as anything other than the little kid who was obsessed with fart jokes." I shrug as Brooks chuckles.

"So, you knew Roddy when he was with Daisy?"

I snort out a laugh.

"I knew Roddy when he fucked things up, and when he came back and blew it again, and again. We'll see how it goes this time. He's a great guy, but I'm not sure he's a great husband. And the verdict's out on his parenting."

Brooks nods and grunts a short, "*Hmm.*" He takes my suitcase out of the back of my van, then closes the door, wheeling it for me along with his gear bag while I push Holly toward the hotel entrance.

I hang back with Holly while Brooks checks in with the team. When he waves me toward the elevator bay, I scurry to catch up. I push the stroller in and step to the side while Brooks moves in behind me. The doors are almost closed when a hand pushes them back open and Jayden and the team's female hitting coach slip inside with us.

"Hey, Brooks," Jayden says, giving his teammate a slight nod.

"Hey." Brooks keeps it short, and I look down at my feet as the elevator moves upward.

"You going to the dinner?" Jayden asks through a yawn.

"I'm pretty beat. Plus, I got Holly. I'd like to give Lindsey a break and spend some time with her." Brooks says it so casually, *I* almost buy his story.

"Yeah, I'm exhausted too. Bus trips suck, man. I'll probably turn in early. Gotta get the legs fresh and ready for tomorrow morning, chasing down all the damn fly balls our fucking bullpen gives up.

"No doubt," Brooks says through a breathy laugh.

The doors open on the fourth floor and Jayden slips out first, holding the door with his hand so it doesn't close while Coach steps out.

"Good night, dude," Brooks says.

Jayden nods and says, "You too."

While I keep my chin down, I lift my gaze and watch Jayden head down the hallway as the elevator doors shut, and though I can't say for certain, I swear he reaches for his coach's hand.

"*Uhh*," I hum.

Brooks turns to face me. "What? I think that went fine."

I huff out a short laugh.

"Oh, *we're* fine. I don't think he was interested in either of us at all. He had his mind on *other things*."

Brooks narrows his gaze on mine, puckering his lips while his mind works, and I see the moment it hits him.

"Oh, shit!" His brow shoots up.

"Yeah, I think he's hitting that. Pun totally intended."

"Yeah, I've had a feeling. That's . . . well, all right. See? You and I aren't controversial at all." He reaches up and strokes his thumb across my nipple through my T-shirt, and I suck in a quick breath.

"Uh, fooling around in an elevator is a little too public," I chastise.

He chuckles, then turns back around while we ride the rest of the way to the eighth floor. Meanwhile, my nipple is now buzzing with heat. And I feel myself getting wet.

I'm not sure how Brooks pulled it off, but we have adjoining rooms at the end of the hallway on the top floor, and my room has a full wall of windows overlooking the river.

I push Holly inside and take in the view while Brooks pulls her out of her seat and lays her on the bed to change her. She's such a good baby, and normally, I'd love spending this time with both of them, playing with her and watching her discover new things. But all I can think about is the buzzing energy Brooks left behind when he touched my breast.

Holly cries as Brooks cleans her up, and I hand him a fresh diaper, then dispose of the soiled one by double-bagging it and running it down the hall to toss it in the maintenance trash. By the time I get back to our rooms, Brooks has already made Holly a bottle, and he's pacing around the center of his room while feeding her.

"I'm going to freshen up while you spend some time with her. Is that cool?" I point with my thumb toward my shower, and he nods.

It's been a while since I've stayed in a hotel. In fact, other than a trip downtown to catch the Thunder game with Brandon when the boys were first born, I don't think I've been in a hotel since before we were married. There wasn't time for getaways, and all our funds went to paying for school, which Brandon attended for six straight years.

A hotel shower is literally one of the world's wonders, in my opinion. An endless stream of hot water, and a large space with fresh towels that someone else cleans at the end of the day. Gah! It's bliss.

I get the water steaming hot, then strip out of my T-shirt and linen shorts, shimmying out of my white lace panties before unhooking my bra. I open the glass door and hold my hand out to test the temperature before stepping inside, then glance over my shoulder to see if Brooks can see me through the open door. He can't at this angle, but I leave the door wide open anyhow, just in case.

I lather my hair with the hotel's shampoo, washing it twice before filling my palm with way too much conditioner. When it's someone else's supply, I don't have to be stingy, and I love the way this particular product smells of vanilla and lavender. I'm massaging my scalp when Brooks suddenly steps into the shower with me.

"May I?" he says, working his hands into my hair and threading his fingers between mine.

"*Mmm*," I hum, leaning back until my back rests on his hard chest. His cock pushes against my ass.

"Holly's out like a light. She takes after her daddy. A full meal and it's time for a nap," he says, chuckling against my neck, then licking the beads of water from my skin.

I lower my hands and reach behind me to feel for his hips, guiding him so his cock slides between my ass cheeks. I've never had anyone that way, and suddenly I'm filled with so many ideas.

"You should eat, then. So you can get a good night's sleep," I say, hinting in the most obvious way.

"I should," he says, nipping at my ear before gliding his hands, slick with conditioner, down to my breasts.

"I fucking love your tits," he groans, kneading my breasts, then pinching my nipples while the water washes away the leftover product from my skin.

I arch my ass as his hands move to my hips, and he lowers himself to his knees as I press my palms against the tile wall. He nudges my legs apart more, then palms my ass with both hands before licking my pussy from behind.

"Oh, fuck," I moan, bending over further to give him better access.

He pushes his tongue inside my pussy while his hands pull my cheeks apart, and when the pad of his thumb teases my asshole, I whimper, wanting more.

"Oh, you like that," he says through a devious chuckle.

"Uh huh," I cry, nodding and bending over even more so that the top of my head is resting on the wall.

Brooks sinks a thumb into my ass to test me out, and my body tightens around him.

"Relax," he whispers, kissing my ass cheek before sliding his thumb in and out a few more times.

His tongue laps at my pussy, licking me with long strokes,

then flicking my swollen clit. Soon, he sinks a finger inside of me, still circling his thumb inside my ass, and the dual sensations bring me close to the brink.

"What do you want, Lindsey? Do you want this?" He works his finger in and out of my pussy, then halts it, leaving me breathless.

"Or do you want this?" He sinks his thumb into my ass a few times, then pulls it out.

I nod, rolling my head against the shower wall.

"I want both," I say. "I need both."

He playfully slaps my ass as he stands behind me, stroking his cock as his palm flexes wide over my skin, locking me in place.

"Then I'll fuck them both," he says, guiding his cock to my pussy first and slowly sinking into me.

"Oh, shit," I whimper, slapping the shower wall above my head as he slowly pulls out and then drives into me again. I squeeze my own breast with my free hand, pulling on my nipple to relieve the building ache.

"Oh, that's too fucking hot, Lindsey. You can't do that," he says, suddenly reaching around my front to straighten my spine while he's still inside me.

He flips the shower fixture off, and I have to stand on the tips of my toes to keep his cock in place, but it's worth it to feel both of his hands on my breasts as he pumps into me from behind. As his hips work faster, his hands slide down to my hips, holding me in place so he can fuck me harder.

He pulls out and steps back, then holds out a hand, urging me to follow him. My body beckons me to follow, and I feel drunk yet totally aware of every nerve in my body. I step over the shower curb and move toward the sink counter. Brooks spins me to face him, then lifts me onto it and spreads my legs so he can step between my knees. He guides his cock into me within seconds, and I lie back so my shoulders and head are resting on the mirror as he pummels into me as his hands hook under my thighs.

He seems practically mesmerized by the way my tits shake with the force of his cock thrusting into me, so I touch my nipples again with one hand, hoping it drives him even more wild.

"Oh, fuck," he growls as I pinch myself. He jerks my knees forward until my ass is nearly hanging off the sink, and I brace myself with my other hand as he pulls out of me, then guides his cock into my ass.

"Relax, baby," he says, pushing his tip in at first, teasing me as he gets me used to his size.

Brooks is thick, and I should be worried about him putting his cock there, but I'm not. I want to feel him inside me everywhere. I want to please him with all of me, to taste him and have his cum paint me inside.

"I'm ready. I swear," I say with a vibrating whimper.

"Oh, yeah?" He slides in deeper, going slow as my body expands to take him.

"Ah!" I cry out, my mouth held open as I look between my legs.

He pauses about halfway—at least I think it's halfway—then slowly slides out before pushing in again, this time deeper. He works my pussy with one hand as he pulls out of me again, then teases me with the tip of his cock, coating his dick with my wetness dripping down before pushing it back into my ass. His slick shaft slides easily this time, and I take him all the way.

"Yes," I utter, my head resting on the mirror again as my eyes roll back with the movement of his hips. He goes slowly at first, teasing my clit while he fucks my ass, but soon, I'm climbing to my peak and begging him to go harder. He does as I say, fucking my pussy with two fingers while he fills my ass with his cock. I come undone, numb from the explosion of nerves throughout my body. Brooks holds me in place as he fills me with his cum, pulling out of my ass and painting my pussy with the last few drops.

He leans over my naked body when he's done, one hand at the arch of my back so I don't slip from the counter, and his forehead lands on the mirror above mine.

"I think I like it when you travel with me," he whispers, shaking with an exhausted-sounding laugh.

"I'm really only here for the hotel shower," I tease.

Brooks laughs out louder, then pulls me up so I'm sitting solidly in front of him. He moves his hands to my face, stroking my cheeks with his thumbs before dropping a chaste kiss to my mouth.

"It's good you like this shower, because you're going to need another one after that. Come on," he says, helping me to my feet.

He washes my body clean, taking care to clean every place he had me before shutting the water off and drying my skin. He walks me to his room, pulling a large T-shirt from his suitcase and slipping it over my head.

He offers to get us room service, but I'm too tired to eat. Plus, I'm too happy lying next to him in his bed while Holly sleeps in the small bassinet next to us. If this weekend is our fantasy, I'm not wasting any moments of pretend on over-priced burgers and fries. I'd rather take more showers with him instead.

TWENTY-ONE
BROOKS

ONE MONTH LATER

I thought the off-season would be hard. I dreaded it when spring ball began, because I figured I would be grinding away in a gym all by myself, hoping to gain that one extra pound of muscle that would make the difference.

Instead, I love the off-season. I'm coaching tee ball to a bunch of four- and five-year-olds, and I'm giving lessons to the high schoolers on the side. And none of it is for the money. It's to keep me close to the game, and close to the girl.

And that muscle I thought I needed? It's probably good. I finished the season hitting three-fourteen, with seven homers and a Sweetwater record for RBIs. I'll never be the slugger Roddy was, but I'm not looking to fade out as a designated hitter. I want to be known for doing it all. And this season, I feel like I did. Texas didn't call me up, but they didn't pull up any position players for the last few games.

I got some looks from the right people. Coach likes me, and he's a direct line to Corey Bustos, the manager in Texas. As long as Corey doesn't get shit-canned before he has a chance to call me up next season, my chances are good.

For now, though, I'm vested in teaching this rag-tag crew how to throw to the chest. If only my two star players were here to use as examples.

I glance over at Lindsey, who is watching Holly roll from side to side on a giant blanket under the tree. My girl is officially a scooter. Her crawl is a bit start-and-stop, but I can tell she's itching to get to places on her own. *Fiercely independent.* That's what Lindsey calls her. I hope so. But also, I hope a little part of her always needs her dad.

I sometimes think that when I see Lindsey talking with her dad, Dale. He was really close with her sister, Renleigh, but there's a kinship between Lindsey and her father that Renleigh doesn't quite have yet—parenthood.

The two of them are yapping beyond third base, her dad rattling on about how kids at this age should master the basics. I bet he was one hell of a high school coach. I bet he goes back to it, in fact. He's doing so well now that his cast is off. When he broke his leg in the middle of stroke recovery, Lindsey and her sister were both worried that he'd backslide. But his injury actually seems to make him work harder. I also feel his second chance with his wife fuels him some. He picked up his balance quickly so the two of them could start ballroom lessons, though she has to lead. And if he didn't need that cane to steady himself when he walks, he'd be right out here with me, shagging balls and rolling grounders. At the very least, he'd be driving his pickup toward the city to pick up his grandkids, who have now missed two practices in a row.

I wander over to Lindsey, and she shifts her gaze to the parking lot. Her soured lips tell me everything I need to know about the disappointment she's feeling. Her ex promised to bring the boys to practice today since he missed bringing them to the last one. He had office hours, apparently. And when Lindsey asked to pick the boys up so they didn't miss out, the guy got super cagey. It's obvious he doesn't want his sons hanging out with me. It's also apparent the woman he was having an affair with is now living with him and watching Deacon and Riggs when he's not home.

"They're too busy playing house," Lindsey mutters.

Her dad coughs out the word, "Asshole."

"I agree," I say.

She twists her body to face me, and her eyes squint as her lips bunch up with a pensive expression.

"I should go get them. Should I go get them?"

I shake my head because I really don't know the right move here.

I wish I could take her hand and kiss it. Her parents have us figured out, so I don't feel the need to pretend in front of them. But also, Lindsey's still worried about her ex using anything he can against her in court. And some of these judges out here are pretty sexist when it comes to separated couples fraternizing before divorces are final. Brandon gets to keep playing house with his mistress, but meanwhile, Lindsey and I have to stick to her carefully crafted script.

It's getting harder to stay out of her room when the boys are home, though. The only good part about them being at their dad's—we don't have to be so guarded. Holly's too young to tattle on us.

"Wait, I think that's him," I say, gesturing to the Land Rover that just pulled into the parking lot near the playground.

The back passenger-side door flings open and Deacon and Riggs come flying out of the SUV. They are each carrying new bat bags and running in bright orange cleats that look like they just came off of the production line. Brandon steps out finally, dressed in khaki pants with the cuffs rolled up, white sneakers, and a linen short-sleeved button down. He looks ready for a cruise.

"I guess they had to go shopping first," I say.

"*Hmm*, always buying their love," Lindsey says, rolling her eyes and turning her back to her ex as he walks up. She busies herself with Holly, and I position myself in front of her, so her ex has to go through me if he wants to make any comments.

I stand my ground, high-fiving the twins when they reach me. I send them off to play catch and warm up, and they give their grandpa a quick hug before racing off and leaving me alone with their father.

"Sorry, we're late," he says, pulling his sunglasses from his face and tucking them in his shirt pocket.

"Yeah, it's best if you can get the boys here for the start. It sets a bad example."

I had *zero* parents around when I was a kid, but I always made it to practice on time.

"They're four," he says, pursing his lips.

"Yeah, and you're twenty-seven." I could take my sunglasses off to match him, but I kind of like that he can't see my eyes behind the lenses. Means I can glare at him all I want.

"Relax. I got them here this time, didn't I?" Brandon moves toward Dale and reaches out a hand. Lindsey's father stares at it for a beat, then looks up at the man who used to be his son-in-law.

"What am I supposed to do with that?" Dale says.

Brandon huffs, then utters, "Fine," and pushes his fists into his pockets.

The three of us stand together and look on while the twins throw the ball back and forth, missing with their aim more often than not. They're laughing, though, which is what I remember most about my first few baseball practices. It was all about the fun for me. It forged a lifelong love affair with the game. I want that great beginning for the twins.

"You want to grab a glove and join us?" I prompt Brandon. The silence had gone on long enough.

"Aww, I wish I could, man. But I just stopped in to talk to Linds about something."

I glance to my right, where Lindsey is still crouched next to Holly. Her shoulders have risen, and I'm not sure whether it's because she's anxious about talking with her ex or because he called her Linds. Both, I think.

"All right, well, I'll be out there running drills. If you change your mind, I have a spare glove in my black bag. I mean, unless you ran out and bought a brand new one." I turn my back on him and shake with a short laugh. That's all I can do to the dude, make jokes about his money and the way he's trying to buy his boys' affection. My jab doesn't seem to faze him. It would be so much easier if I could punch him in the nose.

"Come on, Dale. I could use your help with this drill." I urge Lindsey's father to walk out to the middle of the field with me, and he obliges.

We gather the kids into two lines and walk them through a relay race in which they run to the other side of the infield, then field a slow-rolling ground ball and throw it back. It's going to be chaos, like it always is, but the kids will love it, and they'll start working like a team to figure things out. Plus, it will give me time to keep an eye on the conversation happening between Lindsey and her ex.

"I don't like the way she gets small around him," I say to her dad as the kids get started. Both balls have already been missed, and half of each team is racing to retrieve them.

Dale grunts and covers his mouth, though not well, and leans toward me.

"I hate the way he's standing there breathing on this side of the ground."

I flash my attention to him, a bit shocked and definitely glad his grandsons aren't nearby, then we break into heavy laughter.

He shrugs.

"I said what I said. Never liked the guy. He doesn't like sports. Who doesn't like sports?"

It's a fair assessment, especially from a guy who spent his life coaching and who raised two daughters who know more about baseball than most of the dudes doing color commentary on TV.

After a few minutes, it seems as though the conversation has ceased between Brandon and Lindsey, though they're still standing next to one another. Her arms are crossed over her chest, and I've learned enough about her body language to tell she's either fighting not to cry or holding in anger. I don't know Brandon well, but he reads like a kindergarten book with his posture—smugly relaxed with his hands in his pockets, his sunglasses back over his eyes.

Lindsey bends down eventually, picking up Holly and feeling her bottom to see if she needs a change, and Brandon takes a few steps away to give her some space. My guess is he never changed the boys' diapers, so he doesn't know how to handle what Lindsey's doing.

"Can you watch these guys for a sec?" I say to Dale.

He follows my gaze toward his soon-to-be ex son-in-law, then nods. I drop my hands in my pockets after tucking my mitt under my arm, then head toward Brandon, trying my best not to rush. I don't want it to look like I'm rescuing Lindsey. I'm not. She can definitely take care of herself. But I need this guy to know that everyone is on her side.

Brandon tips his chin up as I approach, and I offer him my mitt.

"Want to join in on the fun?" I know he doesn't. He hates that he's stuck out here.

"Is that what they're having? Fun?" He grimaces, then shakes his head at what seems to have devolved into a game of keep-away out on the field.

I chuckle.

"Looks pretty fun to me."

I drop my glove to the ground and look on with him, standing beside him while Lindsey takes Holly to the van.

"You could have hired a real nanny, you know," he finally says.

We eye one another, and he shakes with a smug, silent laugh, then turns his gaze back to the field. I keep my focus right on him.

"She's great with my daughter. She's pretty great with your boys, too." I stare at him until he finally gives in and glances at me briefly.

"Yeah, that's just it. They're *my* boys. You get that, right?" He swallows hard, his Adam's apple giving away the strain he's feeling.

That's what this is about. He's jealous.

I bend down and pick up my mitt again, this time tapping his bicep with it, and forcing him to give it a good look.

"Then, you should go out there with them. They'd like that." He stares at my mitt for several quiet seconds, and I think part of him really wants to take it, but eventually he pushes it away.

"Like I said, I'm good," he huffs.

I shake my head. He simply can't let me be right about something. He'd rather miss out on a great morning in the park with his boys than give in and take a little advice from a guy like me.

"Whatever," I scoff, turning my back to him and heading toward the van, where Lindsey is wrapping up the waste from cleaning up Holly. I take the plastic bag from her, throwing the trash away while she pulls Holly's cotton shorts back into place.

"You okay?" I ask. She's clearly not.

"He said he thinks it would be too hard for me to be the primary parent while I'm going back to school. Apparently, the boys have told him that I'm too busy at the table most nights, on my laptop or reading. And when I'm not, I'm paying attention to Holly. He told me they feel neglected." She sniffles, and I run the pad of my thumb under her eye to catch the tear that falls. I don't care who sees us.

"First of all, there's no way the boys said that. He either

flat-out lied or twisted their words. And second, don't you dare feel bad about finishing your degree. Just because he couldn't be a parent and a student at the same time doesn't mean you can't. Your boys are proud of you, just like I am."

She forces a timid smile onto her lips and croaks, "Thanks."

I nearly reach for her and pull her into a hug, but I stop myself. Her ex is watching everything we do. In looking over her shoulder, though, I catch a glimpse of someone hovering around the back of my SUV. And when the guy turns to the side, I recognize him immediately. It's the same sketchy dude who showed up at the ballpark a few weeks ago. He's holding a stick with a mirror on the end, scanning the undercarriage for something, and he's drawing a lot of eyes—including Brandon's.

"Shit," I mutter, taking off across the parking lot.

The guy hears my heavy steps and instantly breaks into a run, leaving his mirror device behind so he can leap over a neighboring fence. I chase him for a bit, trying to head him off on the other side of the yard he fled through, but he's gone by the time I round the corner. He probably had someone waiting in a car nearby.

I jog back to my SUV, where Lindsey is standing with Holly, and Brandon has made his way over. I pick up the mirror and cut myself on the jagged crack.

"Dammit," I hiss, sucking the droplet of blood from my thumb as I inspect the busted device in my other hand.

"Who was that?" Lindsey asks.

"I don't know." I look over my shoulder in the direction the guy took off, and nothing looks out of place. No cars racing away. Nobody lingering in a driveway. It's quiet.

"He showed up around a month ago, asking about the Suburban. Said he knew my mom." I forget that I have an audience of two, but Brandon quickly reminds me.

"I don't like that you're putting our boys in unsafe situations, Lindsey. And *you* . . ." He points at my chest. "You should be focused on keeping all of these kids safe. Maybe practice is done for today, yeah?"

He shakes his head at me with a look of disgust, then heads toward the field, where his boys are still laughing and having fun with their team. He calls them over and they race toward him, but as soon as their tiny arms sag at their sides with apparent disappointment, Lindsey hands Holly to me.

"He's going to take them home because of some manufactured concern. I'm putting a stop to this," she says, marching toward him while I hang back with my girl.

I should probably follow behind her, but I'm starting to think I'm weakening her defense. And I'm not so sure that concern is manufactured. I don't like that whoever that man is can easily find my vehicle. But I intend on getting to the bottom of that tonight.

TWENTY-TWO
LINDSEY

I'm starting to wonder if was ever truly in love with Brandon, or simply enamored with the *idea* of him. I think I was attracted to his mind.

We met my freshman year of college. He was three years older than me, a senior about to enter grad school. I went to watch a debate with a few classmates as a way to get credit for one of our undergrad classes. But then I saw him at the podium, and the way he made the room bend to his argument was like watching a wizard harness magic.

I should have known then that he would do the same to me.

Looking back, it's so obvious how he worked every argument to his favor. I never wanted to step away from school, but he didn't want to share in the work of being a young parent. I could have easily succeeded in doing both—raising the boys and continuing my coursework. He was afraid he'd have to help, though.

I'm stewing over the words he said out on the field today, but at least the boys got to stay and finish their practice. And I got to take them home with me, a day early. I'm sure that was somehow Brandon's ulterior motive all along. He probably has a big date with Caitlyn, or maybe another student he's cheating on her with. Joke's on him this time, because I got exactly what I wanted. There's no place I'd rather be than here, in this home, with my boys . . . and Brooks and Holly.

Brooks has called us a family a few times now, and at first, I bristled. Not because I don't want it, but rather, I don't want to lose it. It feels fragile, and we're keeping so much of our lives inside these walls a secret. Even within this house, the side we show the boys is different than the way we are when we're alone with one another. I'm tired of sneaking into his room at night for fleeting moments of bliss.

I need to get through the next month, to my court date with Brandon. Then, maybe he and I can try this blended family thing for real. Until then, I'm not sure I should keep a foot in both worlds. I don't want to hurt him. And I don't want us to hurt my boys.

Hearts are evil bastards, though. And damn it if there's not something about him that simply draws me in. He's been on the sofa with his laptop for a while now, rubbing circles in his temple. I think he's struggling with seeing that man again at the park.

His past still haunts him, and I don't think he's been able to move beyond his father showing up out of the blue. I can't imagine being in his shoes, though, so I wouldn't dare force him to confront that demon. I understand that sometimes the walls we build are really meant to keep out the bad guys. If I learned anything from the years I helped Brandon study for psychology exams, it's that there is no black and white when it comes to taking care of one's own mental wellness. There's lots of gray, and what we choose to do in that space is our call to make, and ours alone.

I pull my laptop closer and open my list of this week's assignments, dreading the new round of algebra lessons. I remember hating this course the first time I took it. Now, more than four years later, I want to stab algebra in the heart.

"Trade you," Brooks says from the sofa. I meet his gaze as he holds his laptop up as if I can read the screen from here.

"Gladly," I joke, but when he doesn't laugh with me, I realize he's genuinely asking for help. I leave the table and move to sit beside him. The boys are in bed, but they've been waking up a lot lately, so I don't sit too close.

"Who's Pen?" I ask, reading the name at the top of the email he's showing me.

"Holly's mom."

His words land in my gut with a thud.

"Oh."

I return my attention to the screen, taking in her full name. Pen Cashun.

"I didn't know her last name," he says.

I nod.

"That's okay," I say in a hushed tone.

Brooks doesn't talk about Holly's mother, ever. While he's told me the details about how Holly showed up at his door, he's never delved into the details of the night she was conceived. I haven't pried. There's not a shred of evidence that what happened between him and Pen was anything more than a night of passion and escape. And it came with consequences that he's fallen in love with—Holly. I've never been jealous of what they had, and I'm not now. But I do think there's a part of him that feels ashamed. And I wish he didn't. I begin to read her email so I can understand.

Brooks.

I have been struggling. That's why I haven't reached out sooner. I'm in a safe place now. I'm clean. For a few weeks, actually. Maybe this time it will stick. I was hoping I could see Holly, just once. I have something for you, too. For her. I understand if you don't want contact, and I really have no right to ask. But if you could find it in your heart to give me this one thing, it would mean the world to me. I want nothing more than the two of you to be happy forever.

Sincerely,
Pen

I read through the email three times, each read leaving a tiny, invisible cut in my chest. I don't know when the tears form, but when the first one slips down my cheek, Brooks hands me a tissue.

"You should read the note," he says, leaving me alone with his computer while he hurries to his room. He comes back with a folded piece of paper. I flatten it against the keyboard and read the shaky handwriting of a young girl in crisis.

"She knew you would take good care of her. She did the right thing," I say, handing back Pen's note.

He takes a deep breath as I close his laptop and move it to the side. I twist so I'm facing him and take his hand. His gaze drops to our touch, and his fingers work their way through mine as if he's afraid I'll let go.

"What do I do?" His top teeth saw at his bottom lip as his gaze flits up to mine.

"What does your gut tell you?"

He quakes with a silent laugh.

"My gut is a liar. It told me my parents loved me for years." His head falls to the side, and I mimic him as I caress his face with my free hand. He leans into my palm, closing his eyes before kissing the inside of my wrist.

"Your parents were sick. Addiction, probably other mental illness, circumstances, do not define love based on what you had growing up. That's not the way love works."

He opens his gaze on mine, and we stare at one another in silence for what feels like several minutes.

"I love you," he finally says.

I saw it was coming. I anticipated this while I swam in the blue of his eyes. I lay awake last night thinking of what I would say when he uttered those words. And yet now that I'm faced with them, I don't know what to do. So rather than saying it back, no matter how much I love him in return, I simply smile softly and stroke his face with my thumb.

Our quiet moment is broken up in seconds by the sound of tiny feet rushing down the stairs.

"Mommy! Brooks! Mommy!"

I recognize Deacon's raspy tone and scoot back, putting a foot of distance between Brooks and me. Deacon stops at the foot of the steps and rubs his eyes with a fist. I move to go to him, but before I can, Brooks cuts in front of me and scoops my son into his arms, hoisting him on his hip.

"What's up, buddy?" He begins to climb the stairs as Deacon rubs his face on his shoulder.

"I had a nightmare," my son says. I move my hand over my heart and trail behind them, but when I reach the landing, I halt and simply watch as a different kind of magic unfolds.

"What was your dream?" Brooks asks, pulling back Deacon's blanket, then setting him on the bed.

Riggs sits up and rubs his eyes.

"What happened?" my other son asks.

"Your brother had a bad dream," Brooks explains.

"Me, too." Riggs climbs out of his bed and crawls over his brother, working his small body into the covers with him.

Brooks chuckles, then tucks the two of them in. But rather than leaving, he sits at their bedside and makes up a story about people made of candy. He never asks them what their dream was, probably because he's had enough nightmares of his own to know that kids don't like reliving them. Instead, he replaces the startling dreams with thoughts of silliness, inviting the boys to help him tell the story, asking them what the candy people do for a living. Naturally, the candy people are baseball players. And the two best players are named Deacon and Riggs. At one point, my boys are giggling.

The story goes on long enough that I eventually sit outside their doorway so I can listen to the end. And when they finally fall asleep, Brooks backs out of the room quietly and helps me to my feet.

He tries to break our hold once I'm standing, but I cling to him. I rise on my toes and swing my free arm around his neck, and I kiss him to let him know exactly how I feel. Even if I can't say it, I feel it. And by the way he kisses me back, I think he knows.

TWENTY-THREE
BROOKS

I don't know if I'll regret this. But I read over Pen's email a dozen times, and there's something about it that feels important. Not for me, but for our daughter.

Holly is mine. She's mine alone. I don't think Pen will fight to get her back, or to have shared custody. I don't believe she would have written the words she did if that were the case. She knows her flaws, and she knows some of them may be lifelong battles—ones she could lose.

That's how Pen and I connected. I was in a low place of self-pity, and we'd talked at the pub from time to time, so she was the willing ear the night I bottomed out. I let out all of my anger over my parents, over the death of my mother, and the fucking vehicle I was living in because of them. Pen understood because she'd been raised in a similar household. Only rather than getting away, she fell in deep.

The night we hooked up, she was several months into a recovery. She said she was feeling proud of who she was becoming. But she was lonely. So was I. And we gave each other comfort. Holly was made from something peaceful, something beautiful amid chaos and heartbreak. I like to think she is everything that is and was good between Pen and me.

I didn't want to force Pen to meet me at Earl's, what with it being a bar and all, and her an alcoholic. There isn't much in this town that's open early besides the coffee shop outside city hall, though, so that's what I went with. Now that I'm waiting for her here with Holly, I'm questioning whether Earl's might have been better. It looks a bit like a set-up or a sting, with cop cars parked outside police headquarters, and town employees grabbing their morning coffee inside. At least the patio's nice.

I stand when I see her familiar green Subaru pull into one of the street parking spots a few spaces away. I clutch Holly against my chest, spinning her around so her legs can kick the air rather than me. She's been busy lately, and she's starting to master crawling. If I put her down, there's no telling how far she'll escape to.

I hold up a hand to wave hello. Pen is sitting in her car, engine off, as though mustering the courage to confront me. Us. I have no animosity, so I wave her to join me and smile, hoping it makes her feel safe.

She finally gets out, pulling a patchwork purse over her shoulder. She's wearing a long denim dress, and her golden hair falls in braids on either side of her face. She looks healthy.

"Hi," I say first.

Her eyes are misty as she smiles with closed lips.

"Hi," she says, her raspy voice a little clearer than I remember it. She's doing well; I can tell.

"She says hi, too," I say, lifting Holly's hand and forcing it to wave. She coos and kicks her feet forward before laughing.

Pen's hand covers her mouth, and her eyes tear up.

"My God! She's so big," she whispers behind her palm.

"She's crawling," I tell her.

She drops her hands, her mouth agape, but her smile creeps back in.

"I'd show you, but she'd be in traffic in no time. She's gotten rather fast."

Pen balls her hands together, and I can tell she wants to hold our daughter. I wasn't sure how I'd feel about this, but now that we're here and I see her, it would be a shame not to let her.

"Do you want to?" I stretch my arms forward, and Pen nods emphatically. We step onto the patio, and she pulls out a chair at the table and situates herself. I hand Holly to her.

"Hi, do you remember me?" Pen turns our daughter so she can kick out her legs, holding her under her arms while she dances.

"Oh, my goodness!" Pen makes exaggerated faces, lifting Holly, then bringing her feet back down to her lap.

"Is she making you fly?" I say.

"She's flying," Pen says, lifting her again as she makes a whooshing sound. Holly giggles, and Pen brings her in to hug her close.

"She's a healthy baby. She has an entire team of uncles, and I think maybe half of Sweetwater," I joke. Though it might not be far from the truth.

"Thank you for this." Pen's gaze rests on mine, and for the first time since I've known her, she seems content.

"Of course," I say.

We spend a few minutes catching up. Pen tells me about her work in rehab and how she's moving to Austin, Texas, to stay with an aunt. It sounds like a good thing. It's a relative who once tried to get custody of her when things got bad with her parents, so maybe now that Pen is an adult, she'll get a second chance at having a loving family experience. I fill her in on all of the little moments she's missed with Holly, including the time I met Lindsey in the diaper aisle, clueless. I bring up Lindsey a lot, and eventually she calls me on it.

"She's a good friend," I say, not wanting to label us without consulting Lindsey first. We're more than friends, but what that looks like exactly has yet to be fully discussed. Things are more than physical now. Well beyond that. They're real. For both of us, I think.

As our conversation dies, Pen shifts in her seat, motioning for me to take Holly back. Our daughter fell asleep amid our conversation. She's had a busy morning so far, so I don't blame her.

Once Holly is nestled in my arms, Pen unhooks her purse from the back of the parlor chair she's sitting in and pulls out an envelope. She lays it in front of me, pressing her palm on top for a beat before pulling away.

"It's everything she might—or you might—need to know, from my side of the family. Medical stuff, a little genealogy, my blood type, addresses and phone numbers for the good people I know in case you ever need to reach someone in an emergency. My number is in there too, but I don't expect phone calls or even letters, really. I'd love a photo from time to time, but again . . . I don't expect it."

"I'll send some," I commit.

Her soft smile tells me she's grateful.

"I wrote a letter in there, too, and that's for you to decide. If you think she needs to read something from me one day, give it to her. And you can read it if you'd like. It's nothing angry, nothing sad, but it's the truth. I want her to know that I love her more than anything on this earth, and that's why I left her with her daddy. I knew . . . I *know* her life is going to be amazing with you. Because of you. I sense the love in your heart. And she deserves all of it."

I suck in my lips and nod, tears pooling in the corners of my eyes.

"I'll save it for her. I don't need to read it."

Pen reaches for my hand, and I place my palm against hers. We squeeze each other and lock eyes, sealing this agreement in our own way. I trust Pen. And maybe that's strange, given how Holly turned up at my door, but I believe every word she's said. She's never lied about anything to me, and I would know—I was raised by liars. I can smell them.

Pen stands, so I take the envelope and carry Holly to Pen's car. I hug her goodbye, and she kisses Holly's head before getting in. I see her start to cry as she backs out of her spot, and I could too right now if I let myself.

My world works in balance, though. All good things seem to come with rotten ones on the other side, and when I turn to head toward my vehicle, I catch sight of the same man who has been harassing me for a month as he races by in a beat-up Chevy pickup.

My chest inflates with a deep breath, and my veins fill with a little extra blood as I hold Holly close and take long strides to my SUV. I lock her into her seat, double-checking the clasp as I scan the street through the window. Clearly, that guy has no interest in *me*. It's something about this car.

I close the door and inspect the outside of my vehicle, walking the perimeter and kicking the tires. I get down on my hands and knees and shine the flashlight from my phone up into the underbelly, but nothing seems out of sorts. I feel it in my bones, though. Something is off. It's not this SUV he wants. It's not sentimental. There's something *in* this thing, something I don't want to show up when I trade it in for a fresh ride.

Knowing I won't be able to rest until I figure out this mystery, I go see Roddy, the only person I can think of who might be able to help me take this machine apart. I call him on my way, and he's waiting in his driveway when I pull up, his German Shepherd ready to work.

"She's really trained for this, huh?" I ask as I pull Holly out and move away from my car. His dog's nose is working overtime, nostrils flaring and teeth showing.

"Got Izzy from a state trooper. She's technically retired, but you can't unteach a dog tricks, it turns out." Roddy unclasps the hook on her leash, and Izzy races to the driver's side, barking and growling at the inside panel of my door.

"Pretty sure we need to start there," Roddy says, holding up his drill.

He whistles, calling Izzy off, then gives her a Milk-Bone to reward her for her work. He feels around the door panel, finding a few screws holding the inside paneling in place, but it doesn't take long for him to pop it open, and when he does, more cash than I have seen in a lifetime spills onto the concrete.

"Fuuuuck," I say, stepping in closer.

Izzy rushes over, sniffing wildly at the bundles of hundred-dollar bills. Roddy looks up at me as he nudges one of them with the tip of his drill.

"Pretty sure these things are coated in narcotics. Don't touch a thing."

My stomach bubbles with acid, and I think I'm going to be sick.

"Take her for a minute," I say, handing my daughter to my teammate as soon as he stands. I rush to the gravel along the street and hurl my morning coffee into some weeds.

"Guessing you weren't aware this money was in here when you bought this thing?" He laughs through his words, but I'm suddenly flooded with all of the terrible memories my mind worked overtime to suppress.

This money is definitely saturated with drugs, and probably blood too. I remember the men in our house counting these stacks, piling them into boxes, and moving them to trucks to haul across the state for the cartel to pick up at the border. My mom wasn't small-time. She was *big* time. My father started the business, but when he went away, she took it over. If she weren't such an addict herself, she could have risen to kingpin. Instead, she overdosed after hiding her worth for her only kid to inherit.

Blood money.

Drug money.

I slept with this shit for a year.

I pinch my brow as I pace Roddy's driveway, and he seems to understand that this is something serious for me.

"Do I want to know?" he asks.

I shake my head and utter, "I'm not sure. I don't really know fully. Just . . ." I stop and look up to meet his gaze. "My mom died of an overdose, and this Suburban is the only thing she left me."

Roddy studies me for a beat, likely piecing this information together with the bits about my past that I've shared with him, such as my dad went to prison and my mom was a loser. He nods finally, then sets Holly back in her car seat before pulling out his phone.

"Roddy, I don't think we want more people—"

He holds up a finger, stopping me as he presses his device to his ear.

"Hey, I know we need to talk, you and me. But right now I need some help. It's for Brooks. Can you come watch Holly for an hour or two? I have to help him with something."

Roddy's gaze lands on mine as he listens to the other side of his call. My guess is it's Daisy.

"Thanks. It's for him. This favor isn't for me." He ends the call with that. One day, I hope the two of them can work out their beef.

"You can't call Lindsey in on this. Keep her safe," Roddy says. His eyes widen, and he drops his chin, as if he's waiting for me to agree. I nod, but I also wonder if I should get out of here. I'm not sure what he's thinking of doing.

Roddy heads into his garage and grabs a garbage bag meant for lawn clippings. He puts on a pair of work gloves and scoops the money into the bag. I search his garage for a second pair, and when I can't find anything, I grab two more garbage bags and cover my hands in the plastic. Together, we get the cash into the bag in less than two minutes. Roddy triple-bags it, then knots the end before throwing it into the back of my SUV, along with two shovels.

Fuck.

Daisy pulls up a few seconds later, and my pulse races even faster.

"Let me see that sweet baby," she says as she gets out of her pickup truck and skips over to Roddy and me. I pull Holly back out of her car seat and will myself to mind my expression. I don't need to be showing my panic, no matter how much I'm sweating under this long-sleeved T-shirt and jeans.

"Thanks, Daisy. I'm having an issue with the car, and I don't want her riding in it while Roddy helps me work it out. And Lindsey's studying for an exam. She only has so long before those boys start demanding attention." I chuckle, really selling it, and Daisy waves me off as if it's no big deal.

"You guys go do things with car parts and oil. Meanwhile, Holly and I are going to visit the goats in the back."

She marches through the garage and into the house as if it's her place. Perhaps at one point it was.

"You have goats?" I ask Roddy.

"I have everything," he says. He whistles for Izzy to jump into my vehicle, and she obeys, leaping into the back seat with ease.

"Let's go," Roddy says, sliding into the driver's seat. Before I question why he's driving, he gives me a look that I obey about as quickly as Izzy did his command. I hold up both hands and make my way to the passenger side, and in less than a minute, we're out of his neighborhood and hitting the highway at eighty.

"There are a lot of places to hide things out here, Brooks." He glances at me as he speaks, so I nod.

"Have you hidden things out here?" I ask after several seconds pass without him saying another word. He glances at me again, and when our eyes meet, I sense that's not something he will answer. Ever.

"Okay," I say, swallowing hard.

After we drive east for about twenty minutes, Roddy pulls onto an unmarked dirt road that winds along a dry riverbed, pulling into some thick brush that shields my car from view. It's barren land, and we've traveled far enough away from the highway that I can't hear the traffic, even if I hold my breath and try really hard.

"Let's dig," Roddy says, walking a few paces and glancing around the area.

"Are you expecting someone to be spying on us?" I ask.

He meets my gaze and shakes his head before pointing to the massive boulder lodged next to a petrified tree stump.

"About forty feet south of that. Remember it, just in case." He drops his gaze to the earth, then stabs the dirt with his shovel.

"Why don't we just burn it?" I ask.

He doesn't look up, and he keeps moving the shovel, so I join him, moving dirt to the side as we dig into the soil.

"When money like that shows up in your life, odds are high someone is looking for it. You never know when you might need to give it back, and if you don't have it to give—"

He pauses his shovel but doesn't look me in the eyes.

He doesn't need to. I'm pretty sure I understand. If it comes down to my life, Holly's life, Lindsey's life . . . or the cash. I want to have the cash to give to whoever is asking for it.

We dig for thirty minutes, making a hole about four feet deep. The clay is hard once we break through the topsoil, so if many years pass, I wonder if I'd even be able to dig this cash back up once the dirt solidifies on top of it again.

We pat the earth down, then kick some brush around to mix up the terrain and cover our tracks. Roddy has me pull the SUV out and turn around as he destroys our tire tracks for several feet. He has me back up and form new tread marks that lead into the open field to my right, and I stop before my tires get too lodged in the mud.

I'm heavy on the pedal once we reach the highway, and Roddy clears his throat when I creep close to one hundred miles per hour.

"We don't need to be pulled over right now," he says.

I nod, easing off the gas. My heart is still pounding so hard I think it's chipped my breastbone. My pulse doesn't slow until we pull back into Roddy's driveway. I follow my teammate into his garage, hooking my shovel onto the wall next to his, then stomping dirt from my shoes on the large rubber mat just outside the door that leads to his kitchen.

When we step inside, it's as if the world turns to color once again. The scents of vanilla, cinnamon, and maple permeate the air, and Daisy is standing at the griddle, humming a classic rock song while Holly plays with a stuffed bear on a quilt in the center of the room.

"Is that . . . yours?" I point to the bear. Roddy glares at it for a second, then looks at Daisy.

"She needed a toy. You need to learn how to share," she says, holding out her finger, which is covered in what looks like sugar and syrup.

Roddy sucks it away, and my eyeballs nearly fall out of my head, so I head to the blanket and sit down to play with Roddy's bear. I guess he and Daisy are making progress.

TWENTY-FOUR
LINDSEY

I've missed my sister. I think Brooks has also missed Hunter. When Renleigh called to let me know they're coming to town for a few days, he lit up like he hadn't in days.

Meeting with Pen was hard on him. He came back from his breakfast meet-up with this invisible weight on his shoulders. He was gone for a while, so I'm not sure how intense their conversation got, but he doesn't seem to want to talk about it. At least, not for the last three nights that he's snuck into my room. He just wants to hold me to his chest and stroke my hair. I'm not complaining. But I still feel this vice grip on my chest, like something's wrong.

It's probably my anxiety leading to my divorce being finalized. Brandon has been radio silent since I chewed him out at the ballpark and told him to stop taking his jealousy out on our boys. He didn't deny he was jealous. But he also made sure to tell me that Caitlyn was not living with him, despite anything I'd heard.

I hadn't heard that, actually. I simply assumed since the boys always described her being in the house, sleeping in daddy's bed with him, waking up in one of his T-shirts, and walking around in her underwear in front of them. Good thing they're four!

Thing is, I don't even care if Caitlyn is living there. Not anymore. What I care about is the hypocrisy, that he can behave one way, yet I can't. Truthfully? All of it is wearing me down. And all I want to do is tell my sister about Brooks, and what he said, and how I may be in love with him, too. But on the chance my battle with Brandon gets uglier, I don't want my sister to have to lie for me. Right now, she has plausible deniability. As far as she knows, I'm the nanny. Full stop.

I'm not happy about how comfortable I've become with lying, myself. It makes me feel dirty, and not in the fun way. I suspect that's why I've had a few panic attacks lately. I start thinking about what people see, what they assume, and the stories I need to make up to cover it all. It's too much. All of it.

Which is why this glass of wine and my sister's company is the single greatest birthday gift I could dream of. The big two-seven. It's not a milestone number, but for me, this year is significant. It was a year of change, and a lot of growth. I've found my voice in many ways, and I've started saying yes to the things I want. Not just Brooks, but school, and the idea of maybe getting a job doing stuff my mom did for years.

I sit back and prop my feet on the wooden table as my sister does the same.

"You remember how we always wanted to live in this house when we were kids?" she says.

I chuckle and glance around the porch space. I've made a few improvements, even though it's just a rental for us. The woven rug, the potted plants, and Dad's old wind chimes. Brooks can't stand them, I can tell. When we're out here at night, he takes them down and tells me it's because he can't concentrate on me fully with the distraction. He always hangs them back up, though, because he knows I love them.

It's the little things. And he does so many little things.

"You know, he's probably going to get called up next year,

then this dream house of ours goes—" I mouth the word *poof* and fan out my fingers.

"*Hmm*, we'll see," Renleigh says, eyeing me over the rim of her glass. I match her glare with my own.

"What? You don't think he'll get called up?" My chest tightens a bit. I fear she has heard a rumor, such as him getting cut. I know that's unlikely given his stellar season, but still . . . this game is also a business. It would devastate him.

"No, nothing like that. I'm sure he will. I just . . . I think he kind of likes this place. Hunter does, too. I have a feeling he'll want to make some roots here, is all."

I nod, keeping my eyes on her so I can read how her expression changes. My sister isn't stupid. She has to see beyond the surface when it comes to Brooks and me. But she's always been better at bluffing. And right now, she's not giving me a clue.

We sip from our glasses, and she fills me in on life in Texas and what it's like to sit with the wives at the stadium. I bet she becomes one herself before too long, and I love that for her. My sister didn't believe in love for a long time. She resented our mom for leaving us to spread her career wings. It's a little fucked up, sure, but also, having been put in a box and limited myself, I sort of admire her for knowing she wouldn't be fulfilled as a stay-at-home mom.

"I'm thinking of going into campaign work. Sort of like Mom. After I graduate, of course." Renleigh's gaze tightens, and her mouth pulls in. "I know how you feel. Complicated shit for you; I get it. But I've been learning about some of her early campaign work, talking to her a lot, and it kind of excites me."

Renleigh leans back as she exhales, and I can tell she's still disappointed. I drain the last drops of wine from my glass and set it on the table before moving to the cushioned outdoor loveseat next to my sister. I put an arm around her and squeeze her to me, which I realize while in the act is another thing she's not really hip on—being hugged. Unless it's by Hunter. I hold on anyhow because pissing her off is my job. So is pushing her to do things she's afraid of.

"You should spend some time with Mom while you're here. I'm not saying you have to forgive the shit she did. But maybe you'll understand it a little. It might be good for you. Help you pack away some raw feelings and find closure and shit."

Renleigh laughs at my side, then tilts her head until it rests on mine.

"Closure and shit. I'm going to use that in a toast to Mom when they celebrate their wedding anniversary," my sister says, and I know that it's really a promise.

"You can credit me in the footnotes."

We giggle, and my sister rehearses her pretend speech, blasting through a few favorite sore spots from her childhood, including the time our dad joined her for the Muffins with Mom event at our grade school. By the end of her monologue, she does admit that she's been talking to Mom more than I realize. I don't pry, but I'm glad to hear it. One of these days, that boyfriend of hers is going to propose, and she needs to be in a good headspace to say yes.

Holly starts to cry, so I head into the house to check on her, and Renleigh cleans up our glasses, rinsing them in the sink and stowing our bottle of wine away for her next visit, which I hope is soon.

"Where are my rugrats, by the way? Are they at the asshole's place?" Renleigh, like my father, has never really loved Brandon.

"No, they have preschool. It's been a blessing. I can't wait for all-day kindergarten. I mean, I love being super mom, but those two exhaust me. When they get home, we're going to the park to celebrate my birthday, and that somehow means I'm going to have a sunburn and loads of sand in my hair."

Renleigh chuckles as she slides up next to me, leaning over

Holly while I check her diaper. She's being fussy but she feels dry, so I pick her up and bounce her at my side a bit. It seems to settle her.

"You're great with her. With all babies, really. It's one of your many superpowers, Sis." Renleigh squeezes me with a hug she initiates, and I revel in it for the few seconds it lasts.

"You know, I would make a great aunt one day . . ." I begin. My greatest superpower is nagging my sister.

"And we're done here," Renleigh says, blowing me a kiss as she leaves the house.

Brooks went down to the river with Hunter. The two of them are fishing, which is amusing since they both suck at it. But my father set them up with his old gear, and I think the trip was more about getting in some quality guy time.

I turn on some music since Holly seems ready to play, and bop around the living room with her on my hip. We pretend to dance, and I try to two-step on my own with her affixed to my side. I'm lost in the moment when I spin around and come face to face with Brooks's father, standing in the foyer with a gun held at his side.

I scream and immediately step back several paces, holding Holly to my side and turning my body to shield her. I feel like I might pass out, but that wouldn't help either of us, so I lean my weight against the kitchen table and scan my surroundings for anything sharp, or pointy, or heavy.

"I'm not here to hurt you. I just need to know where the money is," he says.

My eyes lose focus, and I swallow the instant dry lump in my throat.

"What money?" Is he talking about Brooks's signing bonus? He can't possibly think that's how this works.

I reach for my purse, and he lifts the gun, waving it at my hand.

"Don't do that. You stay still."

I nod, my entire body vibrating.

"I was going to give you my wallet. I don't have much, maybe forty bucks. But you can take my bank card. And there's a nice watch in there. One of those that connects to your phone. It's not a name brand; it's a cheap knockoff. You can have it, though. Maybe sell it?"

My eyelids flutter as fear pricks at the corners of my eyes. I feel the tear form.

"Oh, God. What do you want?"

"I need Brooks to give me the money. Where is he?"

His father's pupils seem larger than normal, and he keeps scratching at the arm holding the gun. If I didn't have Holly, I could maybe take him down, or at least run away. But I can't risk anything happening to her.

"He's out. But I can call him. I just need my phone," I say, glancing at my purse.

His father takes a few steps toward me, and I flinch, but he ends up dumping my purse on the table and pulling my phone out to hand to me.

"Call him."

I nod, my hand flailing as my fingers try to work. I consider pressing the emergency button, but again, that gun is probably loaded. And his dad isn't right in the head. I'm pretty sure he's in withdrawal or having a full-on meth-induced delusion.

I manage to press Brooks's name, and his father snatches the phone from my hand, putting it on speaker. Brooks answers after two rings.

"Hey, what's up?"

"It's your dad. I'm here at your house. And I want my fucking money."

He ends the call and tosses the phone toward the kitchen sink. It bangs against the counter and lands in the iron basin, and I'm pretty sure I heard the screen crack.

"Now, we wait," he says, fanning the gun at Holly and me. I think he's telling me to sit down.

I pull the closest chair out and sit in it, and Holly wails as if reading the fear emanating from my body.

"Shut her up," he barks.

I nod and cry, wishing I could yell back that babies don't work like that. Instead, I hush her and do my best to smile through my pained face. My phone vibrates against the sink, and I'm sure it's Brooks calling me back. I mentally calculate how long it will take him to get home. Too long, for certain. But I can survive this. I will keep Holly safe. What's forty minutes when a full life is waiting on the other side?

TWENTY-FIVE
BROOKS

This is what Roddy meant.

I knew it when he said those words, but I thought I'd have years before I came head-on with making this choice. And I never thought it would actually be Lindsey and Holly I was saving. I assumed it would be my own ass. It would come down to the stranger and me. That the guy would finally hunt me down when I'm old and haggard, and he's barely hanging on to life. I'd give him the money and spit in his face before he killed me.

I haven't slept well in days, not since Roddy and I found that cash. I thought about calling the detectives who have been working on our break-in, but they haven't done shit since they inspected the house. And Roddy was right—when someone hides that kind of money in a vehicle, they aren't fucking around. Calling the cops would only put me on the map with the wrong guys even more than I already am.

There are at least two people after that stash: my dad and the stranger. What a fucking gift Mom willed to me. I laugh out in anger as I tear down the highway. Hunter had already left for the afternoon when Lindsey called, and I was just packing up her father's gear. I left it all by the river, but I think her dad will understand.

I continue pressing Lindsey's contact every ten seconds. She's not picking up, and my mind is racing with the worst thoughts. Roddy and I estimated there was about ten million in those stacks. I'm no expert in counting drug money, so it could have been more. It was definitely not less.

I should have fucking called the cops.

I finally reach our street, and I peel around the corner so fast my tires skid across the gravel road. It's not easy to fishtail in an enormous SUV, but I manage to spin out and snap the rear axle, sending my car skidding at fifty miles per hour into a thicket of wild brush.

I kick the door open and race the rest of the way to the house, flinging the front door open and coming face-to-face with Lindsey as she sits perfectly still in a chair in the center of the kitchen, her eyes red with terror and tears. Holly is asleep against her chest.

My head swivels to my father, and I see the gun in his hand a second too late, kicking him in the hip and knocking him back several steps before he grips the revolver in both hands and points it at me.

I shove my hands in the air and position myself between him and the girls.

"What do you want? They have nothing to do with this, so they're going to go. What do you want? Tell me!" My heart is pounding so hard it drowns out all sound, but thankfully, I'm able to read my father's lips.

"Money," he says.

"Only if you let them go," I demand. My mouth tastes of bile.

"If I let them go, how do I know you'll follow through?" His voice is an eerie type of calm, and the marks on his arm tell me he's been shooting up something. Probably a lot of things. I remember those marks, and those hands, hurting me when I was a kid.

"I'll take you to the money. I don't want it. I don't want you. And I never want to see you again," I growl.

My father holds my gaze, his pupils so big they look like black holes ready to swallow up everything alive. He leans to the side and spits on our floor.

His gaze shifts as he stretches to peer around me, but I move to block his view. I don't want him setting eyes on Holly. He might recognize the shape of her chin. He doesn't deserve to know he has a grandchild. She's safer that way.

"Let's go," he says, waggling the gun in my direction.

"I need your keys," I say to Lindsey over my shoulder, keeping my eyes fixed on the man who helped make me.

"They're on the table," she says.

My dad nods toward Lindsey's purse, the contents spilled on the tabletop. I hold one hand up while I sift around with the other, feeling her lip stick tube, then her wallet. I finally land on her keys, and clutch them.

"Let's go," I say, shuffling toward the front door. My father follows a few feet behind me, but pauses, turning around.

"We're leaving, I said!" I growl at him, but he doesn't listen. Instead, he moves into the kitchen. He pulls what I assume is Lindsey's phone out of the sink, then smashes it with the butt of his gun.

"Now, we're leaving," he says.

I turn and continue my way out the door. I press the unlock button on the van key fob, and my father moves to the passenger side while I get in to drive. He keeps the gun fixed on me without bothering to buckle up, and I indulge in a one-second fantasy that involves me ramming the side of the van into a tree and killing him. The variables are too massive, though. And I keep replaying Roddy's words.

There are a lot of places to hide things out here, Brooks.

I pull away from the house and head toward the south

highway. I've replayed the route in my mind a thousand times, instinct telling me I would need to know this one day. Turns out one day was only a few days later.

Once we hit the highway, my father buckles his seatbelt. I glance at his gun hand, and he hisses at me, the same noise he used to make when I caught him smoking behind our old shed. Memories flood back. We did have a yard. And I had a swing. And Mom, she wasn't so broken and ugly. That was when it all started.

"Why?" I ask, not even realizing my words are aloud until my father begins to answer.

"Because I've got nothing else," he says.

He's tucked into the corner, his back resting on both the seat and the door so he can keep his eyes fixed on both me and the road. I wonder how many times he's held someone at gunpoint like this. This isn't something you do on a whim. He's too good at it.

"That's your fault," I mumble.

"Shut the fuck up," he barks.

I shake my head but forge forward. Good ole Dad.

I slow when I recognize the landmarks that precede the unmarked road, and when I spot it up ahead, I turn off the roadway but grind to a stop.

"It's here? Right next to the highway? I'm not stupid. Take me all the way there," he says. His breath smells of rotten teeth and candy. He always liked peppermint. I think when he first started smoking a lot, he ate the candies to cover the stench of cigarettes. Then he moved on to smoking other things, shit that smelled like burnt plastic and cleaning fluid. How the fuck is this man alive?

"This is as far as I go," I say, my body trembling and rebelling against my brain. Why am I being brave? Why now?

Because of Holly. And because I don't know what he'll do once I show him the spot where his money is buried. I think he'll kill me, and then I won't be able to see her grow up.

He stares at me and chews at his dry lips, then breaks into a demonic laugh, stopping abruptly before lunging at me and barking like a dog. I flinch and press my body against the driver's side door, but I stay inside the van with him. He's fucking mad.

"If you walk about four miles that way, you'll come to a massive rock wedged against a tree stump. There are some wetlands to the left, so watch your step. About forty feet due south, the ground is still loose enough for you to dig with your hands."

"Why don't you dig for me?" He lifts his chin.

I shake my head, forcing myself to be brave.

"Because I don't fucking want to," I growl. I must be mad, too. I've certainly snapped. But I have to draw this line and cut him out completely. He needs to disappear, and I only know one way to make sure of that.

"Four miles?" His eyes bore into mine, but I hold steady.

I nod.

"And if you're lying to me?"

"I guess that's the gamble you're going to have to take. Shoot me now, and you'll never know, or take me at my word, and start walking."

I'm so scared, I've surpassed physically shaking. I'm catatonic. I think my heart has stopped. I can't feel a thing. I just have to hold on for a few more seconds.

"If you're lying to me, it won't be me you'll have to worry about. There are dangerous people after me, son. And if they don't get paid . . ."

I blink slowly. I realize a lot of people are looking for that money. It's why this is the only way. There's no way in hell my father will ever give it up when he gets his hands on it. He's not paying off dangerous people. He's running. The only thing he has ever loved more than getting high is stacks of hundred-dollar bills.

"Don't call me son."

His lip sneers, but creeps into a full smile, and he breathes out a laugh. He pulls the handle on the door, pushing it open a few inches while holding the gun up enough that I'm forced to stare into the barrel.

He finally pushes the door open wide and sets one foot on the ground. I'm tempted to hit reverse and race away, but that would only make him doubt me. He needs to believe me. He should. I'm not lying. The money is right where I said it is, and he can go get it.

Once he's fully out of the van, he pushes the door closed but keeps the gun pointed at me. I hold his stare and wait for him to start walking, giving him nothing in my expression. But when his mouth curves into a sinister smirk, my body begins to feel things again. He lowers his weapon and fires at the front passenger-side tire, and the van leans to the right as the tire quickly deflates.

Fuck!

My eyes dim as he laughs at me, waggling a finger as if he's taught me some great lesson. Thing is, I still have my phone. He never once asked for it, even after he smashed Lindsey's to pieces. I keep my hands on the wheel as he walks away, and I don't move them until he's at least a hundred yards ahead with no chance of seeing my mouth move when he turns around, which he has, repeatedly.

I work the phone out of my pocket and press the emergency call button. The nine-one-one operator answers immediately.

"I'm at mile marker thirteen off Highway 183. I was carjacked, and the man forced me to drive him here. He had a bag full of money and what looked like a brick of white powder. I'm sure it was drugs. He took off and ran into the field just south of the highway."

I hang up before she asks any more questions, and when the callback rings, I toss it behind me, and push the transmission into reverse. I won't make it far on just a rim, but I should get a few miles away if I drive slowly. I begin to roll backward, toward the highway. My father's form is barely visible in the distance, but I swear he's pointing the gun at me. I keep the tires moving regardless, and eventually, he continues walking to what I hope is the end of our relationship.

I somehow get seven miles away before the rim becomes undrivable, and as the unmarked police cruisers race by me headed the other way, I start to breathe again. I pull to the side of the road and walk to the back of the van, getting out the jack and the donut so I can try to make it the rest of the way home. I'm sure Lindsey's called the cops by now. People are no doubt looking for me.

I wanted more than seven miles between me and the final scene. Not because I feel guilty in any way for turning in the man I loathe. I just don't want this van, or my name, mentioned in the same breath as what I suspect will be a major headline in the local news.

I start to change the tire and am nearly done when a siren chirps and a state trooper pulls up behind me. I hold my hands up and tell him my name, and also alert him that I'm alone. He searches the van anyhow, doing his job. He frisks me, too, ordering me to the ground and pressing a knee into my back. He pulls my wallet out to check my ID and calls my name and license number in the radio attached to his shoulder. When I hear the command officer utter, "All clear," he moves his leg and helps me to my feet.

"Sorry about that. We needed to make sure," he says.

I'm emotionless. I can't thank him even if I maybe should. I don't want to be living through any of this. Even the end, which I hope this truly is. And it's probably because I can't help but focus on the inevitable outcome waiting for me when I get home.

Lindsey needs to leave. She isn't safe with me, not until I know for certain that nobody else will come looking for my criminal inheritance. I can't be the thing Brandon uses to prove she isn't fit to keep her boys. She can't lose primary custody. The three of them need one another. Those boys need a parent who puts them first. Who will put her life on hold to make sure they get to live theirs. Brandon isn't that guy. He's a weekend dad, and I doubt he'll even keep that up for long.

Holly and I need to leave Sweetwater for a while, at least until the new season starts again, if I even continue to play. Maybe having my name out there is too dangerous for her. Maybe I don't need to give her a life with riches. Lindsey grew up as a coach's daughter, and look how she turned out. *Incredible*.

That's Holly's fate, no matter what my job is.

TWENTY-SIX
BROOKS

Nothing happened exactly as I thought it would. Probably because my plan came together under great duress in the short amount of time it took me to drive forty-seven miles to a remote location outside of Payne County.

I knew that even if I was able to get away from my father, others would inevitably follow. The stranger who kept showing up was likely one of many. And if I turned in the money myself, I'd constantly worry that I'd be labeled a snitch by people I've never met. Whoever truly owns that money would come looking for me to pay it back, with interest. As it is, I worry about my last name being the same as his. I'm connected to it no matter how hard I try to sever the ties. Jared Callahan had only one son. And fuck me, I'm him.

I'm sure my fears sound like wild conjecture to Lindsey, but I know better. I've seen horrible violence play out for a few thousand dollars. I can't fathom the horrors someone would be willing to commit in the name of millions. It's enough for a father to hold his son at gunpoint. Not that he's much of a dad. Or that I consider myself his son. Blood, that's all we share. DNA. Everything else I've scraped together from life.

Good and bad, it's been built on the acquaintances and friends I've made along the way.

Nobody has made me a better human than Lindsey. And that's why I have to walk away.

Drugs and money. I grew up in that life, without any of its riches. Even at the end, my dad had a mouth full of rotten teeth and drove a car with a rip in the front seat and bullet holes in the trunk. I'm still not sure whether those bullet holes were there because of him or whatever sad sack he got the car from. It doesn't matter. It's merely a symbol of a life not worth much in the beginning, middle, or end.

"Okay, Mr. Callahan. I'm sorry to ask, but one more time, can you walk us through what happened?"

I take a big drink from my bottle of water and nod, straightening the story in my head to make sure the details align. The same story I've told three times in a row. Some things are exactly like they are on TV. Police interviews are one of them.

"My client is tired. Is this really necessary? His father died today." The lawyer my agent hired for me is a shark. He's going to walk away from this day fifty grand richer, so he better be. But if it ends this all, here and now, then it's money well spent.

"It's okay. I can go through it one more time."

"Okay," my lawyer says, folding his hands over his notebook but keeping his pen ready.

"My father first contacted me around the start of my season. Late spring, around the time I found out I had a daughter."

"Go on," the detective says, reading along as I talk. He's taken notes on each version I've told. I haven't veered once. I also haven't slept in two days. And in that time, I've done nothing but brand this story in my mind. This is how it went, even if it's not *quite* the full truth.

"He sent a few emails at first, then text messages. I ignored them because I wasn't sure if they were real or if someone was phishing. And even if they were from him, my father and I haven't spoken since he went to prison."

"And that was . . ." The detective looks through his notes, but I finish it for him.

"Ten years, seven months ago."

"Right." The detective nods.

"He showed up at the home I'm renting in Sweetwater on June first. We had a brief exchange, and I told him to leave and never come back."

The detective pushes his glasses down his nose and meets my gaze over the gold rims. We've been through this part three times too.

"I did not know he was breaking parole when I saw him," I say.

It's no surprise that my father lied about getting out early for good behavior. He evidently never checked in with his parole officer either when he was really free. He fled, finding out where I was after tearing through the last shithole my mom lived in before she died. I guess when he didn't find the money hidden in any of the usual places, he came looking for me.

I walk the detective through the series of events before that final visit, when my father showed up at my house with a gun. I explain how we met for breakfast and he demanded money, but I cut him off from my life. Then I relive the terrifying phone call Lindsey made, my walking in as he held my daughter and her hostage. I never say a word about the buried money, though, or that I knew where it was. This is where the lie begins, because I never want that money linked to me.

"He had a bag of something; I figured money and drugs because . . . well, my father is a drug dealer. I thought I saw some cash. He demanded I drive him somewhere, so I took the keys to my nanny's van since I wrecked my car racing home. I drove at gunpoint where he told me to go. We got on

Highway 183, and then he started to get paranoid. He made me pull to the side of the road, so I did. He got out of the van, and I took off. He shot out the front tire as I sped away, and I nearly lost control of the van, but managed to turn it around and head the other way."

"You were going back home," the officer says, reiterating what I've told him twice before.

I nod.

"I wanted to get to my daughter, and to our nanny. I wanted to make sure they were safe."

"And you called nine-one-one at that point."

I nod again.

"Yes. I was in a panic, and I said everything I could remember about where he was when I left him. I lost the grip on my phone, though, so I kept driving, hoping I gave them enough information."

"And you told the operator he was a man. You didn't say *father*."

I nod. Upon reflection, that could be a miscalculation. I wanted to build distance between him and me. And I didn't want a public record linking us other than the birth certificate filed in California.

"Like I said, I panicked. And I was ashamed. That's my fucking dad. I'd rather nobody know that. You know what I mean?"

I hold the detective's gaze for a beat, and while the first time I walked him through this part, he scrutinized every detail, this time he seems to take my word. Good. Because this part is the truth.

I finish out my version of events, about the trooper finding me while I was changing the tire, and him bringing me to the substation where Lindsey and Holly had been taken. He turns the camera off this time, and I exhale as I push my chair away from the table.

I still don't know the details of what happened when I left

my father in the field. I know what I picked up from local news, that police seized a great deal of drug money after a lethal shootout with a man named Jared Callahan. He was forty-six years old, and his wife died of a drug overdose while he was in prison. He appeared to have been acting alone, trying to bury the cash to come back for later.

Anyone looking for that money will see this story when they search online. The stranger likely knows already. That cash is being transferred to the feds, and my father will be cremated at the expense of the state once the medical examiner makes her final report. I am nothing but a footnote, a local ballplayer making league minimum, and the unfortunate son of a really bad man.

The sky is gray when I leave the substation for what I hope is the final time. It smells like rain is on the horizon. Maybe a tornado will rip through this land and erase the bad things that happened here. Too bad a storm can't erase the images in my mind.

I shake my lawyer's hand, and he reassures me that he doesn't see any reason they'll need me for further questioning. The trail died in that field with my father. I'm sure his past connections will take them somewhere else. What's important is that wherever the story goes from here, it will be far away from my daughter and me.

Lindsey is waiting for me in the rental car, a modest sedan with heated seats and tinted windows. She doesn't know this, but I'm going to buy her a new van before I leave. And maybe I'll get a car like this when my insurance comes through. I don't need much. Just a safe ride for Holly.

Lindsey steps out of the driver's side when I approach, and slides her arms around me, pulling me into a hug. I want to squeeze her and never let go, but that will only make it harder when I have to. I've been holding back, and I know she can feel it. We've both blamed the trauma. And truthfully, that's all there is to blame. Trauma, and Jared and Rachel

Callahan. If I were anyone else's son, maybe I'd be free to have love in my life.

Once she's in the passenger seat and buckled, I pull us out of the substation lot. Holly is in her new car seat, still reversed but growing fast. Her feet nearly reach the back seat as it is.

Lindsey moves her hand to the center console, her fingers curled up and waiting for mine to fill in the gaps. I do, because I won't be able to tomorrow.

Lindsey called Brandon and asked him to pick the boys up from preschool when shit went down. He hasn't used it against her yet, but it's only a matter of time. We both know that. Nothing needs to be said.

I knew we couldn't hide everything from him, but I really hoped to limit the damage done. Instead, inevitable decisions have been moved up in my timeline, and hers. And it seems she's made the first one already.

The moving truck is waiting in the driveway when we pull in. It isn't mine.

I squeeze her hand and roll my head to meet her eyes. She isn't crying, but I know she will. The tears are waiting in the queue.

"Are you going to your parents' place?"

She nods.

"They've already made room. My dad can get upstairs now, so his office will be where the boys stay. If I'm even allowed—"

"Shh, don't think that way. You're not the one putting them in danger."

Her first tear falls. I touch the side of her face and catch it with my thumb.

"You don't put us in danger either," she says, and we both laugh out pathetic, breathy sounds.

"Really, Brooks. None of this is your fault. I have never felt safer than when I'm with you." She swallows hard, and her lips form a trembling smile.

"You must have walked through life terrified all the time," I joke.

She shakes her head, not even bothering to laugh.

"I felt stifled, and diminished. And betrayed. You make me feel beautiful."

"Because you are."

She leans her cheek into my palm and closes her eyes for a moment.

"Maybe I can come back when the season starts. I need to get through the court date, and then perhaps . . ."

I shake my head, and her mouth hangs open, but her expression doesn't show surprise. She knew I'd do this. She shakes her head anyway.

"Don't," she says.

"Your ex lost his mind when I was his sons' tee ball coach. You think he'll be fine with me being your boyfriend?"

"He doesn't get to say who I love," she says, and my heart stops. It's the first time she's uttered that word. I tremble as she grabs hold of my wrist.

"I love you, Brooks. So much. I love *us*. Our weird little family. It's what I want."

My chest quakes, because me, too. It's *all* I want.

"Where will you go?" she finally asks.

I draw in a heavy breath and shift my gaze to the windshield, glancing up at the mirror to catch the reflection of Holly in the back. She's chewing on her fist, drool coating her chin and soaking the front of her shirt. She's teething.

"Texas, maybe? I can think there, see what the future holds. And if baseball is still a part of it—"

"Baseball will *always* be a part of it. You'll be back in the spring. Just a few short months."

I look her in the eyes, and it kills me to see how much hope is suddenly in them.

"We'll see," I say.

She shakes her head, then leans over the console and pulls

my face to hers. She presses her lips to mine, then presses our foreheads together.

"You'll see, you mean. You'll be back. You're meant to be here, and to play this game. And you'll be one of the great ones. I feel it."

I smile as she strokes my jaw with her thumb, and close my eyes to picture the future she sees. It feels impossible, and the truth is, I'm not sure I want that life if she's not in it. Everything about this place and this game reminds me of her. But she probably thinks I can be with her, too.

Maybe. In another time.

TWENTY-SEVEN
LINDSEY

ONE MONTH LATER

I FaceTime my sister from the Earl's bathroom. She couldn't come home for my court date, but I feel her support from afar.

She picks up on the first ring.

"Are you ready?" she asks.

"You tell me?" I hold the phone up to show her my reflection in the mirror. I borrowed one of our mom's pant suits, and it's a little snug up top. I'm more of a full chest, whereas Mom and Ren are cute little B-cups.

"Wow, you look hot. Is the judge a man?"

I snort laugh, but then bunch my lips, taking her thought seriously for a moment. My judge is, in fact, a male. I unbutton one notch on the light blue blouse under the blazer, and Renleigh laughs through the phone.

"Not bad. I mean, not as good as you look in your Earl's shirt, but not bad."

I look at the black and red Earl's shirt folded on the sink.

"It's probably not the look I'm going for in court," I say.

"Fair," Renleigh replies.

I've been working at Earl's for three weeks. Daisy took me

on without question. It's the one gig I know will work around my classes, and despite the nonstop chaos that's been my life for the last several months, I plan to finish my degree. This job —this stop in life? It's temporary.

"Have you talked to him?"

Ren and Hunter have seen Brooks. He and Holly moved to Austin, and he's been working at a baseball hitting facility during the off-season, giving lessons. Holly goes to a nearby daycare.

"Yeah, he seems good. He still won't commit to going back, though. His agent works with Hunter's, and they've been talking a lot. Hunter is going to hang out with him today, try to convince him to stick with it. Linds, they're going to call him up this season. Hunter's agent told him."

I smile, unable to help but feel proud. Of course he's getting called up. He can't quit now, not when his dream is so close.

"How soon?" My question is selfish. I want him to spend time in Sweetwater first.

"Probably not right away. Are you considering nannying for him again? You know Daisy would let you leave and come back. We're like family around that place."

Of course, my sister thinks I'm interested in the job aspect of his return. I've been guarded with our relationship, especially after everything that happened.

"Maybe," I say after a short pause. I lean in close to the mirror and rest my phone on the sink, forcing my sister to view the Earl's women's restroom ceiling while I touch up my lipstick.

"He thinks he traumatized you, I guess. But I told him there's nothing we haven't seen in Sweetwater."

My sister and I both had wild times when we were in high school, nights filled with lights-out drag racing and jumping off cliffs into rocky water. Our youth was reckless. That's different from what happened with Brooks. That was actual danger. It was out of my control. And while my heart still wants to be with Brooks, I'm having a tough time reconciling what I went through with keeping my kids safe. I'm sure he is, too.

"Yeah, I'm fine," I finally respond.

I'm not.

"Hey, good luck today. Remember, you're an incredible mom. He's a cheater. And he doesn't know how to fish!"

I laugh, loving my sister's assessment of my divorce hearing. I blow a kiss into the phone and end our call.

I give myself one more once-over, rolling my shoulders and evaluating my cleavage. I decide better and button my blouse again. I march out of Earl's like I own the joint and drive my new van to my parents' house so I can pick up my dad and kiss my boys for good luck. They have no idea what's going on. They just know that their dad is buying them anything they want, and their mom has been overly affectionate lately. I suppose all is as it should be in their world.

My lawyer is waiting at the front of the courthouse when I arrive. Suddenly, everything feels high stakes, and I doubt every detail we've worked through. Even this stupid white pantsuit that suddenly feels even more snug.

I pull the jacket off before my dad and I reach the ramp next to the steps.

"Linds, you need to calm down," my dad says. "Your pits are sweating like mine."

I glance down and note the dark blue circles ringing my undersleeves.

"Dammit," I curse, handing my jacket to my dad so I can flap my hands at my pits like a crazy woman. I breathe through my nose and walk in circles, looking up at the sky, then closing my eyes.

"Lindsey, you got a minute?" My attorney clearly can't see. Because no, I do not.

I open my eyes at him, but continue to air-dry my silk blouse. I think it's beyond hope. I may as well shove my arms back into the damn jacket.

"We have a new proposal from your ex. I think we should discuss it before we head into court."

My eyes pop out. I feel my brow touch my hairline.

"What kind of new proposal?" My stomach drops. I've been anticipating something like this for weeks. Since Brandon learned about Brooks's father. I did everything right. The boys were always safe. But Brandon kept grilling me about the *what ifs*. He's not wrong. Those same questions have kept me awake almost every night since it happened.

What if the boys walked in when Jared had a gun pointed at me?

What if he kidnapped me instead of his son?

What if I was shot? Or killed?

"Okay, let's take a look." My father and I follow my lawyer through the security checkpoint, then duck into a meeting room on the first floor.

Brandon should be waiting upstairs in the trial room, along with his judgmental parents and a handful of his colleagues who will testify about what a good man he is. They're all liars. They covered for him when he was sleeping with Caitlyn. None of them can look me in my eyes.

"Okay, lay it on me. How bad is it?" I brace my palms on the table and study the grain in the wood.

"It's not bad at all, Lindsey. He's withdrawing his custody request."

I lift my gaze as he slides an updated parenting plan across the table, and my first observation is how short it is. Two pages, to be exact.

"What is this?" I scan it, looking for the trick. There must be some language in here that catches me in a *gotcha.*

"It's yours. It's what we filed originally. You get primary custody, and he gets every-other weekend, with a contingency to waive any weekends he has to travel for work. I mean, it does put a burden on you, but—"

"Take it," I say, popping my head up and meeting his eyes.

"You won't have guaranteed weekends without the boys," he explains, but I already get it. How is that any different than what I signed up for when we had kids?

"I know. I agree. Sign it. Stamp it. Tell his lawyer, or whatever we need to do."

My dad pats my knee and says, "Hot dog!"

I shake my head and start to laugh when I meet my father's gaze.

"How is this happening? I mean, I usually say that when shit falls apart, but for once . . . and how?"

My dad laughs, and our straight-faced lawyer even gives in with a chuckle.

"You're due some good luck. Maybe we all are," my dad says.

I have to agree. Between his strokes, then broken leg, and my mom and him throwing my sister and me for a loop with their weird-ass marriage, he's already built a bank full of good fortune that should come our way. And that's not even touching my own bullshit. A cheating husband, a contested custody, and being held at gunpoint.

Meeting the perfect man, and the universe not letting me have him.

I sign the document where my lawyer taps his finger, then he shoves it back into the envelope. We filter out of the meeting room and head to the elevators. We manage to snag an empty one, and once the doors close, I ask for one more reassurance that this is really going the way he says it is.

"Unless they pull something out of a hat when we get in there, it's a done deal. This should be a short and sweet trial. I hope you have something to do for the rest of your day." He chuckles, and I shake my head, still in disbelief.

"I don't. I don't have a thing. And that's okay, too."

My father's hand weaves into mine, and he gives my palm a squeeze.

"Why in the world would he do this?" I say as we step out of the elevator. I'm not really asking anyone in particular, but my lawyer answers.

"Hard to say. Sometimes it's a financial thing. Maybe it's work-related. Hell, I've even seen it where the other party is suddenly expecting a new baby, which changes all kinds of plans."

I come to a hard stop right outside the courtroom doors, and my father stops alongside me.

"Holy fucking shit," I mutter.

My lawyer looks at me with a hint of concern, his brow drawn in tight. I smirk on one side of my mouth, though, then glance at my dad.

"He knocked her up," I say.

My father's head falls back with a roaring laugh, and I immediately cover his mouth with my palm.

"*Shh!* They're going to hear you," I say, struggling to contain my own manic laughter.

"I couldn't give a rat's ass. Let him," my dad says.

"Can we go in now?" Our lawyer is ready to get this over with.

I place a hand over my chest and measure my breath, stifle my amusement, and once my giggles are under control, I nod. We step inside, and the courtroom is rather empty. Everyone in my entourage rode up in the elevator with me. On Brandon's side is a petite blonde I recognize from last year's faculty holiday party. Oh, and from the photos I had a private investigator take of her at dinner, and checking into a hotel with my then-husband.

I stare at her, willing her to look up, just once, so I can

litmus test her eyes. She keeps her gaze lowered, though. Brandon's parents sit on one side of her, and a woman who looks like an older version of the adulteress sits on the side closest to me. I'm pretty sure that's her mom.

"Give me one second," our lawyer says, signaling something to Brandon's attorney. Both men approach the bench, and the judge leans in close as they speak. It all takes less than a minute, and before I know it, my lawyer is standing next to me, and the judge is reading everything I just reviewed on the cover sheet of Brandon's proposal.

He gavels us out after both sides agree. All that's left is for me to wait for a piece of mail. A divorce decree, which I can staple on top of my marriage certificate and stow away in some box that I'll likely store at my parents' house and never need to see again.

It's hard not to notice the smile on Brandon's face as we leave. I get that he's excited to have a new baby coming into his life, but nothing about how we got here should make him happy. I stop at the door and consider walking up to him and offering a passive-aggressive congratulations, just to fish for confirmation. But before I make that mistake, my father grasps my bicep and meets my determined stare. He shakes his head.

"I know you want to, but it won't do any good. Just because you're wearing her pant suit doesn't mean you have to act like her." He arches a brow, and I let a smile slip in.

"You're right," I agree. And he is. My mom would have interrupted the judge and taken over her own form of questioning to get to the bottom of Brandon's reasoning. She would have fired our lawyer and put Caitlyn on the stand. And then she'd probably get herself banned from Payne County courtrooms for life.

There's value in that. And it's tempting. But right now, I get to walk out of here with almost everything I want. And my attention is better spent on getting that last piece.

TWENTY-EIGHT
BROOKS

SPRING

I thought it would feel different coming back. I also knew it would feel the same.

This town is woven into my soul. My best memories bloomed here, but also some of my worst. I've spent the last few months reconciling my past with my present, and the only thing I know for certain is that Holly, Lindsey, and her boys are the most important people in my life. I'm still not sure I can keep all of them safe, though. And I question whether I deserve to.

I put Lindsey and my daughter at risk. What they went through was due to me and my decisions. I could have done more when someone broke into our home. And burying that money with Roddy, and not telling Lindsey what I had done, was foolish. I thought I was protecting her by burying the truth along with the drug money. That hole was too shallow.

And yet she forgave me, almost instantly. And she still calls, even when I don't answer. Her messages are kind, her wishes for me genuine, and there's always this glimmer of hope in her voice.

When she called last week, I finally picked up. She asked if I was coming into town soon and if we could talk. Hunter and Renleigh tell her everything, and they likely told her I am thinking about hanging up my cleats. My agent disagrees. And so does Hunter. But he doesn't know what it's like to live in my head. Baseball was a given for him, but I'm not sure I can drum up the same fire required to get to the next level. I lost some of my fuel after everything went down last year, and I haven't exactly kept up with my training like I should have. It would be easy to get back, though. I just need one reason. Maybe three.

And that's why I'm here.

The golden Earl's sign flickers against the periwinkle sky. Dusk hits differently in this part of the world. Flatlands and windmills broken up only by the few places like Earl's, where trucks pile into the lot, and beer flows freely, and in the distance, stadium lights glow above the horizon.

I'm here to see both. Either to say goodbye, or . . .

Lindsey's van is pulled up right by the door. Her shift ends in an hour. I'm early, but I drove straight through, and once I crossed the county line, I had to keep going.

Holly is spending the weekend with her Uncle Hunter and Aunt Ren. I think the two of them want to see what it would be like having a family. Hunter bought a ring already; I saw it. He doesn't think Renleigh is ready for him to ask, but sometimes you just have to take a leap of faith.

Kinda like the one I'm about to take.

I get out of my car and straighten the denim button-down I changed into at a gas station four miles back. I want to look nice when I see her, which means I couldn't show up in the same shirt I wore for three hundred miles. I like to eat on the road. And I'm a messy dude.

I roll up each sleeve, then glance down at my jeans to make sure I'm not covered in crumbs. With a deep breath, I roll my shoulders back and head to the heavy metal door branded with Earl's famous tagline: Good beer. Good people. Good times.

I add one more in my head.

Good luck.

A round of laughter hits my ears as soon as I step inside, and I glance to my right to spot this season's new batch of rookies piled around one of the pool tables, probably losing lots of cash to one of the locals. I learned really quick not to bet on pool games here. For some of these folks, pool is like a second language.

Daisy spots me over the crowd gathered around her at the bar, and she nods with a smile. I move in close enough to order a drink, but she's already got a Coke waiting for me.

"I might need a little rum in it this time," I say. I don't drink much. She got that right. But I could use a dash of courage.

She tops it off, then slides it my way.

"This one's on the house. She'll be right out."

Daisy winks, then heads to the other end of the bar to bark at a few men getting rowdy. She has bouncers at this place, but Daisy can usually break things up before she needs to call on the muscle. She's a woman in charge. Turns out, that's my type.

When the curvy waitress rushes by with a tray filled with shots and two whiskey sours, I track her movement with my eyes. Lindsey looks different in this element, and seeing her puts a boyish grin on my face.

"All right, gather round, fellas. Time to toast," she says as she lines up the drinks on one of the high-top tables in the back. It looks like someone is having a bachelor party. Either that, or it's rush season for the university fraternity, and one of these dudes got in. I never did any of that shit, so I'm not sure if it's the right season for it.

Lindsey's hips sway as she maneuvers her way through the crowded tables, picking up empty glasses and stuffing tips into her apron pocket. I'm starting to wonder if she's even interested in going back to a nannying gig, given how much cash I see her tucking away.

Her gaze lifts after she clears her last table, and when our eyes meet, I remember why I came. I need to know if I can live without this girl. And if I can't, I need to convince her that she needs me just as much.

"You're early," she says, sidling up to me with a full tray propped on her palm.

"Not a lot of traffic heading this way, I guess." I scan along her side, tracing the curve of her breast and her hips. "You can really rock an Earl's T-shirt, by the way."

Her head tilts, and she gives me side eyes. All I can do is shrug.

"I have very good taste. What can I say?"

Her lips slowly pucker into a tight smile, and she steps into me, giving me a kiss on my cheek.

"Yes. You do," she says.

I watch her hips sway as she sashays around the bar, dumps her dirty glasses into a bin, then tucks her tray behind the counter.

"You good if I take off now, Daisy?" She holds up a hand, and Daisy gives her a thumbs- up from the other end of the bar. It's packed in here.

"I'm fine waiting if she needs your help for a while."

"Daisy? Help?" Lindsey spits out a short laugh as her eyes pull in. As if on cue, Daisy whistles loudly enough that the entire bar gets quiet and looks her way.

"Someone lost their keys. Who's Mikey is a bad boy?" she reads aloud from a keychain. The razzing comes from the table of rookies in the back, and they shove some poor dude side to side as he makes his way to the bar like a kid getting called to the front of the class.

"Mikey is indeed a very bad boy," I tease under my breath.

"You're one to talk," Lindsey jokes. Heat rushes down my neck, mostly from the way her gaze flirts with me.

"You're a little too good at this gig," I warn.

She unties her apron after pulling out a fistful of cash, then settles in next to me on a seat at the end of the bar.

"You should see me nanny," she teases. Her smile isn't quite as big this time, and her gaze lingers on me for an extra beat.

"Renleigh told you I'm thinking about . . ." I lift a shoulder, unable to say the word *quitting*. Perhaps that's the only sign I need. I can't even say it. I just can't seem to say I'm coming back for good, either.

"She says a lot of things. I'd rather hear what you have to say. Here, help me count." She pushes the pile of money to the bar space between us, and I help her flatten out the crinkled ones and fives.

"This looked like a lot more when you pulled it out," I admit.

"It always does," she says with a sigh. She glances at me with a faint grin, then moves on to her copies of tabs while I take over counting her cash. We both end up with eighty-seven dollars for our total when we count, including the credit card tips. That's not enough to cover groceries for a week.

"It'll pick up when the season starts. Plus, I won't be taking classes over the summer, so I'll have more time to work."

"School is going good, then?"

"I didn't fail algebra, so yeah. I'd say it's going well." Her lips bunch with a short laugh, and she breathes on her nails before rubbing them on the center of her shirt to mark her accomplishment.

"What I hear is you're thinking of switching to a math major," I tease. She shoves my arm, and I brace myself for the impact. Because I don't move, she ends up leaning into me, and her hands stay on my arm.

"Politics, actually."

My eyebrows raise.

"Politics. Okay." I hold on to her gaze for a few extra seconds, and see the spark behind her eyes.

"My mom ran a lot of campaigns, and I've gotten really interested in that work."

"I remember," I say, still stuck on her eyes.

Her head pivots a tad, and her mouth pulls up into a suspicious smirk.

"Why are you looking at me like that?" she asks.

"You just look really happy, is all. It's . . . it's nice to see you that way." I drop my gaze to her hand as it curls around my bicep. I wasn't sure how she would look. The last visual I really have of her is one where she was incredibly frightened. And that was my fault.

"It's nice to see you happy, too," she says. "You are, aren't you, Brooks? Are you happy?"

I let out a short, breathy laugh and suck in my lower lip, finally peeling my focus away from her perfect face. I lean back, holding on to the edge of the bar as I stretch my back. Her hand slips from my arm at the same time.

"That's a really hard question. Am I happy?"

"It shouldn't be," she says.

I nod.

"You're probably right," I admit, blinking my focus back to her.

She leans into me again, her hand tipping up my chin. It takes all my self-control not to grab it and kiss the inside of her wrist.

"I'm always right, Brooks. Every. Single. Time."

The way her lips part with a tiny breath takes me spiraling back to the first time I kissed her. Her mouth is intoxicating, but I can't let that alone sway me into making such a monumental decision.

"How are you, really? Are you . . . okay?" I sink into her gaze, and breathing gets harder all of a sudden. This is what I came here for. To know for sure. To read her eyes and tell one way or another if I stole her glow with my dumb fucking life. If I broke her spirit. "Or did I . . ." My breath stutters, and I spin on my stool to face her head-on.

Before I can get out another word, she rests her other hand on my face. I hold her wrists and try not to drown while looking at her.

"I miss you. I miss *us*. But other than that, Brooks. Yes, I'm really, *really* okay."

I nod, my movement tiny. "Yeah?"

Her lips curl up slightly. "Yeah."

I match my breathing to hers, and slowly my hands glide down her arms, stopping at her elbows. I can't seem to remove them completely. I'm afraid if I do, she'll disappear.

I don't know why I'm so afraid. She's right here. All it would take is one *yes* from me. One ask—*let's start over.* But what if that was our end, and she's better off now that she's okay? That missing us is beautiful, and something we can both do without me fucking up her life. What if that wasn't the end of everything, and there's someone out there still looking for something my father stole? Or my mother stole? The baggage they left behind for me to clean up. If only I had one sign.

"I'm staying with Roddy. Maybe . . . maybe tomorrow we can talk more. I'd love to see the boys, and—"

"Brooks, I don't want to do anything just a little. I need to know if you're coming back. All of you. All in. I'll be okay, but I can't get my hopes up again that there's something here when it's not."

"But there is something," I say, suddenly feeling the fight in my own chest.

She slides from her stool and steps between my legs, closing the distance between us until it's nothing more than a few inches.

"Prove it."

My universe, it always balances out. And I've had a lot of

shit roll down the hill and bury me this last year. I'm due something good. I'm due a sign, a not-so-subtle nudge.

Perhaps the man was sitting across the bar this whole time. Or maybe I conjured him out of thin air, and he isn't even real. Whatever the manifestation, real or not, I'm compelled to walk toward him and see.

"One second," I say, squeezing her hands and slipping off my seat to talk to the man sitting alone at the other end of the bar.

"Uh, okay?"

I meet her eyes briefly and point to the man, who is busy watching a game on the TV plastered above the top-shelf liquor.

"You see him, right?" I ask.

She squints a little but nods.

"Yeah, Brooks. I see the man minding his own business." She chuckles, but sounds a bit worried.

My chest is quaking, but I'm not scared seeing him there. He's not wearing the ragged clothing I saw him in before. And he doesn't look like he's tweaking out, or after me. He looks like a regular man from Sweetwater. Blue collar. Or maybe . . . *a cop.*

I clear my throat as I approach him, and he twists in his seat, pulling a beer bottle away from his lips. His eyes flicker with what I think is recognition. I don't say a word. I simply stare into his eyes. He pulls his wallet from his back pocket, then unfolds it on the bar top for a brief second. The gold and blue of the badge hits me first, and I take a mental snapshot of the ATF before he closes the billfold and returns it to his pocket.

"I'm sorry. I thought you were someone else," I say.

He nods, and I leave him behind me, and suddenly everything makes sense.

When I get back to Lindsey, she's cashing out her tips for bigger bills, and gathering her purse to leave. I block her steps as she moves to round the bar again, and her miffed expression is the last thing I see before I run my hands into her hair and press my mouth to hers.

She hums into my kiss, and her impatience dissipates almost instantly. Daisy's whistle draws too much attention to us, but for once, I don't care. I lift Lindsey, and she wraps her legs around me while I kiss her in front of a bunch of rookies who I will have to convince to keep their mouths shut when the season starts. If Lindsey and I are doing this, for real, I want us to do it slow and do it right.

We'll build the story everyone else gets to think is true: a single dad and his nanny slowly falling in love. It's nobody's business how fast we actually fell.

EPILOGUE

BROOKS

I always swore that if I found someone like Lindsey, I would do things right. I would do it right *all the way*.

I had no idea that my best friend would be asking his girl to marry him on the very same weekend I planned to ask mine. And Hunter's plan has me asking Lindsey's father, Dale, for his daughter's hand a bit of a challenge.

I've been pacing in the parking lot of our crappy two-bedroom apartment for an hour, waiting for him to get seated at the Texas game where Hunter plans to pop the question. He flew their parents in, and Lindsey is waiting for Hunter's mom to call and FaceTime the entire proposal for her to see along with Hunter's sisters.

The timing for *my* call has to be perfect, so when Lindsey's phone rings and she rushes in from the balcony, my heart starts to pound. I stare at the phone in my palm.

"Come on, Dale. Don't forget about me." My hand buzzes with a call from Lindsey's father.

"Hi!" My breathless answer makes him laugh.

"You'd think you're the one popping the question. What's up? What has you so frazzled?"

He has to be kidding. A few seconds pass, and I can tell he's not.

"Well, sir," I clear my throat, and that seems to help him get it.

"Well, shit. Are both of my girls getting married?"

"What?" Lindsey's mom says in the distance.

"Hold on, let the boy ask me," Dale says. "Go on."

"I was hoping, Mr. Blackwood, that you would give me your blessing to ask your older daughter to be my wife. I promise I will treat her like a queen. And I will protect her with my own life. I love her, sir. And nothing would make me happier than to know you are okay with me doing so."

I think I'm going to throw up. The few long seconds that pass nearly make me piss my pants, but soon, Dale is chuckling on the line.

"Never thought you'd get the balls to ask," he teases.

"Oh, ha," I breathe out a nervous laugh. I rub the back of my neck and glance at the balcony. Lindsey is still inside.

"Now, I have to go. It's time here in Texas. See you in a few days, yeah?"

"Yes, sir. Thank you, sir."

"It's Dad," he corrects. My pulse skips. I don't know if I can say that word out loud to him yet, so I simply say, "Okay," instead. His insistence, however, means the world to me.

I pull the ring out of my pocket and pinch it, giving it one more good look before I black out from sheer panic. She has to say yes. She'll say yes, right? God, I hope she says yes.

The boys come home tonight, and all five of us are travelling to Texas for the next two weeks. I've been called up for the end of their season, and my agent feels really good about what that means for my chances of starting for Texas next year.

It will mean a big move for all of us, and another negotiation with Lindsey's ex. Now that he has a baby with his girl-friend, though, he's been less focused on taking his shortcomings out on Lindsey. He's also been less engaged with his boys. And that pisses me off. I've really tried to step up with them, but they still need to feel the love from him. I know all too well how much it hurts when that support is missing.

Even if we move to Texas for half the year, I think our roots will stay here. I've never really had a place to call home. Inglewood was . . . *Inglewood*. I had more than a dozen addresses there, and when I was in Iowa, I called a former drug-pin SUV home for a little while. I kind of like the idea of saying I'm from Sweetwater. It feels nice in my chest, like a full breath and a good cup of coffee.

Plus, I know how much Lindsey loved the Quinn house. I think leaving that place hurt almost as much as us breaking up. So when I get my first big payday, that property is the first thing I intend on buying.

Before any of that can happen, though, I need to get one more *yes*.

I take the stairs two at a time, then head into our apartment and step in behind Lindsey. Holly is taking a nap, and I let her go a little longer than I probably should have because I don't want to take a break in the middle of my proposal to change a diaper.

Lindsey has her hand over her mouth, an effort to keep her squeals inside as she stares at her phone screen.

"Is it happening?" I whisper, kneeling behind the sofa, nuzzling the crook of her neck. Tiny goose bumps cover her neck, and she twitches.

"*Shh*, yes. It's happening," she whispers behind her palm.

"Okay, got it. Lips zipped."

She hushes me again, and I chuckle. I'd better not push my luck. Now is not a time to be trifled with. Plus, I have to admit, there's something pretty sweet about getting to watch your best friend tee up his dream life. As Hunter gets down on one knee, Lindsey gasps, and a tear slides down her cheek.

"Don't cry, baby," I say against her ear. I slide the side of my thumb along her cheek to wipe it away.

"It's a happy cry," she says, no longer needing to hide the fact she's watching this all unfold. Hunter's sisters are on the video call, too, and between the three of them, it's a happy cry fest. I can't lie, though, if I weren't so damn nervous, there's a good chance I'd be tearing up, too.

"Oh, my God, Mom. Thank you for videoing this for us. Did you record it too?" Hunter's oldest sister asks.

Lindsey glances over her shoulder at me, and I kiss her lips softly.

"How the hell do I know if I recorded it? Is that how live-streaming works?" Hunter's mom says.

"Mom, it's a FaceTime, not a livestream," his other sister explains.

"Same. Thing!" his mom screams.

Lindsey starts to giggle, and we both get comfortable, listening closely while Hunter's family has a generational tech-nology spat after his proposal. It's some truly funny shit. But not a woman to be one-upped, Lindsey's mom has to kick the confusion up a notch.

"Did Brooks ask her yet? Do you know?" she says, just a little too close to Hunter's mom's phone.

Lindsey's eyes widen, and mine flutter closed. All of this preparation. I was going to do something cute, like hide it in her favorite strawberry cupcakes that I have chilling in the fridge, or maybe put on her favorite song, "Crazy Love," and ask her to dance. But that wouldn't really be us, would it? This —a blown surprise and scrapped plans in favor of quick and simple. That's us.

"Will you?" I hold the ring between my thumb and index finger and rest my elbow on the back of the couch. Lindsey's gaze flits to the pink diamond, then back to my eyes. If I get one thing right today, it will be picking out the ring of her dreams. She's only pointed it out a dozen times everywhere it pops up—social media ads, famous influencers on the red carpet, Marvel movie marriage proposals.

"You got the ring," she says, a tiny smirk playing at her lips.

"I did." I slip it on her finger, then take her hand in mine and kiss her knuckles as I look up into her eyes.

"You also got the girl," she says.

My grin spreads like a fire in the wind, and I pull her over the couch so she's sitting on the floor with me, straddling my lap as I kiss her face—every square inch.

I didn't just get the girl. I got the whole entire dream. And I am never letting it go.

THE END

Ready for more Sweetwater Springs?

See where it all began with Easy Tiger.

Coming May 21, 2026 - Book 3: Chin Up Champ - a forbidden, friends-to-lovers small-town baseball romance - preorder now!

If you enjoyed Sweetwater Springs, I have several other sports romance series you might enjoy. Check out the following:

VARSITY HEARTBREAKER - BOOK 1 in the VARSITY SERIES
READ NOW IN KU: Varsity Heartbreaker

Lucas Fuller is a lot of things.

He's the boy next door.

He's the first crush I ever had.

He was my first kiss.

He's also the only person who has ever broken my heart.

For two years, I've wondered what happened to the us I used to know.

We were best friends, and then suddenly…we weren't.

I tried to run away from it. I even changed schools just to make the hurt disappear.

But no matter how hard I tried to not think about Lucas, I

just couldn't stay away from the high school quarterback with perfect blue eyes and so many secrets.

I'm back. We're seniors now. We've grown—all of us. And Lucas Fuller might be different, but I'm different too.

This is my time to take risks, to experience life and to fall in love for real.

I want Lucas Fuller to be a part of my story, but I know for that to happen, I need to know the truth about our past.

THE TOMBOY AND THE CAPTAIN Book 1 in the FINAL SCORE SERIES
  READ NOW IN KU: The Tomboy and The Captain

It was supposed to be my year, but then he made a bet that I couldn't refuse...

A star senior on the Tiff U volleyball team, it's been my goal to come back strong after an injury that nearly took me out of the game. But I'm Laney freaking Price, and I'm taking my shot to make it on the new pro women's team, despite the lack of support from my father.

The problem? Cutter McCreary. He is the Captain of the Tiff U hockey team, all-around loveable guy, and a total player. And did I mention a complete thorn in my side since freshman year? Yeah…that guy. His charms don't tempt me.

Until…a mix up with our housing situation forces us into a bit of a predicament. We were both promised a room. The same room.

His proposal? A bet. We split the room in half—for now. Whoever falls in love with the other first has to move out. The winner gets to stay. But when strategic glances turn into late night talks, and fake kisses start to feel real, I'm finding myself without a game plan. And winning suddenly doesn't feel like the only thing that matters.

ACKNOWLEDGMENTS

This series is so much fun to write. Thank you for taking the journey back to Sweetwater Springs with me. This book and series comes from my baseball-loving heart. And I would never be able to pull off the stories I write without the help of some very important people in my life. So, as always, thank you Autumn for holding me together in all places of life. Thank you Brenda for editing my words to make me sound my very best. Thank you mom for your eagle eye, and Tim and Carter, for standing behind me and believing me always.

I'll keep this one short and sweet, but I would be remiss if I did not thank you, my reader. You are the reason I do this. Thank you for your time. I never take you for granted, and I will appreciate you always.

If you enjoyed Hey There Slugger, please consider leaving your review anywhere you would like. It is the best way you can boost an author, and the difference it makes is enormous.

Time for me to dig into the next couple to fall in love in Sweetwater Springs. I wonder who it is . . .

ABOUT THE AUTHOR

Ginger Scott is a *USA Today, Wall Street Journal* and Amazon-bestselling author from Peoria, Arizona. She has also been nominated for the Goodreads Choice and RWA Rita Awards. She is the author of several young and new adult romances, including bestsellers Waiting on the Sidelines, The Hard Count, A Boy Like You, This Is Falling and Wild Reckless.

A sucker for a good romance, Ginger's other passion is sports, and she often blends the two in her stories. When she's not writing, the odds are high that she's somewhere near a baseball diamond, either watching her son swing for the fences or cheering on her favorite baseball team, the Arizona Diamondbacks. Ginger lives in Arizona and is married to her college sweetheart whom she met at ASU (fork 'em, Devils).

FIND GINGER ONLINE: www.gingerscottbooks.com

facebook.com/GingerScottAuthor

instagram.com/authorgingerscott

tiktok.com/@authorgingerscott

ALSO BY GINGER SCOTT

The Boys of Sweetwater Springs

Easy Tiger

Hey There Slugger

(The full 6-book series coming soon)

Final Score Series

The Tomboy & The Captain

The Wallflower & The Running Back

The Best Friend & The Short Stop

The Boys of Welles

Loner

Rebel

Habit

The Fuel Series

Shift

Wreck

Burn

The Varsity Series

Varsity Heartbreaker

Varsity Tiebreaker

Varsity Rule breaker

Varsity Captain

The Waiting Series

Waiting on the Sidelines

Going Long

The Hail Mary

The Waiting Series - Next Generation

Home Game

Game Face

Final Down

Like Us Duet

A Boy Like You

A Girl Like Me

The Falling Series

This Is Falling

You And Everything After

The Girl I Was Before

In Your Dreams

The Harper Boys

Wild Reckless

Wicked Restless

Standalone Reads

The Older Brother

The Moon and Back

Southpaw

Candy Colored Sky

Cowboy Villain Damsel Duel

Drummer Girl

BRED

The Hard Count

Memphis

Hold My Breath

Blindness

How We Deal With Gravity

www.ingramcontent.com/pod-product-compliance
Lightning Source LLC
Chambersburg PA
CBHW011926050726
47591CB00009B/2357